By

Bow, Daggers

&

Sword

BY

BOW, DAGGERS

&

SWORD

Part 2
A Ranger's Tale

MARC ALAN EDELHEIT

By Bow, Daggers, and Sword: A Ranger's Tale Part 2

First Edition

I wish to thank my agent, Andrea Hurst, for her invaluable support and assistance. I would also like to thank my beta readers, who suffered through several early drafts. My betas: Jon Cockes, Nicolas Weiss, Melinda Vallem, Paul Klebaur, James Doak, David Cheever, Bruce Heaven, Erin Penny, April Faas, Rodney Gigone, Tim Adams, Paul Bersoux, Phillip Broom, David Houston, Sheldon Levy, Michael Hetts, Walker Graham, Bill Schnippert, Jan McClintock, Jonathan Parkin, Spencer Morris, Jimmy McAfee, Rusty Juban, Joel M. Rainey, Jeremy Craig, Nathan Halliday, Ed Speight, Joseph Hall, Michael Berry, Tom Trudeau, Sally Tingley-Walker, James H. Bjorum, Franklin Johnson, Marshall Clowers, Brian Thomas. I would also like to take a moment to thank my loving wife, who sacrificed many an evening and weekends to allow me to work on my writing.

Editorial Assistance: Hannah Streetman, Audrey Mackaman, Brandon Purcell

Cover Art by Piero Mng (Gianpiero Mangialardi)

Cover Formatting by Telemachus Press

Agented by Andrea Hurst & Associates, LLC www.andreahurst.com

Marc's Website: http://maenovels.com/

Other books by Marc Alan Edelheit

Chronicles of a Legionary Officer
Book One: **Stiger's Tigers**
Book Two: **The Tiger**
Book Three: **The Tiger's Fate**
Book Four: **The Tiger's Time**
Book Five: **The Tiger's Wrath**
Book Six: **The Tiger's Imperium**
Book Seven: **The Tiger's Fight (Coming 2022)**
Book Eight: TBA (Coming 2023)
Book Nine: TBA: (Coming 2023-4)
Book Ten: Conclusion (Coming 2024)

Tales of the Seventh
Part One: **Stiger**
Part Two: **Fort Covenant**
Part Three: **A Dark Foretoken**
Part Four: **Thresh (TBA)**

A Ranger's Tale
Part One: **Eli**
Part Two: **By Bow, Daggers, and Sword**
Part Three: **TBA**

The Karus Saga
Book One: **Lost Legio IX**
Book Two: **Fortress of Radiance**
Book Three: **The First Compact**
Book Four: **TBA (2023)**

Born of Ash:
Book One: **Fallen Empire**
Book Two: **Infinity Control (Coming 2022)**
Book Three: **Rising Phoenix (Coming 2023)**

The Way of Legend: With Quincy J. Allen
Book One: **Reclaiming Honor**
Book Two: **Forging Destiny**
Book Three: **Paladin's Light (Conclusion)**

Nonfiction:
Every Writer's Dream: The Insider's Path to an Indie Bestseller

TABLE OF CONTENTS

Chapter One

Eli lowered himself to a knee beside a large boulder. His legs burned from the climb and his breathing was slightly labored. The exertion to reach the summit had felt good, invigorating.

For the most part, the top of the ridge was bare rock, surrounded by pockets of eroding soil and a scattering of trees.

He placed a hand on the boulder. It had yet to warm under the direct light of the morning sun, which had been fully up for less than an hour.

The valley that stretched out before him was filled with trees and hemmed in by low but steep ridges. A wide brown river snaked its way lazily through the valley. To the north, the river appeared to cut through a forbidding notch. There was another notch on the south side of the valley too.

The view was quite breathtaking, and for a moment, Eli forgot his worldly concerns. That in and of itself was a blessed relief, especially after the events he and Mae had just involved themselves in.

Motion above drew his attention. Barely a speck in the vastness of the blue sky, a hawk soared high overhead. Squinting, he eyed the raptor for several heartbeats, following its flight, then turned his attention back to the valley, which appeared isolated, and thoroughly unspoiled.

Though they were still in the Kingdom of the Castol, he saw no evidence of civilization or settlement below. They were moving through a region, west of the town of Brek, that was sparsely populated.

Eli had never been to this valley before and felt the urge to explore. He liked the thought of that, putting aside his worries for a time, discovering new things. The forest in these parts was ancient. It called to him. Perhaps that was what he and Mae needed?

When he closed his eyes, he could hear the forest singing to the joy of life, celebrating the coming of the change in seasons, the great cycle. He sucked in a breath and let it slowly out through his nose, thoroughly savoring the moment.

He wanted it to continue, to let the link fully form. Eli almost allowed himself to go, to open his mind to the Mother of the forest. Instead, regretfully, he pulled back and shifted his gaze to the ground and what had initially caught his attention, necessitating a halt in their travels. As if a cloud had moved across the sun, Eli's mood dimmed.

"That is a beautiful view," Mae'Cara said. She had been trailing a few yards behind him and had caught up.

Eli did not reply.

"What did you find?" Mae asked.

He glanced back at her. She held her unstrung bow lightly in her right hand. A bundle of arrows was secured by a simple leather tie just above her pack. Her left hand was loosely holding onto one of the pack's straps. Mae's face was flushed with the exertion of their climb up the back side of the ridge, which had included some serious scrambling. Reflecting morning sunlight, a sheen of sweat beaded her brow. She wiped it away with the back of her arm.

"A partial print," Eli answered as he turned back to what he had discovered. "It is faint, but a solitary footprint no less, maybe three or four days old."

"Interesting." She joined him and studied the print for a long moment. "This is the third mark we've found in less than a day, and along the road too."

"Yes," Eli said.

"Do you believe it belongs to them?" Mae asked.

"In 'them,' you mean the fugitive Mik'Las and Sariss'Sa the Atreena?"

"You know very well that is who I mean."

"I suppose it is possible."

"You are not thinking that is the case, though," Mae said as more of a statement than question.

"Mik'Las is quite skilled," Eli said. "He was trained as a ranger."

"Right then. He would not make such a basic mistake." She waved at the print.

"No," Eli said. "I would not expect him to do so."

"Perhaps it is that he has grown careless. He might feel, with the recent rains, we have lost his trail."

Eli considered her words, then shook his head firmly. "No. Not so soon. He would not become so lax either. Not him, especially since he now knows we are after him and on his trail. Mik'Las will be extra careful. His purpose is flight and escape."

"The Atreena, then?" Mae suggested. "Could this be a cry for help?"

"As in Sariss'Sa is intentionally leaving signs for us to follow?" Eli looked back down into the valley. He turned his gaze to the northeast and pondered her words. "I suppose that is possible."

"You are not wholly convinced."

"Are you?" His tone was harder than he had intended. She was reaching for the long straw, the easiest to grab, and he suspected she knew it.

Her brow furrowed slightly. Mae cocked her head to the side, clearly displeased with the game. "No. I am not convinced."

"These are not their tracks, then." Eli rubbed at his eyes. He hadn't slept well this past week. He never slept well after battles. The things he did and saw haunted him, usually for days to come, sometimes even weeks and years after.

He did not enjoy taking life, and yet, when he was forced to, he committed to the act wholeheartedly. There was no point in hesitating or holding back. Still, every time, it bothered him deeply. It was as if each act of ending a life tore at his soul.

Eventually, he knew the funk would pass. That would take time. He blew out a breath and returned his focus to the conversation at hand. "They may not have even come this way. For all we know, Mik'Las has taken a road north or, for that matter, south to the empire."

"Who is using our road, then?" Mae pointed to a marker tree fifty yards ahead, downslope. The tree had been shaped into a horizontal bend before being allowed to grow vertical once again. It was the sort of marker to be noticed by other elves, indicating the direction of travel to be taken, a hidden path set in plain sight. "And why are they using it?"

"That is the question that begs answering." Eli felt a stab of curiosity at that. Still, he found his interest muted to some degree. He glanced over at her and felt a wave of sadness before looking quickly away as she caught his gaze.

"Are we going to talk about it?" Mae asked.

Eli stood. "We should be focused on the hunt. Talking can wait."

"I disagree."

Feeling unhappy, Eli glanced over and fought a scowl. He knew she would not give in. Mae never did when she desired something. And she badly wanted to talk about his feelings. Eli had been procrastinating, thinking about how to broach the subject in a way that would minimize difficulty and complication. For afterwards, they both needed to work together. There was still the mission to be done.

"You have barely spoken a word to me since we left Karenna's camp," Mae said. "Normally, I cannot get you to shut up. Tell me what is wrong."

"After the battle, I have not felt much like talking," Eli admitted, wishing he could change the subject and push this off for another time.

"Talk to me … please." There was a touch of anguish in her voice. It tore at his heart, rending it more than killing ever had.

Eli felt a grimace form. The new sword belted to his side felt heavy, like it was weighing his soul down. He resisted the temptation to put his hand on the hilt. The human he had met outside of Karenna's camp had given it to him as a gift, a memento to a friendship that had yet to come to pass.

The caretaker had arranged for that meeting. It had shocked Eli to his core. It was part of what was bothering him. What he had learned that night, and the consequence of that knowledge, was like eating an undercooked meal, and it was not sitting well with him.

"Well?" she demanded when he did not speak.

"I thought," Eli said, "you did not want to talk about what you saw at the Pool of Reflection?"

"This is about what happened between you and him."

"Is it?" Eli asked bitterly. "You saw it, did you not? I read it in your eyes when Karenna sent me to him. You knew whom I was to meet before I even knew. The pool is the only plausible explanation."

"You warned me not to speak on what I was shown, or did you forget that?"

Eli did not reply. He looked away, thinking. He felt trapped, with no way out.

"I believe you now know, or suspect, some of what I was shown," Mae said after a moment, "especially after you met with *him*, the High Father's Champion."

Eli stilled at those words, then turned his gaze back to her and stared for a long moment. "I—I…" Eli stopped as he gathered his thoughts. "I fear only pain can come from this." Eli sucked in a breath, pausing. He started again. "I have learned I have a duty to our people, one that is greater than I even believed possible."

Mae paled. "Beyond being a ranger?"

Eli gave a slow, grave nod of his own. "And it comes with a heavy burden, one I wish I could set aside."

"Burden? What do you mean?"

"You saw what happened between Karenna and Edgun," Eli said. "Their battle was the opening gambit of the gods. We witnessed something that, to our knowledge, has never happened before on Istros, a coming together of Champions." Eli rubbed at the back of his neck. "The Last War has finally come to Istros's doorstep. We witnessed the first part. What comes next will be worse. Though I do not wish it so, it seems I have a part to play in that." Eli paused, sucking in a breath. "It is my destiny, my fate."

"Destiny?" Mae's voice was scarcely a whisper. "You are one who does not believe in such things."

"I do not." Eli glanced down at the ground. "Until recently, I had not."

"We all have destinies," Mae said. "You have just come to realize that, is all. You are overthinking things."

"This is different. Mine will require sacrifice."

"You are speaking on us now?" Mae's tone hardened. Her gaze had become piercing, as if she was intensely trying to read the meaning behind his words, his intentions.

"As much as it pains me, there can be no us." Eli said the words he had been dreading to utter. He felt his heart shatter a little more. "You will have your own part to play."

"I know," Mae said in a whisper. "But what about the *now*? Can we have the now? There is time yet."

"Is there? We don't know that."

She stepped nearer and searched his face. Though he longed for nothing more than to take her into his arms and tell her it would be all right, he hardened his heart for what he was to do next. It was more difficult than he had expected.

"I—I … do not…"

Tears brimmed her eyes. She held a finger up to his lips. "Do not do this, please … I beg you."

"To let what is between us grow stronger would be a mistake, for that is surely what would happen. We need to end it here and now."

A solitary tear rolled down her right cheek. Mae's tone was anguished when she spoke. "You cannot mean that." She placed a hand against his chest.

"We were meant to be together."

"I do." Eli could not believe he was turning her away. This was perhaps one of the most difficult things he had ever done. He could see no other choice, no clear path that would lead to anything but heartbreak and suffering. He knew he could not handle that. She deserved better than him. "I am decided. There is no us."

"No."

"There is someone out there for you and it is not me, someone who will bring you happiness."

Mae stared at him in what he could only describe as abject horror. Her mouth opened as if to speak, then closed. Her jaw clenched, tightening ever so slightly. A vein on her temple throbbed almost violently. Then she did the unexpected. Mae moved so fast Eli never saw her fist coming. It hammered into his jaw, hard, and sent him reeling. Tripping over a small stone, he fell to the ground, landing on his butt. He sat there for a moment, stunned.

He looked up at her. "You hit me! I cannot believe you hit me."

Chest heaving, she stood over him, gazing downward. Eli reached a hand to his jaw and winced in pain as their eyes met. Hers flashed with a mounting thunderhead of rage. She landed a kick hard into his side. Eli gave a grunt from the unexpected blow. She moved to kick him again. His shock shifted instinctively to action. Hastily, he grabbed her supporting leg and jerked, pulling with all his might. She fell to the ground next to him.

Immediately, she moved to spring back to her feet. Eli lashed out with a foot, knocking her back down before she could complete the move. Mae rolled into him next. A fist lashed out into his stomach before he could block it, eliciting another grunt, and nearly stole his breath. He caught her next attack, forcing it aside, then seized one of her wrists. Trying to break his grip, she rolled into and then onto him. Eli's grip was firm, unbreakable.

"Stop it," Eli said, shaking her. "I—said—stop."

Instead of replying, Mae growled as if she were a wild animal caught in a snare as she struggled violently against his grip. With her free hand, she delivered another hammer blow to the side of his left cheek. Eli managed to grab her other wrist after that. She gave a violent jerk to break free and failed. With all his effort, he rolled her onto her side and then onto her back, until he was atop her. She struggled wildly as he tried to hold her still, to keep her from striking him again.

"Calm down." Eli tasted the strong tang of copper. He spat out a gob of blood onto the ground next to her. He felt like he'd bitten his tongue. "I said, calm down!"

She fought against his grip of steel. He was amazed at how strong she was. A moment later, Mae broke an arm free, and before he could grab it again, she punched him in the nose. Eli's head snapped back. Pain exploded, and for a moment, his vision went white, then she broke free and threw him off her.

Blinking and partially stunned, Eli scrambled to his feet and stumbled backward. She was already on hers. He shook his head, trying to focus and clear some of the fog away.

"Perhaps…" Eli said, taking another step away and touching his nose gingerly, exploring the damage. His fingers came away bloody, but the nose felt sound, with nothing broken. That was a relief, for Eli particularly liked the shape of his nose. He held up both hands to her, palms outward. "Perhaps we should take a moment to talk about us."

"You already had that chance. Besides, your mind is set on the matter. It's my turn to do the talking and I intend to make my point felt."

Eli wriggled his nose slightly as he felt it again. "I think you already did."

Mae's jaw clenched and she came forward on the attack.

Eli blocked a blow aimed at his face and took another step back. She followed after him like an enraged bull. He countered several strikes, then hit back, striking her a hard blow on the cheek.

"Bastard," she hissed, taking a step back and baring her teeth at him.

Uh oh, Eli thought.

"I did not mean that," Eli said hastily as he took another two steps back. "Well, I mean I, ah, sort of meant to hit you, but I did not mean to hurt you."

Mae didn't say anything but followed after him as he retreated some more.

"Hurting you is the last thing I wish to do."

"Oh really?" Mae scoffed.

Eli knew he had to find a way to get through to her, to stop this insanity. He hardened his tone. "I am no longer playing with you, Mae. Besides, you drew first blood. You began this."

"I am not playing either," Mae replied and lunged, renewing her attack. After dodging and countering several strikes, kicks, and punches thrown at him, she landed a solid kick to his side.

It hurt.

Dancing sideways, Eli replied with a kick of his own. It smacked against her thigh. She grimaced but it only seemed to increase her rage and desire to hurt him. After that, they continued at it for some time, strike, block, strike, hit.

In short order, Eli found himself becoming badly winded, panting as he worked to fend her off. She was a fury, relentless, an enraged tempest, and, in truth, one of the most capable opponents he had ever faced. He could not believe how fast she moved.

Short of drawing blades, he did not see how this would end. Despite the pain and exhaustion, he found himself admiring her spirit and passion, her drive, more and more with every passing moment. The funk that had hung over him the last few days had gone. In its place was excitement and something else … desire?

Eli took two hasty steps backward and held out a hand.

"Stop. Please. Let's talk about this some more."

Battered and bloody from a small cut on her forehead, Mae took a staggering step toward him, clearly with the intent to continue. There were tears freely rolling down her cheeks. She lowered her hands.

"You cast me aside as if I do not matter," Mae said. "I gave you my heart, the thing most precious I have to offer, and you broke it."

Mae gave a sob, wiped the tears from her eyes, then balled her fists again and raised them.

"I've had enough," Eli added. "Please, I have had enough."

"I"—she took a deep breath, for she was just as winded as he was—"don't think you"—another heavy breath—"have."

She bared her teeth at him again, like a feral animal, and came forward. Eli backed up farther. He was now becoming alarmed. So far, their wounds were minor and easily tended to. If he allowed this to continue, one of them was bound to become seriously injured. He could not allow that to happen, for they had a mission to complete. But he saw no way to stop it from reaching that point.

"I could have handled this better," Eli admitted as he continued to back up.

"You have that right." Mae only seemed to become more enraged. The tears had stopped, and her eyes flashed with rage. In that moment, he thought her the most beautiful person he had ever seen, and it fired his attraction. With grim purpose, she began advancing again.

"So be it, she-devil," he said, coming to a stop. He flashed her a full-on grin, one he knew would provoke her further. Eli felt a stir of worry at what he was about to attempt, along with terrible excitement. He felt his grin grow wider. "You want to play with fire? Let us play then. Bring it on, warden's daughter. Let us see what you have left."

Murder plain in her gaze, Mae growled and charged. Eli waited until the last moment of contact, then deftly stepped to the side, sticking out a leg. It was an attempt to trip. His leg connected solidly with hers. His move almost succeeded. Mae reacted with lightning-fast speed. As she was going down, she latched firmly onto his arm and, using her momentum, took him with her to the ground.

They hit hard and in a tumble. She seemed stunned. Taking advantage of the opportunity before she could react, Eli rolled bodily atop her. He wrapped his arms around her in a bear hug, pinning her, and once again found himself on top. She recovered and just looked up at him. It seemed, finally, the fight had gone out of her. Eli felt a wave of tremendous relief. Breathing heavily, they both stared at one another for a long moment. Then, Eli leaned forward and kissed her.

At first, she resisted, then she gave into him. For Eli, it was as if time had stopped. After several moments, they pulled apart, Eli staring down at her and she up at him, her eyes wide.

"I love you," he said and meant every word. "I truly do."

"You love me?" Her voice was suddenly dripping with sweetness. "I love you too, you bastard."

A heartbeat later, her knee found his groin and Eli knew pain.

CHAPTER TWO

Eli shifted slightly. Mae's arm was wrapped almost protectively across his chest. It felt good to have her hold him. Gently, so as not to wake her, he lifted her arm off his chest and set it aside. She murmured something softly in her sleep and rolled over onto her side, placing her back to him. Murmuring ever so softly, she pulled the blanket tighter about herself and then fell still once again.

The sky had lightened. Soon, the sun would rise over the east ridge of the valley and the day would begin in earnest. Eli lay there, staring up at the brightening sky, the fading stars, and the moon hanging high overhead, a pock-marked, silent sentinel. Without exception or interruption, every night the moon rose and crossed the sky. It was one of the few constants in Eli's world and, like the sun coming up, he took comfort in it, for the passing of time changed all things.

Eli had hardly slept a wink all night. He massaged his neck. It was stiff and sore, mostly from his fight with Mae, but some of it was from sleeping upon the hard ground. His nose still stung from where she had hit him the day before. Whoever said love hurt had not been joking. She had given him a good and thorough drubbing, one he would not soon forget.

Perhaps, Eli reflected, he had deserved it too—maybe a little. He had acted without fully thinking things through. That had gotten him into trouble on more than one occasion.

It had taken their fight for him to truly admit to himself how deeply he cared for Mae, how much she had come to mean to him. And he did love her. He understood that now. There was no denying it, not anymore. He loved her more than he dared to admit to himself or anyone else. When he kissed Mae, it almost felt like he was losing himself with her.

How had it happened?

That was the part that mystified him. It was one puzzle he was not quite sure he would ever solve. In truth, he wasn't too sorry about that either. Their mutual feelings were a fact, a new reality. There was no disputing that. In the end, how they felt about one another was all that really mattered.

Still asleep, Mae rolled over onto her back. Eli shifted onto his side and for a time watched her as she slept, her chest rising and falling with pleasing regularity. Mae's hair was loose and lay about her. Cast in the growing light of dawn, she was so beautiful, it made his heart ache. And though she had a warrior's heart, in her sleep, Mae looked at peace, like an innocent maiden, or a fabled angel that was spoken of in some religions. He almost reached out to her but stopped himself. Eli did not want to disturb this perfect moment.

Oddly, Eli felt at peace too. The funk that had gripped him over the past few days was gone, vanished as if it had never been. Staring at her, he knew he would well remember this perfect moment, treasure it even, for years to come.

What had he done?

A panic gripped him. What he had done was madness, he knew that. She had to know it too.

What had they done? That was the better question. Even before he had mentally asked it, the rational part of his mind knew the answer.

That his father and Mae's mother, his people's warden, might object gave Eli more than a little pause for thought. Both could cause serious complications for him and Mae. Still, what was done was done. Like water under a bridge, there was no taking it back. Even if he wanted to, which he didn't, he understood Mae would not let him.

Laying his blanket aside, Eli sat up. He took a moment to rub the last vestiges of sleep from his eyes before quietly pulling himself to his feet. The stones he had placed around their small fire, which had gone out sometime in the night, still radiated some heat. Eli poked at the ash, revealing the hot embers underneath, and held out his hands for warmth.

Breath steaming in the cold air, he took a moment to stretch out his back, then stifled a yawn. He felt the chill of the dawning morning through his tunic and gave an involuntary shiver.

Fall was nearly at hand. In just a matter of weeks, the temperature would drop even further, and then it would really get cold. The snow would arrive soon after and everything would freeze hard, until spring.

He glanced around the natural clearing they had camped in. Bordered by thick pines, it was quite secluded. After a search the previous evening, they had confirmed the valley was uninhabited. There had been no sign of hunters or trappers having recently ventured into the valley, at least any they could readily find. A more thorough search during daylight would confirm that, but they likely would not be staying, so there would be no point. They had only needed a temporary refuge for the night and this spot had fit that need admirably.

A few feet away, through a stand of pines, was a good-sized waterfall. The falling water made a pleasant, peaceful sound. It was why they had chosen the spot for their camp, a little hidden paradise, a gem for the two of them to exclusively enjoy.

He looked down at Mae. Her blanket was pulled up to just below the top of her bare shoulders. With his eyes, he followed the form of her body under the blanket and felt a thrill of excitement shoot through him.

So beautiful, so perfect and—he was so lucky, so very fortunate.

The night before they had made passionate love. He vividly recalled her skin pressing closely against his in the throes of ecstasy. The memory of it excited him. Eli suddenly realized, with incredible clarity, he had never cared for anyone more than he did her, now, in this very moment. He found that realization troubling, even frightening, and yet at the same time abundantly right.

Sparing one last glance at Mae, Eli stripped off his tunic and turned away toward the waterfall. He needed a bath before they set out. Moving through the stand of pines barefoot, Eli padded over to the river's edge. He stepped out onto a flat boulder that jutted out into the waterfall's pool. Cold spray cascaded over him, causing an involuntary shiver.

Thinking of the bitter cold that waited, he hesitated, then stepped down into the water. His feet sank into the slimy bottom. The ice-cold water shocked his system, but he forced himself to keep going, moving deeper into the wide and frothy pool of water beneath the falls.

When he was slightly more than waist-deep, he fully submerged himself, then stood up and gasped at the shock, sucking in a deep breath. The cold was invigorating and had the desired effect. He was now completely awake.

"Gods," Eli hissed, "that is cold."

He began vigorously scrubbing at his skin and running his hands through his hair, cleaning himself. Most elves prized cleanliness and Eli was no different than the rest. After he was satisfied with his efforts, he swam out to the center of the wide pool, treaded water for a moment, then dove down to the bottom.

His hand touched a sunken log. It felt slimy with underwater growth and mud. Though he could not see it in the murk and churn of bubbles from the falling water overhead, Eli estimated the depth of the pool to be around twenty feet. He swam back up and surfaced, exhaling a great breath like a whale.

Treading water, he spotted Mae crouched down at the water's edge, silent, watching. Body firm and lithe, she was completely naked and studying him, as a predator might moments before the kill. For several heartbeats, he just admired her perfection and once more thought himself exceptionally, even uncommonly, blessed.

"How blind have I been?" Eli whispered to himself.

"Want company?" Mae asked him.

"The water is cold," Eli cautioned.

"Shall I ask again?"

She did not wait for an answer, but slowly moved into the pool. Eli watched as the water rose steadily up her shapely calves to her thighs. Then the water was to her hips, belly, and finally just above her chest, until only her neck and head remained above the water. She dove and disappeared beneath the surface.

Moments later, she reappeared just before him, her hair slicked back and glistening under the early morning light. They eyed one another for a long moment, then with both hands, Eli reached out and pulled her to him. Feeling her wet, naked body against his, he had a terrible moment of pure desire overcome him. He kissed her with passion. She kissed him back. Then with a laugh, twisting in his arms and using her feet, she roughly pushed him away and dove down again, once more disappearing.

Moments later, she broke the surface by the pool's edge. Mae offered him a sultry smile and then turned her back to him as she began to emerge from the water, slowly walking up to the shore. Dripping wet, her hair trailing down her back, she turned slightly and winked. She laughed again, a pleasant sound, then beckoned with a finger.

Eli did not need to be asked twice. He swam to the shore and followed her out of the water. She stood waiting for him, where they had made camp. Nipples erect from the cold, her body glistened under the first rays of the newborn day's sunlight. He stepped nearer to her and reached out, cupping her cheek with a hand as he gazed into her eyes. They were so deep, he thought he might lose himself.

Unexpectedly, she broke contact and took a step back.

"What?" he asked, confused. "What's wrong, my love?"

"Do you love me? Do you really love me?" Her expression was quite earnest.

"Yes."

"Then, I would hear it said," Mae breathed, softly. "The words of bonding, the custom of our people to formalize that which is between us and always will be."

Eli was silent as he regarded her, thinking through what she was asking.

"I would hear you speak the words," she insisted.

"We have bonded," Eli replied. "No matter what words are spoken, our union has been consummated. You know this."

"True, it has been," Mae admitted, "but every girl wants to hear the words from her lover, and I am no different. With the gods listening, I need to hear you speak them. I want to have the questions posed." She paused and her tone grew rock-hard. "I demand it."

Eli stared at her for a heartbeat. Who was he to deny her wish? Going forward, he would do his very best to see her happy. No, he would *make* her happy. He could imagine himself with no one else, ever again.

"With the gods listening, I pledge myself to you. I pledge my steadfast and everlasting love, my heart, all that I am and will be." Eli fell silent as he sucked in a breath of the cool morning air, then continued with the ritual words. "Mae'Cara, will you take me in union and complete the bond that has grown between us? Will you have me until death separates us both and we are once again reunited in the next life?" Eli hesitated again. It had not seemed quite real, until he had begun speaking the hallowed words, just how permanent things would be between them. "Through marriage, will you join my family and yours in union? I offer myself wholly and without reservation. I promise to love, cherish, and honor you till my dying breath. I ask you to take me. Will you have me?"

Mae did not hesitate.

"I do willingly join my family and yours in union. I accept you, Eli'Far," Mae breathed. "With the gods listening, I accept you with all of my heart and soul. I take you as my husband, for now and evermore. No one will come between us, ever. On this, I swear it so. Will you have me?"

"I accept you," Eli said, "as my wife for now and evermore. No one will ever come between us. Upon my ancestors, I swear it so."

Eyes brimming with unshed tears, Mae moved forward and embraced him, holding him tight. Their lips met and she kissed him with a fierce passion that caught Eli by surprise, but not for long.

When they came up for air, Eli had a stab of pure panic as he gazed into her eyes, which were filled with love for him. He had joined himself to the warden's daughter and made an unbreakable promise. Si'Cara was perhaps the most powerful, dangerous, and feared person amongst the High Born, maybe even the world itself.

What had he just done?

She kissed him again and Eli forgot his concerns, his worries. Then, inadvertently, she pressed his nose hard with her cheek. Wincing from pain, Eli pulled away slightly. She looked up at him as he wriggled his nose and resisted a sneeze.

"Does it hurt?" Mae reached up a tender hand, which stopped just before touching.

"It's not too bad." Eli gave a slight shrug of his shoulders, then could not help himself. "Let's be honest, you hit like a girl."

"I am a girl," Mae said, hardening her tone.

"You make my point for me." Eli grinned at her.

"Would you like me to hit you again?" Mae's tone had become ice-cold and laced with danger. "Do you need another lesson in humility? I think I could arrange that, husband."

"Ah." Eli held up a hand, palm outward. "No thank you. I believe I've learned my lesson just fine. Let us not do that again, ever."

"Good. I was beginning to suspect you would need a reminder." Mae suddenly seemed amused. "Perhaps, after all, an old dog can learn new tricks?"

"Did you just call me a dog?" Eli asked in a scandalized tone. "I'm not sure whether to take offense at being called a dog, or old for that matter. Old is one whose age is advanced, like Rivun'Cur."

Mae grinned at him. "Come, husband. Let us consummate our marriage once more before we set out this morning and continue the hunt."

Then she was pulling him toward the blankets, and he wanted only one thing. Her.

CHAPTER THREE

The lake's water was crystal clear and the surface perfectly flat, without even a hint of a wave or ripple. Standing close to the water's edge, Eli had the feeling that he was staring into another world. In a way he was, he supposed, for he could see right down to the rock-studded bottom.

The sky was as blue as could be, with a brilliant sun hanging almost dead center overhead. Despite the unobstructed sunlight, the air was crisp. Across the lake, the first of the trees had begun to change color, from a light green to a bright yellow. And like a polished mirror, the still water perfectly reflected the far tree line.

Before shedding their leaves, soon, more of the trees would begin their miraculous transformation of color. Just the thought of it, nature's sheer beauty, made his heart ache. If you knew where to look, you could find beauty nearly anywhere, and over the long years, Eli had become a master at it.

He turned his gaze back to the water before him, carefully searching.

"What are you looking at?" Mae asked with interest from a few feet away. With a sigh of relief, she dropped her pack next to a large granite boulder. She leaned her unstrung bow against it as well. She took out her canteen from her pack, unstopped it, and drank deeply.

"The correct question is"—Eli looked over at Mae, admiring her for a long moment before turning back to the lake—"what am I looking for?"

"Well, then, husband of mine, whatever are you looking for?" Mae stopped closed the canteen then dropped it at her feet next to her pack. "Since we are playing games, know that I await your answer with bated breath."

Eli glanced back at her again. Amongst everything he'd seen, she was the most beautiful of all. Almost sheepishly, he admitted, "I was checking to see if there were fish in the lake."

"I am shocked." From Mae's expression, she was none too surprised. With the back of her forearm, she wiped sweat from her brow. She looked back the way they had just come. "The hike up here was brutal. This plateau was really difficult to get to."

"It was," Eli agreed, "and it is. I doubt very many have made the effort to come up here."

"See any?"

"See any what?" Eli asked, suddenly confused. "Other people?"

"No. Why, fish, of course. For the past two weeks, any significant body of water has drawn your interest. You have been dying to look for an opportunity to dig up a few worms and drop a hooked line into the water. Tell me that is not so."

Eli knew she was right. He was always looking for a chance, or really an excuse, to get some fishing in, and the lake before them was no exception.

"So, have you seen any fish?"

"Sadly, no." Eli looked out across the water. He figured it was four hundred yards to the other side. The lake was bordered entirely by trees. It was fed at the far end by a small waterfall, which looked quite scenic. In fact, the entire plateau they had climbed up to was scenic, tranquil even. "I don't see much vegetation at the bottom. I suppose it is possible there are fish"—Eli thought for a long moment—"no ... it is *likely* there are fish here. The trick will be finding them."

"Big ones?" Mae asked, clearly struggling not to grin at him. "Or small ones?"

"You are not into fishing, are you?" Eli asked.

"You already know the answer to that question," Mae chided.

"Do I?" Eli asked innocently. He did. On more than one occasion he had invited her to join him. At each opportunity, she had declined. Mae was more into hunting than anything else.

She gave him an amused nod. "You know only too well that I do not find much enjoyment in the activity. Dropping a hook baited with worms does not seem very sporting to me. Fish just see food and bite."

Eli resisted a scowl. "Fishing can be quite difficult. It is not as easy as you might think. It requires skill and an understanding of fish."

"Is that so?"

"The lake is certainly large enough for good-sized fish." Eli crouched down and dipped a hand into the water, disturbing the surface with tiny ripples spreading outward. The water was terribly cold and made his fingers ache. He cupped it with his hand and brought it to his lips, drinking. "The water seems fresh enough."

Mae glanced over the lake's surface. "Well, our supplies are beginning to run low. Fresh fish would be a welcome treat for dinner. I might even offer to cook your catch."

"Oh?" Eli perked up at that. Mae was an excellent cook, and when it came to fish, she was a master. His mouth began to water at just the thought of dinner, which, at best, was several hours off. They'd had nothing but their dwindling rations for days now.

"That is, if you can catch something."

"Now that," Eli said, "sounds like a challenge to me."

"Perhaps it is. Take it as you will."

"So, if I catch something—you will cook it?"

"If you ask me nicely," Mae said. "I believe you know the word."

As if thinking quite hard, Eli eyed her for a long moment. "You mean, please? That is the word of which you speak?"

"So, you have heard of the power, or should I say magic, of that simple word. Many have not."

"It might surprise you, but I have. My mother raised me with manners."

"That is most excellent news," Mae said. "I believe there is hope for you yet."

Eli rubbed his hands together and glanced over at the lake again, this time eagerly. "If there are fish, I am going to find them. On that I promise."

"Perhaps," Mae said, "I might even help you catch us some of that dinner."

Eli looked over at her again, this time with genuine surprise. "I thought you did not enjoy fishing?"

"Are you declining an offer of not only my company but my assistance?" Mae arched an eyebrow at him. There was a dangerous look in her gaze, a warning. "Really? Tell me it is not so."

"Allow me to rephrase that," Eli said hastily. This was one instance he was unwilling to tempt fate. She might withdraw her offer. Who knew, perhaps she might even learn to enjoy fishing. "Your sudden enthusiasm for one of my passions has simply caught me by surprise. I would welcome your assistance and companionship, oh beautiful and wise wife of mine."

For a moment, amusement danced in her eyes. Then she looked back to the lake. Mae's gaze clouded over like a rainy day. It lasted but a moment, though Eli recognized it for what it was. She was worried about the future, their future, what was to come in the days, weeks, and months that lay ahead.

So too was he.

Mae ran her eyes slowly around the lake. She visibly breathed in the cool air, taking a deep breath. A heartbeat later, she let it out slowly through her nose. She did not speak for several moments, before looking back at him and meeting his gaze.

"This is a pleasant enough spot. I believe I would like to spend the night here."

"Your wish on this matter is my command," Eli said. "We shall camp in this very spot, and you are correct. This is a pleasant place. It is—calming to the soul."

Mae eyed him with suspicion. "Have you been here before?"

"As in, did I bring you to this lake intentionally?" Eli asked.

"The thought had crossed my mind. Well, did you? Tell me."

"I would like to say I did do so, but that would be partially misleading." Eli moved over to her. He shrugged off his pack and dropped it at her feet. He then leaned his bow against the rock, next to hers. He rolled his shoulders and cracked his neck before continuing. "I have not been here before, to this plateau." He pointed off to the east. "I am familiar with the land a few miles from here, specifically a valley. There is a small village there called Arvan'Dale."

"Arvan'Dale?" Mae tried out the name. "That has a nice sound to it."

"Arvan'Dale is a mean place, filled with unhappy and untrustworthy humans," Eli said, then conceded, "at least, it was the last time I was there."

"How long ago was that exactly?"

"Fifty or sixty years—at the least. Given time, all things change. But, when it comes to Arvan'Dale, I think not so much. I have little desire to return."

"Still, we could have gone there," Mae said, "and even though it is unlikely, we might have learned something of those we pursue."

"True." Eli considered making a smart comment to deflect, to get off the subject of the village, then thought better of it. Instead, he settled for the truth. "I really wanted to see what was up here and—to avoid that village. My last visit left me with unhappy memories, ones I have no desire to dig up." He waved a hand at the lake and waterfall. "Besides, it seems my curiosity has been well rewarded."

Mae studied him for a long moment before speaking. "I thought it might be something like that, especially since we've lost their trail." She paused and chewed her lower lip. "We are going to turn back, at some point, then?"

Eli reflected that she was getting to know him only too well. He wondered how long it would be before they were finishing each other's sentences, for surely with time that would come.

"I figure we will travel north a dozen or so miles to a pass that I know. It will help us avoid some rugged terrain. The pass takes us back east a dozen or more miles. From there we will find one of our roads running north and south, which we can easily pick up."

"The Karven Son?" Mae asked. "That is the road of which you speak, yes?"

"You are familiar with it?" Eli asked, knowing she likely was, for learning such knowledge of the wider world would have been part of her training.

"Only by study," Mae admitted. "You well know, until this expedition, I have never been outside the confines of our lands. Everything we see and do out here is new to me. I find that to be refreshing—mostly."

Eli conceded that point by offering her a slight nod. He knew she was haunted by what had happened around the town of Brek. The distasteful things they had both been required to do were not easily shaken off.

"If I recall," Mae continued, "the Karven Son is the oldest road in the region. It was laid down soon after our people came to this world." She paused, as if thinking some. "Mik'Las will likely know of this road as well."

"I believe he would," Eli said. "At the least, like you, knowledge of it would have come to him through his training. There is no telling whether he has ever used the road or seeks to do so to make his escape."

"That is what I thought." Mae fell silent for several heartbeats as a hawk glided down from above and skimmed across the surface of the lake, mere inches from the water. Her eyes tracked the graceful creature. Flapping its wings, the bird climbed slightly and landed in a tree on the southern end of the lake. "And if they avoided the roads in this region? Say they went overland? It is what I would do to throw off pursuit, to slip away."

"Then we will have to think of something else. Do you have a better idea?"

"I do not," Mae admitted. "In truth, we really have no idea where he—they are headed or, for that matter, what their thinking is. Do you disagree?"

"I do not. What you say is true."

"What of the tracks we were following?" Mae asked him. "I am curious as to who was using one of our roads."

"So too am I. For more than a week we have seen no evidence of those tracks either." Eli felt troubled by the knowledge that some unknown person was using their road. "We have lost them as well. There is a good chance we will never know the answer to that particular mystery."

"Some rangers we are," Mae said. "The two of us make quite a pair."

"From the onset, we knew this mission would not be an easy one. We are following someone as skilled as we when it comes to the craft of a ranger. Mik'Las is not so easily tracked, let alone caught."

"I know," Mae said.

"We have come close to Mik'Las and the Atreena, Sariss'Sa. We will do so again. The passage of time will see the truth of that."

"Then," Mae said, with a heavy breath, "we will do as you suggest and check the roads first."

Eli did not bother to reply. In his mind, it was the only route open to them. They needed to rule out the obvious. That would allow them to narrow things down, to eliminate those easy avenues of flight and eventually close in on their quarry. She knew that as well. They were just getting it out in the open, was all, voicing the difficult nature, complications, and concerns each had of their mission.

"Perhaps we might remain here a day, rest, recuperate, and explore the area." Mae's gaze went to the waterfall. "I believe I"—she looked over at him—"*we* might enjoy this place before we move on. Do you see a problem with doing that?"

"As you said earlier, our supplies are low. We need to hunt some anyway," Eli said, glancing around at the trees. "There is plenty of game around, that's for certain."

Mae gave him a pleased smile. "I saw a deer track not too far off. I could go for some venison."

"Do you wish to hunt now? Or later?"

"Later," Mae said. "I believe I would like to explore this enchanting place first, to look around the lake, perhaps even take some time to reach out to the Mother and commune. It has been some time since I have done that." Her gaze traveled back to the lake. "Though the water is likely cold, a swim might be in order too. Maybe I'll take a dip first and wash some of the sweat and grime of the day off."

"Then," Eli said, untying his pack and pulling out his fishing line and pouch full of hooks, "I will get a start on catching us some dinner. That will require finding some worms." He began to look around for a good spot to dig.

Mae's expression turned to one of amusement. "As long as you watch where you cast that line. When I go for a swim, do not hook me while you are at it."

Eli turned his gaze to her and full-on grinned. "There is little fear of that, my love. I believe I already have caught the catch of my life."

Chapter Four

Eli shifted his position, going from kneeling to sitting cross-legged on the partially submerged boulder, which was about seven feet from the water's edge. To reach it from the shore, he'd had to make a series of precarious jumps from smaller rocks. The top of the boulder was nearly flat, raised a foot above the water, and made the perfect perch from which to fish.

He stretched his back out for a long moment. His gaze traveled out across the lake. A gentle breeze had begun blowing some time before, gusting lightly across the surface of the water, creating tiny waves. Sunlight reflected back in a dazzling display of brilliance.

Eli enjoyed the view for several heartbeats, then carefully rolled up his fishing line and tied the end securely in a knot around the rest of the line. There were a couple of good-sized bass lying next to him. He was rather proud of his catch.

Both were beautiful fish and would make a fine meal this evening, a veritable feast after the last few days of bland traveling rations. Mae would be suitably impressed. Well, to be honest, he was not quite sure about that. Nothing was ever certain when it came to Mae. At least, he hoped she would be.

Eli had caught five fish in total and thrown three back. The last three were just for the fun of it. To keep them would have been wasteful and Eli was not about such things.

There was just something about casting a baited line into the water that spoke to his soul. Perhaps it was the quiet peace, the relaxation, the time to think and contemplate matters both large and small—he loved it all. He also enjoyed the challenge, for sometimes the fish, for whatever reason, just did not bite. It required skill to encourage them to do so, and Eli had grown to be a master when it came to finding the best places to cast a line and baiting a hook.

Across the lake, near the waterfall, there was a faint splash. Mae had just jumped from a large boulder. He watched for a few moments as she surfaced, treaded water for a bit, then swam back to the rock. She climbed out of the water before jumping back in.

Watching her, he was reminded of a child playing in the water. She seemed to be thoroughly enjoying the moment. One of the things he loved about Mae was her spirit. It couldn't be suppressed, and it was a quality that helped make her a superb ranger.

Placing both palms upon the rock and continuing to watch, Eli leaned back. The afternoon sun had warmed the rock and it felt good against his hands, not too hot or cold.

Not only was he relaxed, but Eli found himself content, at least for the moment. It had been a long while since he'd felt that way. There was a natural magic to this place that eased one's spirits. He supposed his relationship with Mae also helped with that.

Eli stifled a yawn and decided a nap was in order, a short one at least. Then, he fully intended to set up camp, start their campfire, and clean his catch, hopefully all before Mae returned and discovered him lazing about and napping.

Eli closed his eyes and turned his face to the sun, enjoying the warmth. He let out a long breath that was more of a sigh than anything else. Eli felt his brows draw together. Something was not quite right, and perhaps even wrong. Where a moment before there had been the sounds of birds and bugs, now there was a near deafening silence coming from the trees behind him. It could mean only one thing.

He was not alone.

Resisting the urge to turn and look, he slowly sat up and repositioned himself so that, should he need to, he could spring to his feet. Eli turned his gaze back to Mae, who had jumped into the water once again. He was making it appear as if nothing was wrong and he was simply watching her from across the lake.

Eli was seriously concerned. He was straining his senses and hoping, without giving himself away, to find the location of whoever was there, somewhere behind him.

Was harm intended?

His sword and bow were where he had left his pack. That did not mean he was helpless. Far from it. Eli was deadly when it came to hand-to-hand fighting. He also had his two daggers with him and was equally as lethal with them as he was with a sword. To tangle with him was to flirt with death.

Still, he had not heard anyone approach and that was not a good sign. No one should have been able to sneak up on him. Eli ran his gaze around the lake once more, making a full show of it, as if he was simply enjoying the view and had not a care in the world.

This place was incredibly beautiful and peaceful to the soul. It reminded him very much of the Task'Umaul Holdout. The caretaker was one of the few who could sneak up on him unawares and, now that he thought on it, the two places had striking and uncanny similarities. Both seemed to be refuges. He recalled Karenna's statement that the caretaker had other places where he resided.

Was this one of those special places?

Much like the holdout, it was certainly difficult to get to. The lake was secluded, a hidden gem, and there was not a soul living within miles. If there had been, he and Mae would have come across evidence of someone passing through the area to trap, hunt, or fish. They had seen none of that. The only prints they had come across had been animal tracks. The lake was also quite peaceful, more than most places he'd been.

Eli visualized the terrain behind him, recalling it from memory. If it came to a fight, that knowledge would prove invaluable. There was a small grassy bank, then the tree line, and some brush between them.

Eli gave it some more thought. He suspected that whoever it was was likely hiding in the brush. That would provide the best cover.

"I know you are there," Eli said in the common tongue without bothering to look. He was taking a risk, but felt it was worth it, at least to catch the other party off guard.

There was no reply. Nothing stirred amongst the trees and brush behind him. That gave Eli pause.

"Is this your place, like the holdout?" Eli asked, taking a chance it might be the caretaker.

"It saddens me to admit this pleasant spot is not my place."

Eli went very still. It was a voice he did not know, and it had been spoken in fluent Elven, though with a strange, lilting accent. So as not to alarm whoever was behind him, Eli slowly stood. He turned around and found another elf standing on the bank, just before the trees.

"And this is nothing like the Task'Umaul Holdout," the other elf said, "if that is what you are asking, cousin. For one thing, there is no Gray Field about to guard."

The newcomer wore a well-cut midnight-black robe, which flowed down and around him. His hair was black, combed to perfection, and had been pulled back into a ponytail. A thin gold circlet, encrusted with small blue crystals, rested upon his head. Even in the sunlight, the crystals gave off a dull glow. The circlet reminded Eli very much of the crown the warden wore.

He carried a staff, one of the most incredible things Eli had ever seen. It was a crystalline miracle no mortal hand could have ever crafted, and that included those elves who had the gift to grow and shape crystals to their will.

The staff throbbed with internal light and was etched with arcane runes. The hand that gripped the shaft looked to have been badly burned. To say this newcomer looked out of place standing on the edge of the lake in the middle of nowhere was an understatement.

But none of that was what had caught Eli's full attention. The other's face had. Eli blinked, wondering if he was dreaming. He could not believe his eyes. It was like he was looking into a mirror and seeing himself.

No, that was not quite right.

He was looking at an older version of himself. He could see the age and untold years reflected in the other's gaze. And the eyes were hardened, as if in their time they had seen much suffering, too much perhaps. Eli could understand that. Still, he found he could not look away…for the face was a mirror of his own.

"You seem to be at a loss for words. Is that a first for you?" the newcomer asked.

"What do you want?" Eli asked, deciding to be blunt. He did not feel like playing games, for there was a certain menace about this newcomer that made his skin crawl.

"Now that is a very broad question, for I desire a great many things."

"I'll ask again," Eli said and hardened his tone. "What do you want with me?"

"At this very moment, just to talk for a bit," the elf said.

"You wish only to talk?" Eli asked. "That is all?"

"If I meant you harm, you would already be dead without knowing it. I suspect you sense that possibility."

"You are a wizard?" Eli asked, for in his mind there was no other explanation for how the other dressed. And there was both the circlet and staff as evidence. Both were clearly magical, and Eli had seen other such items in the past.

The elf gave a slight incline of his head as his acknowledgement.

"I did not realize there were elven wizards on this world," Eli said. "At least I have not heard of one. Is the warden aware of your presence?"

"I am sure there are a great many things you have not heard or, for that matter, are even aware of," the elf said. "And no. Si'Cara is unaware of my presence upon this plane, and I would prefer it to remain that way, at least for now."

The breeze returned at that moment and stirred the trees. The wizard ran his gaze across the lake, surface glimmering with reflected sunlight. Eli felt himself tense. The wizard's gaze had stopped on Mae, who was still swimming near the waterfall. Eli doubted she could see the wizard from her current position halfway down the lake.

Did he mean her harm?

"I rarely have the time to enjoy such peaceful settings," the wizard said, breathing out and then seeming to inhale the scent of the forest. "This is such a lovely place."

"Who are you?"

"I am known by many names. The most prominent and one I think appropriate is High Master of Obsidian."

Eli's heart almost stopped. High Masters were wizards of unparalleled power. That one was here speaking with him could not be good news.

"That makes you a direct disciple of a god, yes?" Eli asked.

Obsidian inclined his head once again.

"Which one?" Eli asked.

"Does it matter?"

Eli gave it a moment's thought. "I suppose not. Clearly you represent one of the gods our people honor. At least, I hope you do. It might prove unhealthy for me should you serve a dark master."

There was a flicker in the other's gaze. It was there just a moment, but Eli thought it might be amusement. "In general, your assumption is a correct one. I support *our* alignment. But in the end, I do what I do for our people and our people alone, who have been scattered and broken by war without end. That is truly the heart of my efforts, my focus, and my energies."

"You speak of the Last War?" Eli asked.

"I do." Obsidian looked up at the sky. His gaze lingered there for a long moment, as if he was gathering his thoughts, before returning to Eli. "After the First Ones, the High Born were once the foremost race. Our numbers were numerous beyond belief. We honored and worshipped all gods equally. But that was before we were forced to choose a side—before

the gods bickered and warred with one another. The Great
Mother, Kalelaleen, is gone, murdered by the enemy."

"Kalelaleen was real?" Eli asked before he could stop
himself.

Obsidian was silent several heartbeats. In the wizard's
gaze Eli read sadness. "Kalelaleen is all too real."

"You have been there?" Eli asked.

"I was born there."

That rocked Eli, shocking him to his core.

"It was once a paradise, a place of perfect balance, where
life thrived and there was peace. Now the home world is
only a ruin, an uninhabited monument to what once was.
Ancient trees and forests that sustained your ancestors are
no more. Nothing survives on Kalelaleen, not after the Last
War came calling."

Eli felt a wave of terrible sadness at such a thing coming to pass. To him and many others, Kalelaleen had always
been a mythical place, one he had not thought quite real.
To learn it existed was a shock. What was more shocking was
to hear that it was gone.

"The gods, in their infinite wisdom, did not want such a
thing to happen again, ever, for Kalelaleen is what is called a
Cradle World, the planet where our race was born. They put
in place what you might call rules that could not—well, let us
say—*should* not have been broken. Which is what brings me
to Istros and here to this lovely place—to see you, cousin."

Eli thought for a long moment. "Istros is no Cradle
World."

"She is not, at least not yet."

"You have somehow broken those rules, then," Eli
surmised.

"If you must know, a dear old friend broke them."
Obsidian heaved a sigh and within it was terrible sadness.

"He paid for his transgressions against the gods. In a way, I guess you could say he is still paying for his sins. And yet, his actions may just change the course of the war. Only time will tell us that, a time and place I may not visit or foresee." Obsidian paused. "But I digress. In answer to your question, let us say, in spirit, that I have simply bent the rules in support of a good cause."

"I'm not really sure I understand," Eli admitted.

"No, you wouldn't, not fully—not yet," Obsidian agreed. "Would you walk with me? I must soon leave, before my presence here, my *will*, is detected. That might cause consequences and an escalation I personally would prefer not to come to pass."

Without waiting for an answer, Obsidian turned and started walking into the trees, moving toward where Eli and Mae had left their packs. Eli hesitated a moment, then hastened to catch up. Leaving his catch of bass behind, along with his fishing line, Eli had to jump from rock to rock to reach the shore. A quick jog and he fell in at the wizard's side as they worked their way through the trees.

"You have met him?" Obsidian asked, and it was not really a question. "The man out of time."

"Bennulius Stiger," Eli said. "If that is who you speak of, then yes. I have met him. Like this one, it was an unexpected meeting."

"I should imagine so." Obsidian glanced over at Eli. "He should have given you something."

"A legionary short sword. He said it was a gift of friendship, a future friendship."

As they walked through the trees, Eli noticed that Obsidian's steps were silent. His robes did not even whisper against the ground or disturb the low-lying brush but seemed to pass right through them. And more intriguing, he left not a trace of his passage, no prints.

They emerged into the small clearing where he and Mae had left their packs. Eli's new sword was leaning against a rock, as was his bow, right where he had left them both. The wizard's gaze fell upon the sword, regarding the weapon for a long moment.

"Though he promised not to, the caretaker, as infuriating as he is, has interfered once again. This time, however, he may have done more good than harm." Obsidian did not sound awfully happy. "You see, he has set events in motion that will shake the very fabric of this world for centuries to come."

Eli did not reply. He was not quite sure what this wizard intended. Though he was an elf, that did not make him a friend, no matter what he said. Mik'Las was proof enough of that. Just like humans, elves could go bad too.

"You are a very persistent individual, Eli'Far." Obsidian turned to face him. "Sometimes too persistent."

"I will take that as a compliment," Eli said.

"It was not meant as a compliment. The caretaker chose you for a very specific purpose. So now you are my problem, and I, in a manner of speaking, am yours."

"For what?" Eli asked, not liking the sound of anything he was hearing. "What did he choose me for? Explain yourself."

"I have watched you for years now," Obsidian said. "You are a pain in the ass for many who know and love you. But, I believe you are well aware of that fact."

Eli did not grace the wizard with a reply.

"You love and cherish life but have no qualms taking it when necessary. You are ruthless in achieving your objectives. For your enemies, you are a veritable angel of death, a nightmare come to life—but deep down, you are also good of heart and a worthy choice, though, since I am being honest with you, you are not the one I would have made."

"A choice for what?" Eli was feeling lost, and he did not like that one bit. "What have I been chosen for?"

"My agent upon this world, of course," Obsidian said and looked over at the sword. He gestured at it with his staff. "Having arranged for that sword to come into your possession, the caretaker saw to that."

Eli glanced over at the sword, feeling alarm.

"That *gift* is a unique weapon, at least on Istros. You will not find another like it. Though it currently disguises itself as a common legionary short sword, it has been wielded by many before you and will be carried by many after. In short, you have been gifted a magical artifact from a previous age, one of great power—if handled correctly."

"The sword is magic?" Eli was not sure how he felt about that. His sense of alarm was growing by the moment. In his experience, magical items extracted a price from the user.

"Though it has several names, I, along with a few others, prefer to call your sword Memory."

"Memory?" Eli looked over at the weapon and fought off a scowl. "I'm not so sure that is a good name. In my experience, memory fades with time and that is never a good thing."

"For the High Born the passage of time sees all things change." Obsidian glanced over at Eli. "Still, I think it an apt name for your sword. With time, you may come to feel it appropriate too."

"Why?"

"All who have wielded that sword have been exceptional warriors, fighters, killers—a cut above the rest. You, Eli, are no different. When you learn to use Memory, she will impart a measure of the skill, or really knowledge, of those before you. This skill does not relate just to swordplay but other things, making you slightly better, faster, more skilled at fighting and killing. Think of it as a tool to help you get the job done, nothing more, nothing less."

Eli eyed the blade for a long moment. Could he trust this wizard? Did he dare? Though the weapon had been given as a gift, a show of friendship, he had suspected there was more to it. Now, he knew for certain there was, and that made him uneasy. Like one of the fish he had caught, Eli felt hooked, trapped.

"What is the catch?" Eli asked. "What is the price the sword will extract for such a gift?"

"Utter exhaustion is one such catch, as you call it," Obsidian said.

"There are others?"

"Given time, you will discover them."

Eli scowled as he gazed at the sword. "What if I choose not to use it?"

"Then your job will prove more difficult."

"Tell me. What is that job?" Eli asked, tearing his gaze from Memory. "What is it that you want of me?"

"Amongst other things, to catch a criminal."

"Mik'Las," Eli said.

"Though he is of the High Born, Mik'Las is the enemy of our people, an agent of those who would willingly see us to our doom. It may take time, years even, but you are to see to Mik'Las's demise, for ending him will advance our cause greatly."

This was not welcome news to Eli, and in fact he found it quite disturbing. It also helped to explain the criminal's actions. He had become more than an aberration in elven society. Mik'Las was a Dark Elf.

"Eli, our people are scattered across a dozen worlds. Our numbers pale in comparison to what they once were. The High Born face the very real possibility of the end of our story—extinction. The struggle ahead will determine our people's future—that is, if we have one. Do we once again prosper or fade away into the mists of time? Those are the stakes for which we play the game that is the Last War."

Though he wasn't sure if he could trust him, Eli felt Obsidian was telling him the truth when it came to their people. It scared him terribly to think his people might die off.

"Who are you?" Mae stepped from the trees. Her bow was nocked, the string pulled taut. She had an arrow aimed at the wizard's heart. There was a fierce look in her gaze. "What do you want?"

Obsidian turned slowly to face her. "A great many things, my dear."

"He means us no harm," Eli said to her and held out a hand. "At least, I don't think he does."

Obsidian glanced at Eli. "I see we are making progress here on the trust front."

Eli resisted a scowl. "Lower the bow, Mae."

Reluctantly, she lowered the bow. Mae took a step nearer, her eyes flicking from Obsidian to Eli and back again. She blinked rapidly and her mouth fell open in clear disbelief.

"He," Mae said, "he—he looks like—older—but you."

"I know," Eli said.

"How is that possible?" Mae asked him.

"I don't know," Eli admitted.

"You have no idea how much it pleases me you two have bonded," Obsidian said. "Against all expectations, you have joined your houses in union, two of the oldest families on this world, with the purest bloodlines. It is remarkable, for you both are incredibly stubborn and difficult people—similar in so many ways, yet also opposites in so many others. Just remarkable, truly remarkable."

"If you say so," Mae said dubiously.

"I do." Obsidian fell silent for a long moment as he studied them, looking from one to the other. "Enjoy what happiness you can, for the Last War is coming, and when it arrives, it will be terrible for all on Istros. Ahead lies a test like none you have ever faced."

"Cousin?" Eli asked, suddenly recalling Obsidian's first words. "You greeted me by naming me a cousin. Only family refer to themselves that way. Who are you really?"

"I am Vera'Far, and yes, we are related—a very distant relation. It is why you make an excellent choice. The spark that runs within me is also in your blood, Eli." The wizard paused, his gaze flicking to Mae for the briefest of moments before returning to Eli. "Think of me as your ultimate grandfather, on your mother's side."

Eli stared at Vera'Far. On a day filled with shocks, this was almost too much to believe, so much so he suddenly found it comical. He gave a low chuckle and drew a sharp warning glance from Mae.

"Can I call you Grandpa?" Eli asked.

Vera'Far's eyes narrowed ever so slightly as he studied Eli for a long moment then gave a light laugh of his own. It sounded slightly forced. "It's been a long while since I have been amused—or toyed with for that matter. No one has dared try. We are more alike than you know."

"I guess the nuts don't roll far from the tree," Eli said, "no matter how old it is."

Vera'Far gave an amused grunt, then grew serious again. "In the days, years, and months ahead, never lose your humor, Eli. Both of you. Keep it close at hand, for if you think you have seen terrible things—worse is on the horizon." Vera'Far tapped his staff on the ground. It flashed briefly with light. "Now, my time is up—I must leave you."

"What about the short term?" Eli asked, growing serious. "What is it you want of me?"

"If I told you that, it would spoil the fun, and I know how much you enjoy a little excitement," Vera'Far said with a trace of a smile. "You will know it when you find it, but I would begin searching a few miles to the east. Something is there that you must deal with."

"You mean Arvan'Dale?" Mae asked with a worried glance thrown to Eli.

Obsidian turned his gaze to her. "I enjoyed meeting you, Mae'Cara." There was a long pause. "Welcome to the family."

With that, the wizard tapped his staff once more on the ground. The staff flashed again, this time brilliantly. Eli and Mae were forced to briefly look away. Like smoke dissipating on a strong wind, Vera'Far seemed to waver before their eyes. Then, he vanished into thin air and was gone, leaving them both alone.

Neither spoke for several moments.

"You have to admit"—Eli looked over at her—"that was a heck of an exit. Grandpa has style."

Mae could only nod her agreement. She slowly turned her gaze to him. "You must tell me all he said."

"Whether I like it or not, it seems we are going to Arvan'Dale after all." Eli heaved a heavy sigh. He did not wish to return to that place. "And yes, I will tell you everything."

CHAPTER FIVE

Lying down upon their bellies and concealed by the tall grass and brush, he and Mae were perched upon the crest of a small hill. They were looking down upon Arvan'Dale. It was late afternoon and the sun hung low over the horizon to their left. The temperature was dropping rapidly, and Eli found himself almost feeling chilled. He shared a troubled look with Mae, then turned his attention back to the village, studying it carefully.

Below them and down an easy slope thick with wild grass, the village was three hundred yards distant. Arvan'Dale consisted of two dozen ramshackle buildings, which were clustered tightly together along a single dirt track little wider than the width of a wagon. There was no square or village green. There wasn't even a defensive wall or barricade. Heck, Eli thought the village looked smaller than when he'd seen it last, as if it had shrunk.

Most of the structures were hovels, barely large enough to house a small family. There were a handful of barns of varying size behind the homes, along with numerous animal pens. Near the center of the village was a larger single-story structure.

Eli supposed that building was most likely a tavern. It seemed every human town and village had at least one. After a long day's work ended and the sun went down, most average humans seemed to enjoy gathering to drink, gossip, boast, and play games of chance—at least that had been his experience. Elves had different social customs. Still, he found he occasionally enjoyed such gatherings.

Well off and away from the main roads, isolated, Arvan'Dale had always been a mean place, with the people having little with which to scrape by. In his time, Eli had seen dozens of human settlements just like it. He found such a meager existence, one seemingly without hope of a better future, not only wearying but depressing in the extreme. Even for an elf, life was too short to live under such conditions for long, and Eli had.

"Your Arvan'Dale has been abandoned for some time," Mae said with an unhappy scowl. There was a touch of disappointment in her tone. "No one lives here anymore."

Not taking his eyes from the village, Eli absently nodded his agreement. It did indeed appear as if no one had called Arvan'Dale home for some time, likely years. Where the residents had gone or why they had left, he had absolutely no idea.

Without regular attention, several roofs had caved in. Others, in various states of neglect, were so replete with holes, they were in the process of collapsing as well.

One building had even fallen in upon itself so long ago that weeds and a small tree had grown up inside its ruin. Only a single wall still managed to stand upon the stone foundation, and that was leaning over at a precarious angle.

A short distance away was a sad and tired-looking barn, with boards that had grayed with age. Like an old mount that had seen too much saddle time, the barn's roof sagged in the middle.

With the abandonment of the village, the once cultivated fields that surrounded Arvan'Dale had grown wild with weeds, grass, brush, and young trees. It looked very unkempt to his critical eye, and though he despised this place, it felt somehow wrong.

Eli rubbed at his eyes for a long moment. Here before him was yet another example of the passage of time changing everything. It was an inexorable march that could not be stopped by anyone or any force.

The view below them was a sobering reminder of how time, and nature, didn't stop for anyone, not even elves. With the people gone, the Great Mother was slowly and steadily wiping away the stain that was Arvan'Dale and reclaiming what was hers.

When it was finally gone and the village ceased to exist, would his memories of this horrid place finally, at long last, fade? Eli wasn't sure they would, but he hoped so, for they were painful in the extreme.

Despite its dilapidated and abandoned appearance, surprisingly, Arvan'Dale was presently occupied. Smoke drifted lazily upward from the chimney of one of the intact structures, what he supposed had once been the village's tavern.

A short distance away from the tavern, a dozen saddled horses were picketed and hobbled next to a ruin of a barn. Two human sentries, soldiers both, stood watch just off to the side of the horses. Wearing black leather armor and carrying swords, they were talking amongst themselves.

As if they expected no trouble, both seemed wholly unconcerned with their duty, bored even, for one was leaning casually against the wall of the barn. He was drinking deeply from a skin, which Eli suspected contained wine. The soldier wiped his lips with the back of his arm and passed the skin to his comrade, who took a healthy swig.

"Castol cavalry?" Mae asked.

"Judging from their uniforms and from the picketed horses, they are king's men—I believe," Eli said to Mae, "regulars…likely trained fighters all."

"Meaning they are dangerous."

"And from the number of horses picketed down there, at least a light squadron has stopped here for the night," Eli added.

"More than enough for a patrol," Mae said. "We're pretty far to the south in Castol territory, almost to the border. If memory serves, that is twenty miles, maybe fewer?"

"Fewer, more like ten or fifteen miles at most. Though I have not been out this way in a while, there should be an imperial garrison nearby."

"How near?" Mae asked.

"Within forty or fifty miles I suppose. Last time I passed through, it was occupied by a light cohort of auxiliaries."

"Small then," Mae said.

"I have no reason to expect that to have changed."

"What we are seeing here is most likely a patrol, then."

"That could be their purpose," Eli admitted, but something inside him told him that there was more to it than a simple patrol passing through the decaying ruins of Arvan'Dale. In a remote corner of the realm, the village was well off the beaten path. "The Castol do not typically use cavalry. For the most part their kingdom is forested, especially here in the south."

"I know that." Mae's tone took on a hint of irritation as she shot him a hard look. "Are you questioning my knowledge of the land and the type of terrain that is best suited to cavalry?"

Eli shook his head and, with some effort, resisted a grin. "I would never do such a thing. And frankly, I am truly aghast that you would think me capable of treating my wife in such a disrespectful manner."

Mae gave a disbelieving snort. "Oh, my infuriating husband, you are quite capable of anything when it comes to that warped sense of humor of yours. It is a wonder you managed to live past your first century of life."

"Are you questioning my honesty?" Eli asked, rolling onto his side and looking over at her. He placed a hand to his chest. "I am shocked."

Mae turned her gaze back to the village and gestured at it with a hand. "Get to the point, husband. What is it you were going to say?"

"I have heard others say that, given time, wives can suck the fun out of everything."

Mae slowly turned her head and looked over at him again. There was a dangerous glint to her gaze. Her tone was cold when she spoke. "Is that so? And you have experience with that sort of thing?"

"As we were just joined, I do not per se have any experience with that sort of thing, at least not—"

"Careful," Mae cautioned, interrupting him. Her eyes flashed dangerously, and in that moment, with sudden desire rushing through his veins, he thought her the most beautiful creature in the entire world. "You may wish to rethink whatever clever remark you were about to utter. At least, I would advise that you do."

Like a horse racing out of control, Eli felt a thrill of excitement shoot through him. He loved skirting danger and taking risks. It made life interesting and fun. Playing with Mae was no different. At times, it was perhaps even more exciting. Still, he had the feeling he was pushing his luck…just a little.

"Maybe I have said too much already," Eli said.

As if to reinforce her point, Mae stared at him hard, then after a prolonged moment, she turned her gaze back to the village.

"So," she said after a moment's more silence, "what point *were* you going to make about the Castol cavalry?" She glanced over at him again and there was steel in her gaze. "When it comes to the geography of the land hereabouts?"

Eli considered playing with her some more, then decided he had flirted with danger too much for one day. Almost regretfully, he grew serious. "This far south, there's little need for such formations—cavalry, that is—especially if it is for an ordinary patrol through their own lands."

Mae gave a nod of understanding.

"The imperial province south of here is, for the most part, open prairie," Eli continued, "pasture, and farmland. The kind of ground that is perfect for the cultivation of wheat. It is why the empire seized the region in the first place and declared it an imperial protectorate. The empire has even set up several veteran colonies to help tame it and bring it closer under their control. The province is a veritable breadbasket, from which the senate and emperor feed a good portion of the populace of Mal'Zeel."

"So, it is likely this cavalry squadron was operating in imperial lands then."

"With them being so far to the south, that does seem likely," Eli said. "Still, their mission could have been one of simple reconnaissance."

"Or, more likely, they were and are up to no good," Mae said, a hint of excitement creeping into her tone. "And as allies of the empire, we are obligated to find out what they were and are doing, then take action."

"That is, if they were indeed in imperial lands, which, I might remind you, they are not presently. We also need to consider the possibility they might not have crossed the border and are simply what they seem, a patrol, as you said."

"You do not believe that, do you?"

"No," Eli said immediately. "Castol patrols in this region are generally conducted by entire companies of foot and sometimes they come in greater strength to reinforce the kingdom's authority, that the locals cannot misunderstand."

"Really?"

"Yeah. The tribes around these parts were never the friendliest of peoples to begin with. They have no love for each other and feud often. Still, they like their overlords to the north even less and only remain a part of the kingdom by force. About every fifty years or so they seem to band together to try to throw off the king's yoke." Eli paused and regarded the village for a time. "But since we are so close to the border—as you rightly pointed out—we must find out what that patrol is up to."

Mae gave a nod. "Is that the only reason?"

"Grandpa did point us in this direction."

"Uh huh," Mae said. "More than just a coincidence, us running into them."

"If something untoward is afoot," Eli added, "it might have consequences, not just for the empire, but for our people as well."

Mae was silent for several heartbeats. "There is no way to determine that for certain, without grabbing one of them and thoroughly questioning him."

Eli scratched an itch on his jaw as he considered her suggestion. He did not like the idea of grabbing one of the soldiers. "Such an action might give us away. At the very least, they will conduct a search for their missing man."

Mae gave an unhappy grunt, and with that, they fell silent for several moments and continued to watch the village.

"What do you think happened to the people who lived here?" Mae asked after a time.

"I don't know."

"Whatever occurred," Mae said, "it happened years ago."

"Yeah," Eli agreed and decided it was a puzzle for sure. "Perhaps the residents of Arvan'Dale simply got tired of living such a miserable existence, one far from anywhere of note, and just left?"

"How likely is that?" Mae asked him.

"Not very," Eli said. "Rather than quit, humans tend to hang onto what little they possess. The less they have, the more they will fight for it. In truth, what occurred here is a mystery to which we may never discover the answer."

"One problem at a time, then," Mae said. "Is that what you are saying?"

"Exactly."

"So, let us begin with the biggest problem before us. Why did the wizard point us in this direction? Why have us come here, to Arvan'Dale?"

"I do not know, but I believe he means for us to discover that answer for ourselves."

"Could it have something to do with your prior experience with this place?" Mae asked.

"No," Eli said, firmly. "I do not believe it does."

"You are certain?" Mae looked over at him.

Eli gave a firm nod. "Eminently. What occurred took place a long time ago."

Mae fell silent for a few heartbeats. "What do you want to do? Tell me what are you thinking, my love."

Eli glanced up at the sky. There was at most two hours of light remaining. As the sun climbed toward the horizon, the temperature had already begun to drop, presaging a cold night. "We will watch until it is good and dark. Then, we can go down there and poke around a bit"—he looked over at her—"without being seen or detected. I cannot help but feel their being here"—Eli waved at the village—"is no coincidence. We might learn something useful by eavesdropping."

"And if we don't?"

"Then we will consider a more direct approach," Eli said, "perhaps even grab one of them for questioning."

"All right." Mae's gaze returned to the village. She studied it for a time, then looked over at him, her eyes searching his face. "What happened to you here?"

Eli hesitated a moment, then let out a near sigh. She deserved honesty. "I lost a friend in this place, a very good friend. His loss still hurts to this day."

"A ranger?" Mae asked. "One of our own?"

"No, not a ranger and not one of our own. He was a human friend, and without him, I would not be here next to you this day. It pains me that I could not return the favor."

Mae's face took on a somber look as she gazed back at him. "I would know the name of the human who saved your life, for I owe him a debt that can never be repaid."

"Davik Cole," Eli said, even as he tried and failed to keep his thoughts from going to what had happened so long ago. He gave an involuntary shiver at the memory of that horrid day.

"Davik," Mae repeated, as if trying the name out. She fell silent for a long moment. Her next words came as a near whisper. "How did he pass on? How did your friend die?"

"Are you certain you wish to know?"

"Yes."

Eli sucked in a breath as he gathered his thoughts, then turned his gaze back to Arvan'Dale. The hovel where Davik had died was no longer there, but Eli could picture it just the same. It had been a miserable place, made even worse by his friend's brutal murder.

"Amongst the people living in this village was a dark priest." Eli closed his eyes as he thought back to that terrible time. "They had no idea as to the real identity or the affiliation of their headman. And we had no way of knowing either. He blended in perfectly with everyone else. When I met him, he seemed normal enough, friendly even, helpful. In hindsight, that should have been a warning sign, for no one in this village was friendly, let alone helpful, when it came to outsiders. And make no mistake, we were outsiders."

"A dark priest?" Mae asked. "Whom did he serve?"

"Lutha Nyx," Eli said quietly.

Mae sucked in a startled breath. "The goddess of shadows, darkness, and worse? Truly?"

Eli gave a curt nod.

"I did not think anyone worshipped her, not anymore. It was my understanding our people's arrival upon this world saw that religion thoroughly stamped out."

"Belief in Lutha Nyx was never fully extinguished," Eli said. "The goddess still has a following on this world. It is small, but her flock exists just the same. Where they lurk, I am afraid there is just no telling. Like a venomous snake tucked under a rock, they hide themselves exceptionally well, making it difficult to uncover them safely."

Her expression troubled, Mae ran her gaze over the village again. "Why here? This place is the middle of nowhere, with nothing of importance about."

"Perhaps the priest settled here because it was out of the way and far from civilization. He could practice his dark arts without fear of prying or interference. I never did find out his reasoning."

"What happened to your friend?" Mae asked quietly. "How did he die?"

Eli did not immediately answer. He closed his eyes again, trying to erase what he'd witnessed and fought so very long ago. He failed in holding back the horrific images that sprang to mind. "Davik was taken by what lurks in the shadows. They—they devoured him alive and—and I could not stop it."

"I don't understand." Mae's brow furrowed.

"Pray that you never do," Eli said, "for when it comes to Lutha Nyx and her followers, I would stay well out of the shadows and in the sunlight."

Mae scowled at him. "Stay out of the shadows? The sunlight?"

"It is safer that way, healthier."

"What if it is night? What then?"

"Pray it is not."

"You are not exactly filling me with comfort, husband."

He looked over at her. She was gazing back at him. He found her eyes deeper than the deepest of wells. He could fall into them and be more than content, happy even. He *was* happy. There was no doubt about that. Mae provided a balance he had not known he needed or, for that matter, craved, a soothing balm for a tortured soul.

Were he able, he would willingly spare her from the horrors of this world, and Lutha Nyx was one such horror. At the same time, Eli well understood he could not shield her from such things, for it would prove to be the ultimate disservice and an insult to who she was, his wife, his mate, and a ranger of their people. Just as he had, she needed to see the world for how it was, not how one thought or wished it to be.

"Filling you with confidence was never my intention, for when it comes to Nyx, monsters lurk in the darkness."

CHAPTER SIX

"Wake up." Mae jabbed him in the side. "I said, wake up."

"What?" Eli asked, without opening his eyes.

"Something's happening," Mae said as she nudged him in the side again. "I think they're getting ready to leave."

"Leave?" Eli's eyes snapped open. He was lying on his back. Overhead, through a scattering of clouds, the first of the stars were emerging. He and Mae were still on the crest of the hill, and it was almost fully dark. He rubbed his eyes and stretched. While Mae stood watch, he had taken the opportunity to catch some sleep.

Stifling a yawn, he rolled over and peered through the tall grass. Below in the heavily shadowed Arvan'Dale, men had emerged from the tavern and gone to the picketed horses. They were busy untying their mounts, tightening straps, and checking saddles.

"They're leaving." He'd seen such preparations before. It was clear Mae was right. Eli felt himself scowl as he studied the frenzy of activity below. "Now, that is really strange."

"Strange? How?" Mae asked, glancing over at him.

"Their decision to travel after sunset is abnormal. As you are likely aware, human night vision is not as good as our own, especially in low-light conditions. The road to the north and south travels directly through the forest, and thick tree cover at that. In the darkness, under the cover of the canopy and without adequate moonlight, they will be nearly blind. The road in these parts has never been very good, even when Arvan'Dale was settled. One might even consider such a movement foolhardy, for riding a horse at night on a terrible road, when one cannot see, is not the safest of activities. The animal could easily step in a hole or rut and stumble, throwing the rider."

"Foolhardy." Mae seemed to absorb that. She gave a nod, then looked back over at him. "Unless one had a pressing need to travel at night."

"There is that," Eli said, "a pressing need."

"Time to get moving, boys," came the clear shout from an officer below. "We've got a long way to go before sunrise, a very long way. Keep your eyes open and watch the bloody road before you. Mount up."

Eli's gaze fixed upon the officer, who, holding the reins of his horse, climbed up and onto his mount with a practiced ease that spoke of having spent years in the saddle. The officer's armor was more ornate than his men's. His mount also looked of better quality than the rest.

The officer wore a white-plumed crest upon his helmet and, like his men, a gray cloak. He raised himself in the saddle and pulled his cloak from beneath him, where he had sat on part of it. He carefully arranged the tail end of the cloak across his horse's rump.

Clearly getting comfortable, he took a moment to better position himself in the saddle. Apparently satisfied, he pulled on the reins slightly, deftly backed his horse up from where it had been picketed, and wheeled about. The officer spotted one of his men who, leading his mount by the reins, had walked up and was waiting. The officer fished something out from behind his chest armor and leaned over to hand it to the soldier.

Something was said between the two of them. Then the soldier tucked whatever he had been given into a saddle pouch. He mounted up and crisply saluted. The salute was returned just as smartly.

Pulling on the reins, the mounted soldier turned his horse around and started riding northward at a slow, steady walk. The officer watched him for a moment then looked over his squadron, who had all mounted up. He seemed to be studying them critically, as if assessing their readiness.

"Alright, boys, time to earn our pay for king and country... forwaard," the officer called and raised his hand, pointing down the road to the south. Without saying anything further, he started his horse into a walk. Single file and one at a time, the other riders fell in behind him. Unknown to the men below, Eli and Mae watched as the squadron, heading south, steadily worked their way through and out of the village.

"This is no simple patrol," Mae said.

"No, it is not," Eli said. "That much has become abundantly clear."

"What do you think is going on?"

"I don't know." Eli felt troubled by that. "But they are moving in the direction of imperial lands. Traveling at night, their behavior is ... troubling to say the least, concerning even."

"I bet that one is carrying a message," Mae said, indicating the solitary trooper riding northward along the road.

"We are in agreement on that point."

Her eyes narrowing dangerously, Mae looked over at him. "On only one point?"

"You know what I mean," Eli said.

Mae eyed him for a moment more before her gaze softened and she turned back to the solitary rider. "I wonder where he is headed."

The messenger was riding at an almost painfully slow pace out of the village. Eli scratched an itch upon his jaw as he considered the question. It was a mystery to be sure. The messenger was moving much slower than his comrades, who were riding in the opposite direction, headed to the south. It was as if he had nowhere pressing to be, and yet he was already fifty yards to the north and was just passing the last of the buildings at a slow walk. He was leaning forward in the saddle, carefully watching the ground ahead of his horse.

"Well, he has to be going somewhere," Mae added. "A message or dispatch seems to indicate there are more of them out there, perhaps a larger force a few miles off."

"I am thinking that as well," Eli said. "This squadron's purpose may be that of advance scouts."

"By leaving at dusk, they will be able to cross the border at night, most likely unseen."

Eli gave a nod of agreement. "That does seem to be their intention. There is a good-sized town a few miles past the border. They may be seeking to sneak by it without attracting attention."

"What is this town's name? I don't recall learning about it."

"It is a relatively new settlement," Eli said, "a veterans' colony. I learned about it only recently."

Mae's gaze went to the messenger again. She studied him for a protracted moment. "You can read the Castol tongue, right?"

"I can. Why do you ask?"

"I believe the time has come for a more direct approach." Mae stood and hoisted up her pack. Shrugging it on, she glanced at the messenger moving northward before turning to Eli. "He is alone and without protection. Let us go grab him and see what we can learn. Unless, of course, you have an objection to that?"

"I have no immediate objection." Eli pulled himself to his feet as Mae picked up her bow and bundle of arrows.

"Good that we see eye to eye on another point, husband of mine." She flashed him a grin filled with the excitement of the moment. Then, without waiting, she hunched over and started moving down the slope toward the village, angling after the messenger.

Eli eyed Mae for a long moment. There had been other options to take. That was certain. They could have followed the messenger and simply seen where he was going. Or they could have trailed the squadron. Either move would have ultimately provided some answers.

In this instance, he was not wholly comfortable moving so quickly to action. In his mind, there was no immediate rush, for the Castol had not really done anything yet, other than ride out of the village toward the border. Still, Mae had made the decision for them, and in the end, he saw no real issue with it. They were out in the middle of nowhere and there was little risk, especially when it came to seizing a lone messenger traveling at night.

Shrugging his pack onto his shoulders and grabbing his bow and bundle of arrows, Eli followed after her. As he made his way down the slope and into the overgrown fields, he was forced to pay close attention to where he placed his feet. He did not want to get tripped up in the weeds and brambles that grew wildly about.

Within a span of heartbeats, they reached the edge of the village. Arvan'Dale was as silent as a graveyard, almost eerily so. Eli found the nearest buildings blocking their view of the road north and the messenger.

Mae turned to the right and started off, jogging along the edge of the village, making as little sound as possible as she moved past each building. Eli trailed after her. They went quickly, and the run-down and dilapidated hovels, one after another, flashed by.

They rounded the last of the buildings on the northern side of the village and once again caught sight of the messenger. He was several hundred yards ahead and still following the road. He was near the edge of the tree line, where the road entered the forest, cutting through the trees. If anything, he had slowed his pace to a near crawl and seemed none the wiser that they were closing in on him from behind.

Eli and Mae kept to the overgrown field to the right side of the road. Hunching over to avoid being seen, they advanced rapidly toward their mark. It had become so dark, Eli doubted that he would see them, even if they had been on the road and the man looked in their direction.

Glancing over at the poor state of the road, Eli could well understand why the messenger was traveling so slowly. The roadbed was filled with potholes and deep wagon ruts. It almost would have been better for the messenger had he dismounted and led his horse by foot. And Eli could not understand why he had not done just that, for traveling that way would have been safer. There were times he had difficulty understanding humans.

The messenger, still following the road, disappeared into the darkness of the forest, as if it had eaten him whole, horse and all. After a dozen heartbeats, even Eli lost sight of him. Mae increased her pace, and Eli matched her, until they were both nearly running.

"When we get a few yards into the trees," Eli said between breaths, "you go to the left, and I will go right of the road. We move by him and around him, up the road, then stop and set up an ambush. Look for my signal to break."

"Okay," Mae breathed back to him.

"I'll take his horse down," Eli continued, "then we disarm him. We need him alive, so he can answer questions. Otherwise, this might all be an exercise in futility."

"Got it," Mae said between breaths.

They spoke no more after that. The tree line drew closer and closer. Twenty yards, then ten, five—until they themselves hit the trees and near absolute darkness of the nighttime forest. Just off the side of the road, Eli slowed to a jog, and at his side, so too did Mae. It was so dark that even Eli was having difficulty seeing much beyond a few yards.

The road just ahead of them was dark and narrow, as if the surrounding forest were attempting to close in upon them. It began to climb up the slope of a low hill and then bent away to the left. The forest, like the village, was silent as a tomb.

The messenger was not in view either. Eli judged their quarry was at least twenty yards ahead of them and just around the bend in the road. He signaled for Mae to move to the other side of the road. She gave a nod of understanding, crossed the road, and slipped into the trees.

More cautiously, and cognizant of making no sound, they continued onward, moving much slower but still faster than the messenger had been traveling. Keeping in sight of each other, they worked their way up the slope and to the bend. Eli scanned the trees about them carefully and came to a halt. Something wasn't quite right. He could feel it in his bones. At first, he could not quite figure out just what was wrong. Then … it hit him, like a ton of bricks. The forest was not just quiet; it was too quiet.

There was a whinny from a horse somewhere ahead, followed by a shout of alarm, a curse, and a heavy thud. The horse, in clear panic, whinnied again.

Eli threw himself behind the trunk of a large oak on his right. Even though it was nearly pitch-black, he wanted to get out of sight, to buy himself a moment to get a sense for what was happening and to react.

To his left and across the road, he sensed Mae attempting to do the same, then he heard her give a painful grunt and, out of his peripheral vision, had a flash of her crumpling to the ground. Fear struck at his heart. There seemed to be movement all around, and close at hand too. Dropping his bow, he mentally girded himself for battle and yanked out his sword.

His fear turned to anger, which turned to a burning rage, a rage that his wife was in danger, possibly seriously injured. Whoever they were, they wanted a fight. Eli would give them one. It was time to dance the dance of death and he had long since become a master.

"Don't move," a firm voice shouted at him in the common tongue, from his immediate right. "Don't you fucking move, or I swear by the gods above, I will pin you like a child's target at the village fair."

Eli froze, then turned toward the voice. At first, he saw nothing, then made out the shape of a man no less than ten paces away. He was down on one knee next to a pine and had a bow nocked, with an arrow aimed squarely at Eli's chest. The bowstring had been pulled taut and the weapon held steady. All this man had to do was release the string.

Could he successfully dodge the arrow? Eli did not know, but he was about to try. Tensing, he mentally calculated how fast he could move and how quickly his opponent would react. Could he beat the odds?

"Don't do it," the man cautioned in a hard tone, as if he could sense Eli's thinking. "Be smart and put down that sword."

"I would do as the captain says." Another man stepped from behind a tree to Eli's immediate left. This one also held a bow, with a nocked arrow aimed squarely at him. Feeling incredible frustration, Eli regretfully lowered his sword. He realized both he and Mae must have somehow been spotted as they'd observed the village. An elaborate trap had been laid for them, one of which they had stupidly taken the bait and walked right into. And whoever had laid their ambush had planned it exceptionally well.

"Drop the weapon," the first man said in a tone that was rock solid and full of confidence. "I said, drop it. Don't make me tell you again, son."

Letting out a deeply unhappy breath, Eli let his sword fall to the ground before him. He suddenly brightened, for he still had his daggers. He doubted that, in the darkness, the humans could see them. The dance was just about to begin.

"Good boy." Still aiming at Eli, the man came to his feet and moved forward a step. "At least you have some sense."

"Sense?" Eli asked, in a lighthearted manner. "Can you tell me, what is that?"

"Is the other one still breathing?" the first man asked, ignoring Eli's comment.

"I've got the other one covered," someone said from behind Eli. "She's alive."

Eli let out a huge sigh of relief. Still, these men were about to pay for what they had done.

"She?" the first man asked. There was genuine surprise in his tone.

"Yeah…she's gonna wake up with one heck of a…" There was a pause. "Uh oh…oh bloody no."

"What's wrong?" the first man asked.

"Ahhh—boss—she's…she's an elf."

Eli glanced back and saw Mae's crumpled form on the ground. She shifted slightly and moaned. The man crouching next to her stood. He had a sword drawn, with a bow slung over his back.

"An elf?" the first man said. "Really?"

"Aye, sir," came the reply, this time in imperial standard. "And from her dress, she looks like a ranger too."

Eli felt himself scowl and looked around. What was going on here? Who were these men?

Eli turned back around to face front and looked at the first man confronting him, who lowered his bow a fraction and took a half-step closer, squinting in the darkness.

"Is that you, Eli?"

Though he had not heard it in years, now that he noticed it, the voice was familiar—deeper, older-sounding, but just the same, it was familiar. Eyes narrowed against the darkness, the man stepped even closer.

"Titus?" Eli asked tentatively, while at the same time cursing his luck. Of all the people to be caught by. "Flavius Marverus Titus?"

"That's me," Titus replied, then gave a low chuckle that was filled with dark amusement. "I've always wanted to get the drop on you, Eli. After all these years, I guess I've finally managed it."

"Practice does make perfect," Eli said unhappily. "I seem to recall telling you that a time or two."

"Boys, we've caught ourselves a pair of elven rangers," Titus said, "and one of them's not just any ranger either. We bagged the great Eli'Far. How about them apples?"

"I've heard he's nothing but trouble," the man on Eli's left said.

His frustration increasing, Eli rubbed at his eyes and looked over to his left. "Aventus, I see you are still slumming around with Titus."

"I wouldn't be anywhere else," Aventus drawled, arrow still aimed at Eli.

"I guess that speaks on your taste in companions," Eli said.

"Can I shoot him, Titus?" Aventus asked, his tone hardening. "I believe he's more than earned it."

"It's been near ten years." Titus lowered his bow and stepped even closer, directly up to Eli. "Ten...long...years. You have no idea how long I have been waiting for this moment."

"It hasn't been long enough," Eli said. His unhappiness at their walking into the ambush was only growing by the moment.

"I don't know about that." Titus hesitated a moment, then reached out and enveloped Eli in a bear hug, pounding him on the back firmly. "It's been too long, my friend, way too long."

Eli hesitated a moment, then patted Titus on the back and returned the hug. After a moment Eli broke the embrace as he stepped back and closely examined the man before him. Though it had been more than ten years, Titus had changed little, apart from some wrinkles around the eyes and a short brown beard he was sporting. He had a hard look about him.

Titus stood a little over five feet tall and was fit, with a wiry build. He wore green and brown leathers, along with a pair of supple boots, all perfect for blending into the forest. The three other men were dressed in a similar manner.

They looked just as hard and confident as their leader. Around the bend and through the trees on the road, Eli spotted a fourth man, who was securing the messenger's arms behind his back with a piece of cord.

"Does this mean I don't get to shoot him?" Aventus asked.

"Titus, for an imperial ranger," Eli said, ignoring Aventus, "aren't you a little out of your patrol area? You do realize this is Castol land?"

"The same could be said of you," Titus replied. "Besides, you of all people should know we go where we please," Titus said and hesitated a moment, "as do the elves."

"I would never admit to that, even if it were true, which, oddly enough, it is." Eli glanced at the other two men he couldn't see clearly. "Who else do you have with you?"

"Maran and Lenth," Titus said. "Do you know them?"

"I've not had the pleasure," Eli said, though he had heard of the two.

Mae groaned again. Eli moved over and pushed the ranger who was watching her back and away. Taking a knee next to Mae, he examined her. She had a bruise forming on her left temple but, beyond that, seemed all right. A stout tree limb lay on the ground next to her. It had been undoubtedly used to hit her.

"Did you have to club her?" Eli asked, looking up at the man.

"She spotted me at the last moment and was going for a dagger," the ranger replied with a shrug. "I didn't feel like getting knifed, not tonight at any rate."

"Who's that?" Titus asked curiously from over Eli's shoulder.

"My wife," Eli said sourly, without looking up.

"What?" Titus asked. "Did you say she was your wife?"

"I did," Eli said, his sourness only increasing.

"Your wife?" Titus asked again, to which Eli gave a nod. Titus then became visibly amused, a broad smile spreading across his face. "Eli, you're such a pain in the ass, I can't image the woman that would willingly marry you."

Eli gave a grunt at that.

"Were you forced to bribe her father for the honor of her hand?"

Eli resisted a grin at the dig, for it was quite good. Titus had always been one who could give as good as he got. Keeping his face devoid of expression, Eli looked up at the ranger.

"I might have forgotten to mention something."

"What is that?" Titus asked curiously.

"You met the warden once, right?" Eli asked.

"You well know I had the honor of being introduced to her ladyship. You were the one who presented me and Aventus to her."

"Honestly," Aventus said, "though she was bloody polite, the warden scared the shit out of us both, and that's sayin' something."

Eli looked from Aventus to Titus.

"What?" Titus asked when Eli did not speak.

"You also met her daughter that day. Do you recall that as well?"

"Gods, she was beautiful. How could I forget that?" Titus's grin began to grow larger, then he stiffened, suddenly staring hard at Eli. He turned his gaze to Mae again and stepped nearer, looking closely, squinting as he peered at her before turning his attention back to Eli. Even in the darkness, the ranger's face had visibly paled.

"You married the warden's daughter?" Titus asked, horrified. "You're telling me that we just ambushed and knocked out the warden's daughter?"

Eli did not reply. Instead, he was savoring the moment and finding it terribly difficult not to grin. The moment almost made up for the indignity of being surprised by an imperial ranger team.

"No," Titus breathed, his horror seeming to grow. The ranger took a step back. "No … this can't be happening."

"Oh, it is." Eli could resist it no longer. He felt a grin spread slowly across his face and gave fully into it. "To use one of your human sayings, when Mae wakes up, she is going to be pissed, *royally* pissed. And she has a temper that matches only her mother's."

"Oh shit," Aventus groaned. "Bloody gods."

CHAPTER SEVEN

Wiping blood from his hands with a small, wet rag, Eli stepped from the tavern's kitchen into what had once been the common room. The fire had been restoked and fed fresh fuel, mostly the remnants of the tavern's furniture. Providing the only real usable light, a low blaze crackled warmly in the hearth, the flames sending a cascade of dancing shadows across the room.

Eli's wife was sitting on a stool before the fire. She was holding one of her daggers in her hand, tossing it up in the air and catching it. There was no one else about. The other human rangers had been posted as lookouts on the edge of the village. All were elven-trained, something that made the Imperial Ranger Corps so effective. He had no doubt, if trouble came looking, they would receive advance warning. For the moment, they were safe and secure.

With a thick layer of dust over most everything, refuse and broken furniture lay scattered all about the communal room, which was good-sized for a village as small as Arvan'Dale. Only a handful of stools and tables remained whole and serviceable. The remnants of several broken tables, stools, and barrels had been piled into the left corner of the room. Who had done it and why, Eli had no way to know, and in truth he did not care overly much. There were some things worth knowing and others that were not worth the effort.

There were several holes in the thatched roof, along with one in the right wall. All let in a chill draft. The boards around the hole in the wall were thick with black rot. Amongst the rafters overhead were several old bird nests, with generations of droppings plastered directly below on the decaying wood-planked floor.

A low, agonized moan rose on the air behind him. With a hand on the door, Eli glanced back and into the kitchen at their prisoner. Sitting upon the floor, and with his hands tied behind him to a wooden support post, the messenger was slumped forward. The man—his name was Mago—was trembling. His head hung low over his chest.

A clay lamp, suspended from the ceiling by a hook and chain, had been lit with some oil Aventus had been carrying. Under dim lamplight, blood slicked the floorboards of the kitchen around their prisoner.

With a palm resting on the prisoner's head, Titus squatted next to Mago, speaking in a low, comforting tone. The prisoner moaned again, then mumbled something back to the ranger that Eli could not hear. Titus had drawn a curved dagger with a wicked serrated edge. It was held well away from the prisoner's line of sight. The ranger bowed his head and began praying quietly.

"High Father, forgive us for our mortal sins," Titus said, "and our base and wretched nature. This life is a precious gift, and though we don't always do so, we should strive to be better, so at the end, without shame, we are able to bask in your everlasting glory. Still, you are a forgiving god, and Mago here wishes to atone for the wrong he has done in this world. We beg you hear his plea."

The prisoner moaned again as if in reply. What he said, Eli could not make out.

"That's right, son," Titus said, "we're praying for your soul and salvation. Soon, you will be allowed to rest easy and without pain. You have my word on that, understand?"

Other than giving a miserable nod, the prisoner did not respond. After a moment, shoulders shaking, Mago began to sob. It was a pitiful sound. Eyeing their prisoner and Titus for a moment more, Eli felt regret strike at his heart. It was almost a physical blow that left him feeling discomfort in his stomach, as if he might be ill. That such things had to be occasionally done in the name of service did not make it any easier. It was events like this one that at times kept him up at night.

Titus looked up at him and their eyes met. Both he and the ranger had done terrible things in the name of their peoples. The human ranger seemed to understand his thoughts, for he shifted his gaze beyond Eli and out the door. The message was clear. The door creaked upon its hinges as Eli closed it. From the other side, he could hear Titus resume his prayers over his captive.

Putting the ugliness in the kitchen behind him, he started over to Mae. She looked up at him as he approached and, pushing a strand of hair from her face, managed a weak smile of greeting.

"How are you feeling?" Eli tossed the soiled rag aside and reached out a freshly cleaned hand. He rested it upon her shoulder. His knuckles were bruised slightly and hurt, a direct result of the questioning process and obstinacy of the prisoner.

"My head aches something fierce, but I have had worse," Mae said wearily. "You need not worry, husband. I will recover just fine. In a few days I should be right as rain."

Mae ran a hand through her hair and pushed it back behind her ear, revealing her bruised temple, which was purpling. The injury looked worse than it likely was. Eli did not much enjoy seeing his wife hurt.

"No doubt." He understood she likely had a splitting headache and would have for some hours to come. Feeling a stab of sympathy, he rubbed her shoulder for several moments and then, holding his hands out for warmth, stepped up to the fire.

The temperature had plunged over the last few hours and was hovering near freezing. The air had become a touch more humid as well. Even with the fire going, Eli's breath steamed on the air. The holes in the building did little to help keep in the warmth.

He glanced back at her and felt troubled. He found Mae, at times, difficult to predict. She had a fiery temper, and though it was not apparent, he knew it was currently blazing when it came to the humans and what they had done to her. After a moment, he shifted his gaze back to the fire.

Mae tossed the dagger up into the air once more. The blade flickered with reflected firelight. She deftly caught it.

"Thinking of using that dagger of yours?" Eli asked with a sidelong glance.

She looked over at him, her gaze just as hard as her tone. "I am. There are accounts that need to be settled."

Eli held her gaze a moment, then turned back to the fire. He rubbed his hands together to generate more warmth. The silence grew between them.

"It is a good thing," Eli said softly after a time, almost as if he were speaking to himself.

"What's a good thing?"

"That your skull is so thick," Eli said. "One of the rangers just proved that theory of mine a fact."

"You are the only one with a thick skull," Mae retorted sharply, heat in her gaze. She winced as she turned her head to look away from him. A heartbeat later, her shoulders slumped. "Every opportunity, every chance, you must always poke the bear. I ask you, why? Why do it?"

"It is in my nature," Eli said in a lighthearted manner. "You should know that by now."

"I am coming to see the reality of that statement." Mae fell silent. She sheathed her dagger, then looked over. "Sometimes, though, I wish you would give it a break." A deep weariness crept into her tone. "It becomes thoroughly exhausting, especially now."

"Are you having second thoughts?" Eli asked her.

"Of joining with you? Becoming your wife?" Mae asked, to which Eli gave a nod. "Though I could have done worse, no, I have no second thoughts or regrets... at least for now."

"At least for now? You could have done worse?" Eli asked, acting surprised by the comment. "Who's poking the bear now?"

Mae looked over and offered him another weary smile, or really a trace of one. Though he had managed to pull a smile from her, he wasn't able to dispel the burning anger he could readily sense still hidden just below the surface.

"Learn anything from the human?" Mae asked him.

"A great deal." Eli gazed into the fire's depths and considered how to head off potential trouble with his wife and the humans. Her anger was radiating with heat, like a boulder after a long, hot, sunny day.

"Why not just keep me in suspense, then?"

Eli blinked and shook himself. Not only was he tired from lack of sleep, but he had inadvertently lost himself in the flames and his worries, which he had in abundance, both great and small.

In truth, Mae's response to being nearly brained was the least of his concerns, for the moment any rate. Still, it was something he would have to deal with, and sooner rather than later. And yet, what he and Titus had learned from their interrogation of Mago was a much larger issue. It bothered him greatly. He glanced over at Mae and hesitated a moment more before speaking.

"It seems the Castol have settled on war."

"War?" Mae asked, turning her gaze from the flames and looking up at him. She bit her lip and her brow furrowed ever so slightly. "War with the empire? Really?"

Eli gave her a solemn nod. "We both know the implications, do we not?"

"Foolishness," Mae said savagely as her surprise shifted and her anger came out. "The Castol are hardly prepared for a protracted war. If they were, or were in the process of raising serious levies, we would have heard of such news."

"That still does not change the facts as we know them." Eli jerked a thumb at the closed kitchen door. "He told us all he knew."

"What with their elderly and infirm king, and the coming fight over succession, if anything, the kingdom is unstable and not ready for a war with the empire."

"I know," Eli said. "It does not make much sense to me either. We must be missing some key information. At the very least, Cree'Tol should have sent us word on preparations for such a campaign."

"If they are set on war," Mae said, "it would not bode well for our ambassador to the Castol."

"No, it might not," Eli said. "Still, Cree'Tol has always been resourceful when it comes to that sort of thing. Should the need arise, I am thinking she will have little difficulty sneaking away or escaping captivity. Come to think of it, she might view it as a relief from the tedium of her ambassadorial duties."

Mae looked over at him. "Rivun is heading north to the capital to see what he can do to help the king, to stabilize the situation. He wouldn't even have had time to do that yet, let alone get there."

"That is true. Just as Cree'Tol, he and Jit may also find themselves in a difficult spot," Eli said.

"A war of aggression with the empire will mean war with our people as well."

Eli did not reply. His people were bound by treaty with the empire. They both were aware of that. Whether or not the warden followed through with the treaty was a different matter altogether. Eli suspected, if push came to shove, and events became grave enough, she would, especially if the empire requested help. In the past, such assistance ranged from sending teams of rangers, to full line companies of heavy infantry.

"Why do it?" Mae asked with a scowl. "Why now? War does not make any sense."

"Perhaps the king has died and a new one sits on the throne," Eli said. "Until we have more information, there is no way to know for certain. What I do know is that the Castol have heavy infantry encamped just ten miles from here. That is the reality we are faced with."

"How many?" Mae asked.

"According to our new friend Mago," Eli said, "near five thousand, maybe more."

Mae sucked in a breath. "What about the dispatch he was given? Did you learn anything from it?"

"The cavalry squadron is an advance force," Eli said. "The first part of their mission is to ensure the infantry's line of march is clear, that the road is open and the empire suspects nothing. Any Castol civilians they encounter were to be detained—until after the army passed through."

"What about imperial citizens?" Mae asked. "What of them?"

"They were to be executed."

Mae shifted on her stool.

"The Castol are such a warm-hearted and caring people, are they not?" Eli said.

"And the second?" Mae pressed. "What was their second objective? Five thousand does not seem nearly enough for an invasion of the imperial province, at least not enough for it to be successful. I am certain the empire has more power on hand, more than enough to punch back."

"Scattered throughout the entirety of the province, they do." Eli picked up a stick that had been used to stir the fire. One end of it had been scorched black. He poked at the fire, stirring it up. "Which is why this entire enterprise of the Castol poses many questions. I am not quite certain what their game is, ultimately what they hope to gain." Eli paused to suck in a breath. "But, to answer your question, the cavalry squadron's second objective is to ensure word from Astrix does not get out when the town falls under attack. They will cut the roads that lead deeper into the province and patrol the surrounding countryside."

"Astrix, that is the veterans' colony you spoke of," Mae said, "isn't it?"

"Yes," Eli said.

"So"—Mae hesitated as she clearly thought through what he had told her—"they mean to attack the town, to sack it?"

Eli continued to stare into the flames. "That seems to be the immediate objective. Beyond that, we are not sure what their next move will be. Our prisoner tells us the Castol are not terribly happy with the empire placing a veterans' colony so near to the border. They rightly view Astrix as a threat and want it gone."

"So, they are simply going to remove the threat," Mae said, "and then see if the empire responds?"

Eli rubbed his hands together before the fire for more warmth as a draft of cold air driven by a light wind blew into the tavern.

"It is a stupid thing to do," Mae said, "if that is their reasoning."

Eli looked around and spotted a stool a few feet off. Dragging it over and next to her, he sat down.

"How likely is it the empire will tolerate one of their towns being razed?" Mae looked over at him.

He considered his response for several heartbeats. Mae did not press him. Instead, she turned her gaze back to the fire and just waited for an answer. Patience was one thing all elves eventually learned. Though at times Mae lacked that quality, he understood she would find it, just as he eventually had.

"The senate may deliberate for a while before acting, but act they ultimately will," Eli said. "They always do. Razing Astrix will be a slap in their face, something the senate and emperor cannot afford to tolerate. To do so would demonstrate a weakness and lack of resolve before a potential rival. And worse, allowing a veterans' colony to be razed without a sufficient reply would potentially cause legionary support for the emperor or the senate to waver. The legionaries will demand blood, and the emperor, as the hard and unforgiving man he is, will have to respond."

"The Castol should know this," Mae said.

"They do. Within the last seventy years the empire and Castol have occasionally come to blows, usually nothing more serious than the occasional border skirmish involving secondary units. But this"—Eli sucked in a breath—"this will be wholly different."

"What are you talking about?" Titus asked as he closed the door to the kitchen behind him.

Mae looked around at the imperial ranger as he joined them by the fireplace. At his side, Eli felt his wife tense. Her rage was almost a physical thing, and it was directed squarely at Titus.

"You are talking about the coming war, then," Titus said, when neither spoke.

"We were," Eli confirmed as Mae shifted her gaze sullenly back to the fire. She repositioned herself on the stool, turning herself slightly away from the human ranger.

"I did apologize, lady," Titus said, clearly reading her mood. "We had no idea who you both were. Please understand that."

Mae did not reply but remained stubbornly silent.

"Titus," Eli said, with a glance at his wife, "we were just as surprised to find you and your team in Arvan'Dale as you were us."

Titus eyed Eli for a long moment, his dark eyes glittering in the firelight. "Meaning that you really want to know what we are doing north of the border."

Eli gave a shrug of his shoulders before leaning forward. He grabbed a piece of wood that had been stacked just off to the side of the hearth. Smoothed and rounded, it had once been a leg for a stool. He tossed it on the fire. Sparks flared as it landed, and the fire crackled in response.

"If you must know," Titus said, "we had not planned on being here."

"That makes two of us. We had not planned on being here either," Eli said. "Our bad luck then, bumping into you."

Mae gave a grunt of agreement.

"We were on our way to the east of the province," Titus said. "There's been trouble along the border of Abath. The Rivan might be behind it, stirring things up again, so we were dispatched to investigate and get to the root of the matter."

"The tribes have begun raiding across the border," Eli surmised as he began thinking to what he knew of the wild peoples who lived in the forests of Abath, which wasn't much. "Which tribes?"

"Specifically, the Hannee Confederation," Titus said. "We had no inkling there was trouble brewing with the Castol until we came north and were passing through this area."

"So," Eli said, "they sent four of the empire's best rangers to check on the Hannee's intentions."

"You know how it is," Titus said, "there are always tales of raiding parties crossing the border into the province and causing some sort of trouble, hitting isolated farmsteads, killing the locals, and hauling off slaves. This, however, from the reports I've read, seems more than the usual shenanigans."

"Significant raids, then," Eli said.

"High command wants to be sure before dispatching a more substantial force. Besides, sending us was less expensive than an entire legion." Titus rubbed the back of his neck.

"A legion would be extremely helpful," Eli said.

"After what we've just learned, I am in agreement with you there. An entire legion, along with auxiliary cohorts, would have put the fear of the gods not only into the Hannee, but also the Castol. There's nothing like gazing across the border and taking in an entire legion, in all its menacing splendor, encamped for all to see." Titus blew out an unhappy breath. "In truth, there should be a legion stationed in the province. I don't know why one isn't, but I don't get to make those decisions. I'm only a lowly ranger captain."

"There's nothing lowly about your rank," Eli said. "You are number two in the Corps, and when the rangers speak, the senate, if not the emperor, usually listens."

Titus gave a self-deprecating shrug of his shoulders.

Mae broke her sullen silence. "So, what will you do now?"

Titus shifted his hand from the back of his neck to rub at his eyes, which were red from lack of sleep. After a moment he stretched out his back, then held out his hand before the fire. "I'm gonna remain here with my team. The enemy has to march through Arvan'Dale if they want to get to Astrix. I intend to count them to be sure the information we've obtained is correct. Really the size and composition of the enemy is what is truly important. Once I have that, I will report back."

"To whom?" Eli asked curiously. "To whom will you report this?"

"The nearest garrison," Titus answered, "is Fort Trusk, a little more than thirty miles south of Astrix. The commandant can decide what to do with the information after that."

"I know the place," Eli said. "Trusk is on the smaller side, is it not?"

"It is," Titus confirmed. "The outpost was originally established to support the tax collectors. It has expanded, and now one of their main duties is to police much of the region south of here, beating down the bandits. It is mainly a mixed unit, light infantry and cavalry."

"How many men are stationed there?" Mae asked.

"Not enough," Titus said, "if that is what you are asking."

"There wouldn't be any larger auxiliary cohorts nearby, would there?" Eli asked hopefully.

"Not that I am aware of," Titus said. "The nearest significant force is over eighty miles away, at Governor's Seat, and they will need a few days' preparation before marching."

Eli scratched at an itch upon his arm and felt a stab of deep unhappiness and unease. He glanced around the inside of the tavern. It was a thorough wreck. Within a few years, the rot in the walls and roof would spread, eating away at everything, ultimately undermining the supports holding the roof up. Eventually the structure would fall in upon itself and collapse. Without any maintenance, the same would happen to all the structures in the village. Eli supposed it would be a fitting end for a place that had once seen such terrible evil.

More than anything, he wanted to be gone from this place. The itch to move on became powerful. He did not enjoy being in Arvan'Dale, especially at night. Daylight could not come fast enough.

Eli turned his gaze to Titus, who was rubbing his hands before the fire. That the Castol were marching to attack the empire was not welcome news. If it came to war, and it was looking like it would, many would surely die. The civilians living along both sides of the border would suffer cruelly. He could not see what could be done to stop events. Things had already, it seemed, proceeded too far.

"Would you like some company?" Eli asked Titus. "There are only two of us. Perhaps we might be able to help some?"

Mae cast an unhappy look at Eli and shifted on her stool, which creaked. Her gaze was like the sharp edge of a knife and spoke of danger… danger specifically for him. Eli ignored her.

"You want to go with us?" Titus asked, sounding surprised. "Really?"

"Why not? I have a feeling you could use the help, and if there's something we can do to stop what is coming, all the better."

"I don't know what can be done to halt events at this point, but I won't say no." Titus's gaze narrowed, almost suspiciously. "You've still not told me why you both are out here. What are you doing in Castol lands?"

"You are correct." Eli wasn't quite sure he wanted to enlighten Titus on the true matter of their mission. "We have not told you."

"So, why are you out here?" Titus asked.

"We are hunting a criminal," Mae said matter-of-factly.

It was Eli's turn to shoot Mae a hard look. Just like he had, she ignored him.

"Who?" Titus asked. "What criminal would attract the attention of elven rangers?"

"Though it pains me to admit it, we are after another High Born," Eli said unhappily.

"You're hunting an elf?" Titus repeated. The ranger's disbelief was plain. Eli could read it in his eyes. "That's certainly new. I don't think I have ever heard of an elven criminal. You all seem like you are in lockstep with one another."

"Occasionally," Eli said, "one of our apples goes bad."

"What did this criminal do?" Titus asked.

"He took something that did not belong to him," Mae said, "and killed another doing it."

"A murderer and a thief," Titus said. "You know, recently, this might be a coincidence, but we came across two elves, a male and a female."

Eli abruptly stood. He wouldn't have thought he could have been more surprised than when Titus and his team had jumped them a few hours before.

"Mik'Las." Mae rose from her stool as well and turned to face Titus. She seemed just as stunned as Eli. "Was his name Mik'Las?"

"Yes, that was his name." Titus looked between them. "I thought him a nice enough fellow. His companion was strikingly beautiful. Then again, all female elves are. But—she was different." Titus's gaze and tone became distant. "There was something about her that set her apart... She didn't speak but seemed, somehow, terribly sad, almost like he was taking her to a funeral of a dear friend. When she looked at me... it was... it was... I don't know how to explain it other than there was something about her that made me shiver. There is a power to her that I can't explain."

Eli and Mae exchanged a knowing look as Titus shook himself.

"When?" Eli asked. "When did you come across them?"

"We encountered them more than a week ago." Titus paused, looking between them again. "This Mik'Las is the fugitive you speak of?"

"He is," Mae confirmed.

"They certainly did not seem like they were in flight or running from pursuit."

"Where did you encounter them?" Eli asked.

"On the road south," Titus said. "They were both on horseback."

"Horseback?" Eli asked, glancing at Mae. That was not good news.

"Did they say where they were headed?" Mae asked.

"Actually, they did. Mik'Las told us he was going to the capital to see his cousin, the ambassador."

Mae and Eli shared a troubled look.

"How dangerous is he?" Titus asked.

"As dangerous as they come." Eli wondered if Mik'Las was indeed going to the capital. Or had it been misinformation planted with the human rangers to throw Eli and Mae off his trail? Mik'Las's cousin was indeed the ambassador. So that part was true. Were they in league? Somehow, Eli doubted it.

Titus was silent for a long moment as he gazed down at the fire again. Several heartbeats later, he looked up. "If you want, when we return to the empire, I can spread the word. Our people might be able to grab him and save you some trouble."

Eli thought on that for a couple of heartbeats. It was a generous offer and might help, but they could not afford to risk the Atreena. She might be harmed or even killed were the imperials to attempt to apprehend the two. Eli could not have that.

"No. That is our task, and I"—Eli paused and glanced over at Mae—"we will see it through to the end."

"I don't like having a dangerous criminal, especially an elf, moving freely about the empire."

"This is our job to do," Eli said, looking pointedly at the imperial ranger, "and ours alone."

"Eli," Titus began, "our people are—"

"I must insist," Eli said firmly, interrupting the human. "Please understand, this is a High Born matter and one not for humans to involve themselves in."

"All right," Titus said. "If you say so."

"We do," Mae affirmed. "You and your people will not interfere in any way. To do so will create problems between our nations. My mother will take issue with such interference."

Titus looked over at Mae and under the firelight studied her for a long moment. His lips tightened ever so slowly into a thin line. Eli well knew Titus was one who did not like to be told what to do.

"Once again, lady," Titus said, "I offer an apology for the injury caused to you. I do not wish you to harbor a grudge against us."

"Who hit me?" Mae asked quietly.

Eli shifted his stance. "Mae."

"Do not interfere, husband," Mae cautioned with a hard glance. "Who struck me, Titus? Tell me."

"I'm not sure it matters," Titus said.

"It does to me," Mae said in the same quiet tone. With a hand, she moved aside the hair covering her right temple.

Titus eyed the bruise for a heartbeat before he spoke. "Consider me the one who did the deed. I will take the blame for the injury to your person."

"I know it wasn't you," Mae said quietly.

"And yet, they are my rangers. I bear direct responsibility for their actions. If you wish to vent your retribution upon anyone, do so against me. That is my final word on the matter."

Mae's eyes narrowed dangerously.

The fire took that moment to pop loudly, almost causing Eli to jump. A fraction of a heartbeat later, the door to the tavern banged open. Aventus stood in the doorway. He was out of breath. Behind him, with a bare hint of predawn light, the gloom of night had begun to fade. Eli could see the first hints of color in the sky, which was a relief.

"What is it?" Titus asked as Aventus strode in.

"Light infantry, at least a full company," Aventus said. "They're on the road, two miles out. They should be here in little more than a half hour. I have no idea how many are behind them."

"Well." Eli clapped his hands together. "That's quite helpful."

"Helpful, how?" Titus asked, looking over. "I'm not seeing it."

"At least we will not have to go find them."

Titus gave an absent nod. Clearly thinking, the imperial ranger glanced around the room before stopping on Mae. After a moment, he looked back at Aventus.

"Have Maran take the messenger's horse and ride for Astrix to give them warning. Tell him to keep an eye out and watch for that cavalry squadron. He must win his way through to the town, understand? Prefect Deverex must have word of what's coming."

"Maran's our best rider. He will make it," Aventus said. "And what of the rest of us?"

"We're gonna pull out of town," Titus said, "and observe the enemy as they march by. I want an accurate count on their numbers. The more information we can provide, the better. Now, get Maran moving. Every moment counts."

"Yes, sir," Aventus said and left them, leaving the door open as he went.

Mae's eyes narrowed dangerously as she gazed at Titus for a heartbeat. Eli almost missed the look. Then she made her way over to her backpack, bow, and bundle of arrows, which she had set off to the side.

"The enemy should arrive at Astrix's gates by nightfall," Titus said to Eli. "I wish we could have provided the town more warning on what's about to come down upon them."

"Wishes are like daydreams," Eli said. "They frequently have no substance. You know that."

"You know, I've missed that fine elf wisdom of yours."
Titus's tone brimmed with irony. He made his way over to a
table where his own pack and bow lay. A bundle of arrows
was secured to the pack by thin leather ties. Hooves from a
horse could be heard pounding away outside.

"There is wisdom and then there is wisdom," Eli said.

Titus gave an amused grunt and almost seemed to smile.
"Though you were a pain in my ass, I missed you, my friend."

"I can only imagine how droll your existence has become
without my company," Eli said.

"Droll?" Titus gave another amused grunt. "I am
impressed, oh master ranger. You're using big words today."

"What of the prisoner?" Mae asked as Eli moved to
retrieve his own pack from where he had set it upon a dusty,
ramshackle table that had seen better days. There was a
carving of a phallic symbol upon its dusty top. "What do
you intend to do with him?"

Instead of answering, Titus made his way over to the fireplace and grabbed the end of the stool leg Eli had thrown
in. It was partially burning on one end. He tossed it into
the corner, amongst the pile of broken furniture and empty
barrels. As if the pile had been doused with flammable oil,
the fire immediately spread. Smoke began to fill the common room.

"Regretfully, the prisoner's soul has gone onto the loving embrace of the High Father," Titus said, "where he will
be judged for his life's actions and receive his eternal due.
There is no coming back from that."

Frowning, Mae glanced toward the kitchen door, which
Titus had closed.

"By burning down the tavern," Eli said, before his wife
could speak, "you will keep them guessing as to what happened here. With any luck, the Castol won't overthink it,

especially with their own cavalry having stopped here a few hours before."

"Dead men tell no tales, especially those you can't find." With that, Titus glanced briefly at Mae and made his way out of the tavern.

"We kill prisoners now?" Mae asked unhappily after Titus had left.

"When needed." Eli hoisted his pack up onto his shoulder and grabbed his bow.

"I do not like it," Mae said.

Eli was about to turn for the door. He paused, looking back at her. "For our people, we rangers sometimes must do distasteful things. You don't have to like it, but that is the world in which we operate. It is best you learn that now, for the day will come when you will be called upon to do the same."

As if to stop a sharp reply, Mae bit her lip.

Eli turned and, with Mae behind him, made his way out and onto the street. They found Aventus and Lenth waiting a few feet away. Both eyed Mae warily as the two elves approached them. Behind Eli, smoke had already begun to pour from the open door and roof of the tavern.

Mae stared down the road that ran south for a long moment.

"It was Maran, was it not?" Mae rounded on Titus. Holding her bow loosely in a hand, she pointed at him with the end of it. There was fury in her eyes. "That is why you sent him away."

Titus returned her gaze with a flinty one of his own but said nothing.

"Tell me who struck me," Mae demanded, taking a step closer. "I must know."

"No," Titus drawled, "I don't believe I will tell you, my lady."

"Why not?" Mae took another step nearer. Her temper was becoming a powerful thing in its own right.

"You well know why," Titus said. "I've already explained myself."

"It was me," Lenth announced firmly, stepping up before her. "I was the one who clubbed you. Look no further, nor seek to blame my comrades."

Eyes narrowing dangerously, Mae turned toward the other ranger. Her fury, if possible, seemed to only grow, and with it, her hand traveled to one of her daggers and came to rest upon the hilt. To Eli, his wife seemed like a coiled spring, just waiting for the moment of release. Preparing to intervene, he tensed himself.

"I will not permit you to harm him," Titus said.

"You won't permit it?" Mae asked, without looking over. Her gaze was fixed wholly upon Lenth.

"When you spotted me in the forest," Lenth said to her, "you started to draw that very dagger. Were you in my position, would you not do the same as I or worse?"

Staring hard at Lenth, Mae became still for several heartbeats. Then, as if she were in physical pain, which Eli knew she was from her injury, she grimaced. But it was more than that. Eli could tell Lenth had made his point with her and it really pissed her off. She would not seek vengeance. That much was clear to him. Eli suddenly felt a bubble of amusement.

"He said he would willingly do it again," Eli said, drawing both their attention. "Did you hear that, Mae? He said he would do it again."

Lenth frowned at Eli.

Her anger blazing, she looked back at Lenth, then shifted her gaze to Eli and jabbed at him with a savage finger. "Do not start with me, husband. Your attempt at levity might serve to provoke me further."

Eli kept a straight face as he looked over at Titus. "I occasionally enjoy playing with fire."

"As if you needed to tell me," Titus said sardonically. "Seriously, Eli, I don't need this drama right now."

"If you are not careful, this is one fire that might just burn you, husband of mine." Mae's jaw flexed. She spared him one more heated look, then turned away and gazed up toward the hill to where they had originally observed the village. She started off. Over her shoulder she called back to the rest of them. "Unless you want to be the welcoming committee as the enemy marches into the village, I suggest you start moving those sorry lumps you call your asses and get out of sight."

All four of them watched her for several silent heartbeats as she drew farther and farther away. Then Titus, looking over at Eli, broke the silence.

"I am thinking that is a dangerous girl you married," Titus said.

"Oh yes." Eli flashed a grin at the ranger. "Is she not magnificent? It is a quality I have dearly come to relish."

"You married her because she's dangerous?" Aventus asked in a disbelieving tone. "Most people marry for love."

"I find her—shall we say—exciting," Eli admitted.

"She scares the piss out of me," Aventus admitted.

"For a moment, I thought she might kill me," Lenth added.

Eli looked over at the ranger. "The day's still young."

"You're joking, right?" Lenth asked, then looked at Titus with serious concern in his eyes. "He's not serious, is he?"

"Oh, I never joke about such matters." Eli clapped the ranger on the shoulder in a friendly manner as he started after Mae. That elicited a laugh from Aventus. Titus chuckled softly, seemingly more from relief than anything else.

In an effort to catch up, Eli picked up his pace to a light jog. Mae was already thirty yards ahead and working her way quickly up the rise. He glanced back and saw the three human rangers jogging a few steps behind.

Sending a great column of smoke into the rapidly brightening sky, the tavern had begun to burn furiously. Eli could feel the intense heat pressing against the cold air of the morning.

He turned his gaze northward and felt his heartbeat increase. Somewhere up the road and near at hand, the enemy was approaching Arvan'Dale. Feeling the cold morning breeze against his face, he inhaled deeply. The crisp fall air sent energy coursing through his body. With the heat of the burning tavern behind him, the wind smelled of the promise of excitement.

Eli had a war to stop. That was, if he *could* stop it. And if he could not do that... well, there was a war to join.

CHAPTER EIGHT

Amidst the tall grass and under an afternoon sun that provided little warmth, Mae was lying upon her back, sleeping peacefully at Eli's side. She was so close they were almost touching. With her chest rising and falling rhythmically, Mae looked so peaceful and beautiful, his heart ached, and Eli wondered if it might burst in his chest from love alone.

Mae was everything he needed in this life but had not until recently known he wanted. He longed to reach out to her, to caress her face, to run his hand through her hair. It was an intoxicating thought, a powerful impulse, but one he pushed aside. She needed the sleep, and he would not disturb her, not after what she had been through.

Concealed by the high grass, they, along with the three human rangers, were lying upon a medium-sized hill that provided a good vantage point from which to gaze down upon the town. It was farther away and taller than the one he and Mae had used earlier. It was also closer to the forest. Behind them rose a steep, forested ridge that climbed three hundred feet higher. If it came to it, they could climb the ridge in quick order and disappear into the trees.

Titus lay to Eli's left. Aventus, a few feet away, was on his belly next to Titus. And like Eli's wife, Lenth was catching some sleep and lying just beside Mae, off to Eli's right.

"Another company," Titus breathed, "heavy infantry this time."

Almost regretfully, Eli looked up and away from Mae, peering through the tall grass and down into Arvan'Dale. Unfortunately, he had been wrong. The hours since they had left the tavern had passed slowly and without any hint of real excitement. The tedium and inactivity had been terrible, but Eli had been through worse and, like always, would endure.

He focused his gaze on the enemy down the slope. A pair of officers at its head, yet another infantry company was marching through the village. The order of march was spaced out, relaxed even, and the men moved at their own step. Even at a quarter mile distant, Eli could easily hear the low thrum of hundreds of boots.

Over the course of the last four hours, the tavern had obligingly burned to its stone foundation. As if angry, the ruin, now only a confused tangle of charred beams and ash-covered refuse, sullenly smoked.

No effort had been made by the soldiers marching through the village to extinguish the blaze. There had been no point. The village had long since been abandoned.

The fire had ultimately spread to four other buildings, each sending plumes of smoke into the morning sky. Those too had now burned themselves out and, like the tavern, smoked lightly. And yet, the acrid stench of smoke was still heavy on the air, as if the blaze were fresh. Gazing unhappily down upon Arvan'Dale, Eli wished the entire village had burned. It would have been one less blight under the gods' eyes.

"They're king's infantry." Titus was squinting down at the enemy. "Bloody king's infantry, all right."

"They look sharp, and their armor is well maintained," Aventus said, "which means they have discipline. We have to assume they are well-trained."

"See that standard?" Titus indicated a red, squarish banner with the image of a black stag. The bearer was walking just behind the two officers, the standard resting upon his shoulder at an angle. "They are a company from the crown prince's own, picked men all. So, yes, they are good."

"At least we've not seen any more cavalry," Aventus said. "I don't like horse soldiers."

"Horses are expensive and difficult to maintain, especially while on campaign." As he spoke, Titus never took his eyes off the enemy. The captain waved a hand before him. "For each horse, they would need to haul with them at least fifteen to eighteen pounds of feed a day. Multiply that by a few dozen, let alone a hundred or more, and your supply requirements not only increase, but begin to become a burden. Skimp on what you need, go a few days without proper feed, and a horse will go lame. Now consider that, coming through the heart of the great forest, there is little forage to be had, especially for large animals…" Titus fell silent. "Well, let us just say it's much easier to bring an infantry heavy force south, where the men can haul precooked rations and reduce the need for an extensive baggage train. Following me so far?" He looked over at Aventus.

"I am," Aventus said.

"Good," Titus said. "Their supply train, which we have yet to see, is probably struggling to accommodate that squadron of troopers we saw earlier."

"Why, Titus," Eli said, "you are just full of useful information. Has anyone ever told you that?"

"Maybe that's what made me such a good student. I listened and learned," Titus said with a straight face.

"Is that what you call it?" Eli asked, intentionally dripping innocence. "I thought you were just buttering me up. What elf would not want that from a human?"

Titus grinned at Eli. "If I had thought that would work on you, I would have tried it. You are immune to that sort of thing."

"Still, sir," Aventus said, "I'm grateful there are no more cavalry. Once we cross back over the border, you know the terrain. It's all farm and pasture country. There's not much cover to be had. I'd not want to get caught out in the open and ridden down."

"Yeah," Titus said, returning his attention to the enemy. "That wouldn't be good."

"No, it wouldn't," Aventus said.

"You know… once they cross the border, they're probably planning to live off the land," Titus said. "That country is rich with pickings."

"How many companies so far?" Eli studied the infantry making its way through the village. Wearing chainmail shirts and steel helmets, they carried medium spears and large oval shields. Each soldier was armed with a short sword. All wore heavy packs.

"Fifteen companies so far." Titus glanced down at a small pad lying before him in the tall grass. He had a charcoal pencil in his left hand. "Ten light and five heavy infantry companies, say somewhere near three thousand foot, perhaps even thirty-two hundred at most, if we're being generous. But when is a company of infantry ever at full strength?"

"And there's more coming," Aventus said.

"Always looking on the bright side," Titus said to Aventus, "aren't you?"

"I pride myself on keeping a positive frame of mind," Aventus said.

Titus spared Aventus a glance before refocusing his attention on the enemy in the village. "They are bringing some serious power south, that's for sure. All the units we've seen so far look first-rate. I am afraid the Castol mean business this time."

"It's a good thing we chased down those rumors," Aventus said, growing serious. "Otherwise, we'd never have found out they mean to attack across the border and strike at Astrix."

Titus gave a grunt. "By the blessed gods, we got lucky here."

"Fortuna loves rangers." Aventus glanced up at the sky. "She does this day, at any rate."

Eli felt himself scowl slightly and out of the corner of his eye, he caught Titus making the sign of the High Father with a grimace on his face. Eli had never much enjoyed tempting Fortuna either. Then what Aventus had said registered. He looked over at the two rangers. "Wait—what do you mean?" Then it clicked, and with that, he focused directly on Titus. "You came north for another reason then, at least at first."

"We did," Titus admitted. "As I told you, we were passing through the province, heading west toward Abath. We heard some disturbing stories. It seemed like everyone we met was telling some version of the same tale. So, I decided to take a slight detour and check things out before continuing on to Abath."

"Slight?" Eli asked. "This seems pretty out of the way."

Titus gave a shrug of his shoulders. "We go where the need is."

"What stories?" Eli asked, for he had become interested, especially so if it had drawn Titus's attention. "What did you hear that concerned you so?"

"Tales of towns and villages along the border being abandoned," Aventus said.

"Like Arvan'Dale?" Eli asked, his gaze going back to the village. In a loose column of two abreast, the infantry company was still snaking its way through the village. Behind them and nearly overburdened with sacks trailed four company mules. At the edge of the forest to the north, yet another column of infantry had begun to emerge from the tree line. "As in the people residing here just got up and left the town?"

"The stories we were hearing seemed like there was more to it than that," Titus said. "People had gone missing on both sides of the border, and not just a few either, from the accounts."

Eli found himself intrigued by what they were telling him. It seemed some sort of mystery was afoot, and if there was one thing Eli loved tracking down and solving, it was mysteries. "So, you decided to investigate? That's really why you came into Castol lands?"

"Aye," Aventus said. "At first, we found nothing out of the ordinary other than more exaggerated tales. You know how things get in the telling."

"They grow," Eli said, "at least they do with you humans."

"Yeah, well, we poked around the villages and towns off to the east, even looking over some of the more isolated homesteads, and found nothing really out of the ordinary. People were still there. Then we checked on both sides of the border. Eventually, we moved west, and as we neared Astrix, the tales became more than just stories."

The wind rustled the tall grass around them. The sun had brought some warmth, but the air was still cold. The wind made it even more chill.

"The settlements just south of the border were overrun with refugees," Titus said. "They had given up everything and fled from the north. Even Astrix had a goodly number of Castol refugees."

"The Castol sought shelter at a veterans' colony?" Eli asked. "I find that surprising."

"So did we," Aventus said. "Prefect Deverex did as well."

"Deverex?" Eli asked. "I have never heard of him."

"Former Camp Prefect Deverex of the Seventh Legion," Titus explained. "He settled in Astrix and is really the unofficial leader of the town. He's a good man."

"I see," Eli said, then decided to move the story along. "What of the refugees?"

"They were frightened," Titus said, "with wild stories of an evil magic, shadowy creatures hunting in the night. We also heard tales of a Castol army being assembled and that war was on the air, with many fleeing on word alone of what was coming." Titus turned his gaze back to the town. "Seems those rumors were true too."

"So," Eli said, "people were disappearing then."

"We went farther north to track things down," Aventus said. "We learned nothing from the first couple of empty villages. The people there simply upped and fled, taking whatever they could carry with them and leaving the rest behind. It seemed like the entire region, both north of the border and a few miles south of it, had been thoroughly abandoned. Even the bandits had hoofed it."

"Fear is a powerful thing," Eli said.

"Yes, it is," Aventus agreed.

"Then"—Titus blew out a breath—"we came across an isolated farm, six miles off the road and just over the border. It was in the middle of the forest. The family who had lived there had been killed. All we found were their bones."

Titus and Aventus shared a look.

"They had been gnawed upon," Aventus said.

Eli went still as a cold sensation slithered down his spine. "Like animals had gotten at them?"

"I've seen where people have died and animals came across the remains, scattering them about," Titus said. "This was—this was different."

Eli was almost afraid to ask. "Different, how?"

"Their bones had been chewed and broken, the marrow within sucked out," Aventus said quietly.

"Whatever it was that got them," Titus said, "the creature clawed its way inside the farmhouse and killed the family where they slept. Near as we could tell, it was a husband, wife, and two young children."

Eli's stomach clenched uncomfortably. He was not much enjoying what he was hearing. In fact, he did not want to hear it at all.

"It got them all," Titus continued. "Then, it went outside and killed the animals, their horse, sheep, and cow as well. I've never seen anything like it."

His horror growing by the moment, Eli inadvertently returned his gaze to Arvan'Dale. He sucked in a cold breath of air and let it out through his nose. He knew he had to ask the next part. "You found such things elsewhere too, didn't you?"

"We did … dozens of farms, villages and settlements." Aventus waved down at the town. "Even here in Arvan'Dale."

BY BOW, DAGGERS & SWORD

"Here?" That surprised Eli. "Well, that does not make sense. This place has been abandoned for several years."

"That's right," Aventus said. "We don't understand it either. But it happened here just the same."

"We arrived just before that cavalry squadron and explored the town," Titus said. "In all my years, I've seen nothing like it. Eli, the people of this village never left. They were killed and then eaten, near as we can tell, every single person. We found their bones. All had received similar treatment."

"The animals too," Aventus added.

"By what?" Mae asked in a horrified whisper. "What ate them?"

Eli looked over at her. She had awoken and had propped herself up on her elbows. It was clear Mae had been raptly listening to what was being said.

Titus shook his head. "We don't know. But they were devoured. That much is clear, and across the region it happened within the last few months … recent-like, except for here in Arvan'Dale."

Eli closed his eyes and was silent for several heartbeats. He had thought the nightmare over, but no, it wasn't. Though he had never ever wanted to come back here to Arvan'Dale, he was here once more. Providence had brought him back. It seemed there was more work that needed doing.

"It was a very long time ago, but I have seen such things before." Eli opened his eyes and shared a sad look with Mae. He could see the realization dawn in her eyes at what they faced and desperately found he wanted to spare her that.

"You have?" Titus asked. The scout shifted onto his side to face Eli. "You know what did this? Tell me."

Eli's gaze was still locked with his wife's. Her cheeks had paled, but there was also a sense of resolve there. Mae gave a nod for him to proceed. Just as he once had, it was apparent she would face whatever lay ahead with resolve. With that, he turned his attention back to Titus, and still Eli found himself hesitant to speak, as if that would delay any future horror.

"I've got a feeling I am not going to like this," Titus said. The human ranger's gaze was grim, as was his expression. "Am I?"

"No," Eli said, "I do not believe you will."

"Well, then, hit me with it."

Still, Eli said nothing.

"Come on, Eli," Titus encouraged, "get the bad news over with and then we can come up with a plan, not only to face it, but deal with it."

"This is not the first time I have been to Arvan'Dale. My last visit was not a pleasant one. Decades past, I had thought I had ended the madness here. I guess I was wrong."

"Ended what?" Titus asked. "What madness? Just tell me."

"I encountered a priest of Lutha Nyx here, in Arvan'Dale."

Titus had gone still as Aventus sucked in a startled breath and stared hard at Eli. "You're joking, right?"

Eli shook his head.

"Tell me that's not what we are dealing with," Titus asked finally, his tone horrified.

"When it comes to Lutha Nyx," Eli said, "I never jest."

"You are sure about this?" Titus asked.

"There must be a priest somewhere nearby, perhaps even a clutch of followers...considering how many have been killed and are missing."

"Lutha Nyx," Titus said. "High Father, keep us safe from such evil."

"We've got a bigger problem," Mae said in a hushed tone, interrupting them.

They looked over at her. She was gazing to the north and behind them, up on the forested ridge. Eli looked. It took him a moment, but he spotted a soldier on the ridge about a half mile away. The man had stepped from the trees and was standing upon a large outcropping of rock. He was gazing down upon Arvan'Dale. Joining the first, another soldier emerged from cover.

"This is just great," Titus said and looked over at Aventus. "You just had to jinx us with Fortuna, didn't you?"

"Me?" Aventus asked. "How did I jinx us?"

"Yes, you," Titus said sourly. "Next time, don't mention the goddess of chance in passing."

Ignoring them, Eli was still watching the two soldiers, studying them carefully. Both carried swords, along with bows, and they looked to be wearing black leather armor. They were clearly light infantry. He could see additional movement in the trees behind the two. It looked like there was a good number of them and they were moving southward along the ridgetop.

"Skirmishers," Lenth said. He had awoken.

"Most likely," Titus said. "I don't think they've seen us yet."

"Soon as we start moving, they will," Eli said, suddenly eager for what was to come. "I suppose things are about to become exciting."

"Only you, Eli, would become excited at the prospect of action," Titus said with a heavy breath laced with deep unhappiness.

"He is not that bright," Mae said.

"Oh?" Eli asked, looking over at her. "Really?"

"He does not seem to learn either," Mae added.

"Yep, you two are definitely married," Titus said.

"As if that was ever a real question," Eli said, looking at Mae. He shot her a wink and got an exasperated eye roll in return.

"We need to make a decision, and soon." Aventus eyed the enemy up on the ridge. "Do we move or stay? I vote move."

Eli's eyes went back to the ridge. The two soldiers who had appeared on the rock outcropping had moved back into the trees. He could see flashes of the group as they worked their way southward along the ridgeline. They would soon be right behind them, meaning he, Mae, and the human rangers would be trapped between the enemy in the village and those on the ridge. All it would take was for someone up there to look down and spot the small group lying in the tall grass below.

"I don't see that we have much of a choice," Mae said. "Whether we move or not, they are bound to spot us."

"There's gonna be a pursuit," Aventus said.

Eli felt his heart quicken at the prospect of action. "Let us hope it is a spirited one, eh?"

Titus gave Eli a long look that was far from happy. Then, with a grunt, the ranger stood. He shrugged on his pack and picked up his bow. The others got to their feet as well.

"Come on," Titus said and started into a jog down the back side of the hill, angling for the tree line to the south. "Time to hoof it."

A heartbeat later, there came an indistinct shout from the enemy on the ridge.

"We've been spotted," Aventus said as he too moved into a jog.

"And so it begins," Eli said as he jogged after Titus.

"Husband," Mae said at his side, "one day soon, you and I are going have a serious talk."

CHAPTER NINE

Eli stopped and placed his back to the trunk of the oak tree. He was breathing heavily. His legs burned from the run up the ridge and into the forest. He could feel the rough bark rubbing against his back.

Around him, the smell of the forest was strong. It was familiar, comforting, and Eli felt completely at home here. The trees grew tall, with some being quite old. There was also a lot of undergrowth, for a fire had at some point within the last few years swept through the area. He could see the blackened scars on the oldest and tallest of the trees that had survived.

Someone shouted in a firm tone, encouraging others forward. They spoke in the Castol tongue. It came from around the other side of the tree and was not too far off. Bow in hand, Eli nocked an arrow, one he'd made himself. He prided himself in his arrow-making skills. There was a subtle art to it that, if done correctly, could mean the difference between making a difficult shot or missing by a mere hair. Skill was also required when it came to bow work, but you could not ignore the arrow either.

Taking a calming breath, in an attempt to steady himself and slow his rapid breathing, he brought the bow up to chest level, then leaned partially around the side of the tree so that only a small portion of him was visible.

Thirty yards away were two men, both Castol soldiers. They were carrying horn bows. They had stopped and were studying the ground before them. One of the two knelt and peered more closely at the ground. He said something to the other, looked up, and pointed in Eli's general direction. Without having to overhear what was said, Eli well understood the meaning.

In the haste of their flight and the enemy's pursuit, little effort had been made when it came to concealment. There just had not been time, for the enemy had immediately set off in pursuit, which had turned out to be much closer than Eli had expected.

Eli leaned farther out from behind the tree and brought his bow to bear on the enemy. Pulling the string taut and holding his breath, he drew a careful bead on his target.

Eli breathed out, and as he did, he released. The bow's string twanged in a satisfying manner, and with it, his arrow hissed away, flew cleanly between the two men, and hit a third, who had just emerged from cover ten yards behind the others. Eli's arrow slammed into his chest. The strike drove him forcefully backward and to the ground, where he landed hard.

Before Eli could duck back under cover, or the first two enemy could react, another arrow took the kneeling man in the side of the head. The arrow made a cracking sound, like two rocks being smacked together, as it hammered home. The soldier's head jerked to the side violently. He crumpled to the ground a heartbeat later, with only his legs twitching.

The last man threw himself hastily behind the nearest tree. Then, he hollered, nearly screaming at the top of his lungs, "They're over here! Over here. Hurry."

Eli ducked back behind the tree as the man kept screaming. He looked over to his right and saw Titus nock another arrow. Mae, Lenth, and Aventus had continued onward and were ahead somewhere in the trees. He could not see them, but he knew they were out there.

"That was a fine shot," Titus said to Eli as he peeked rapidly around the side of his tree.

"Thank you," Eli replied, pleased Titus had recognized the difficulty of the shot he had taken.

"Mine was better," Titus said after a moment, then grinned full-on at Eli. "The target was smaller."

"Oh really?"

"Yes, really," Titus replied and then, as more shouts rang out, the human leaned around the trunk of the tree, brought his bow to bear, aimed for a heartbeat, and released. "Go," Titus said to him, just as a scream rent the air, a clear result of the shot he had just taken. "Go now."

Eli did not hesitate. He ran, sprinting for all he was worth. After twenty feet, he glanced back and saw Titus release another arrow, then he too turned and dashed after Eli.

An arrow flashed by Eli's head, hissing as it passed. The missile hit a thick branch just ahead of him and punched its way right through the limb. The end of the arrow quivered with unspent energy, and the strike set leaves cascading down from the branch. Ducking, Eli passed under the branch and through the shower of leaves.

Glancing back again, he saw five more of the enemy pounding after them. One had stopped, knelt, and with his bow, taken a shot. He was in the process of drawing an arrow from a bundle strapped to his back. His eyes were clearly on Eli.

Then Eli, with Titus close behind, flashed by Mae, who was concealed behind a tree with her bow at the ready and an arrow nocked. He caught her gaze for a fraction of a heartbeat. Time seemed to slow and his eyes were drawn to hers. She winked at him. Time sped up again and then he was past her. Lenth was concealed by a tree to her right and Aventus to the left.

"Titus," Eli called as he threw himself behind a tree, "get under cover."

There was a solid thud as an arrow hammered into the back of the tree, just a heartbeat later, as Eli got behind it. And as if in reply, bowstrings twanged in rapid succession. This was followed by a meaty *thwack*, a heavy grunt, and the sound of at least two bodies crashing to the ground.

Hastily nocking an arrow, Eli leaned around the tree and took in the scene before him in an instant. Three of the five enemy were down. One was still up but had stopped running and was looking, stunned, at his comrades. He appeared young, even for a human soldier, a mere youth.

Eli released the tension on the string of his bow.

The kneeling man had just released the arrow that had struck Eli's tree. He was reaching for yet another arrow as Eli's hammered home into his collar, biting wickedly deep. Falling back, amidst a gush of blood that fountained into the air, he cried out. He rolled on the ground in clear agony. Another arrow smacked into his neck and then he fell still, his lifeblood pumping out onto the forest floor.

The lone standing man, the youth, had turned and seen what had just happened. He stood, seemingly frozen, for a protracted moment before glancing all around. Then his nerve failed. He broke, running back the way he'd come.

A fresh arrow nocked, Aventus took a step forward, emerging from cover, and brought his bow up. He aimed at the fleeing soldier, tracked him for a moment, then took his shot. The missile flew true and slammed home, square into his target's back. The strike spun the youth around. Eli saw the tip had emerged from the chest, right where the human heart was located.

The youthful soldier stumbled a few steps toward them, eyes impossibly wide, as if in disbelief. His hands went to the arrow protruding from his chest. Gasping and struggling for breath, he took another step before his legs gave out and he fell to his knees, then wavered there for several moments before pitching face forward to the forest floor. He thrashed about, then fell still.

All was suddenly, unnaturally quiet.

Breathing heavily, Eli lowered his bow and attempted to catch his breath. The others looked just as winded.

"That was quite a chase," Aventus said as he moved to the nearest body and, with his foot, rolled the Castol soldier over and examined the dead man. "Skirmisher gear, all right. There's likely an entire enemy company after us. If we're lucky, just a section."

"Perhaps after the others see this scene, they will have second thoughts," Titus said.

"I doubt it," Eli said. "Numbers give people courage."

"What are they doing off the road?" Lenth asked.

"Honestly, I should have expected something like this," Titus said unhappily, as if he blamed himself, "the enemy securing their flanks as they marched. It's common sense. We'd do the same."

"Hindsight is always a bitch," Eli said.

Pursing his lips, Titus stared hard at Eli but said nothing.

"You know that," Eli said. "There is no looking back because you can't change things. Look forward and learn."

Titus gave a nod.

Kneeling, Aventus began searching the enemy soldier, rapidly patting him down. In the far distance, there was an incoherent shout, someone clearly calling to someone else, for there was an answering reply. Aventus did not even bother looking up as he tore the seam of the man's tunic and revealed several copper coins, along with a larger silver one.

"There's more of them coming for damn sure," Lenth said. Despite the chill air, his face was sheathed with sweat. As with the rest of them, he was winded and breathing heavily, though he and the others were beginning to recover. "And they're proving surprisingly persistent."

"Yeah," Titus said sourly. He had pulled out his canteen and taken a quick swig. He stopped it and returned the canteen to his hip, tying it one-handed back in place. "Too persistent. They've chased us for four miles at least, maybe five. These dead buggers, I'd wager, the High Father rest their souls, were the fittest and most eager." Titus ran his gaze over the dead. He expelled a heavy breath that reeked of unhappiness. "And the enemy now knows they've been discovered. They will stop at nothing until they either catch us or see us dead."

"We need to lose them," Mae said, "to throw them off our tracks."

"Agreed," Eli said as another shout rang out, this one closer. "Titus, as fun as this has been—and you know how much I love my fun and excitement—I am in agreement with my wife. It is time to stop playing with the Castol, break off contact, and slip into the forest."

"Fun? Playing?" Aventus asked as he stood. "You thought that was fun and we were just toying with them?" Aventus shook his head as he simply stared at Eli in clear astonishment. "Of course, you thought it was fun. You've always been a little twisted like that." Aventus paused, as if something had occurred to him. "Perhaps that's why we got along, I guess."

"Why, my dear Aventus, I have absolutely no idea what you are talking about," Eli said, managing finally to get his breathing under control. "I really do not." Eli looked over at Titus in question. "Titus, whenever did he and I get along? You know, I do not even like him."

"You've always been full of shit, Eli," Titus breathed, the corner of his mouth turning up. "You know that, right?"

Mae gave an amused grunt herself, which drew Eli's attention and a frown.

"Did you hear that?" Eli asked Mae in mock outrage. "Did you hear what he just said?"

"I did," she said, "and I believe they are onto something."

"I can't believe you are taking their side," Eli said, aghast. "I feel betrayed, cruelly betrayed by my own wife. And after what Lenth did to you, I find that just shocking."

"Eli," Titus warned, "I've already told you, I don't need that."

"I don't need it either," Lenth said with a nervous glance thrown at Mae. "In fact, I would really like to put that bad business behind us."

Mae shot Eli a scowl, grew serious, and turned to Titus. She had clearly tired of the game. "I might be stating the obvious here for you humans, but while we waste time chatting, they are drawing closer."

"I think they went this way," someone shouted, as if to emphasize her point. The shout seemed to come from somewhere down the slope, below them and not too far off.

Titus briefly glanced in the direction of the shout, then looked around, studying the forest and the rising slope that led to rugged terrain. He pointed to a small gap in the tree canopy off to their left, which showed a steep, rocky ridge hanging three hundred feet above them. "We go up there, then down the other side."

"That will require some scrambling, perhaps even climbing," Mae said, eyeing the rocky slope, "and it is more than a little exposed. Again, I will state the obvious, because someone needs to. We could easily be spotted, and they have bows." She pointed to one that lay discarded on the ground.

"It can't be helped," Titus said as he started off in the direction of the ridge, beginning to work his way up the slope and push through the brush that grew all around. "We climb. Now, come on. Leave as little evidence of our passage as possible. If we're careful enough, perhaps they will even go in the wrong direction." He stopped and looked back on Aventus, sparing the human ranger a long, hard look. "And, Aventus, don't tempt fate by invoking *her* name or mentioning luck, will you? You have a bad habit of doing that."

"I do?"

"Yes, you do," Eli said. "It's one of the reasons I don't like you."

"Uh-huh." Aventus looked between them, then gave a shrug of his shoulders, and with that, Titus turned away and continued on pushing through several thick bushes.

"I believe I would like them to do that, go in the wrong direction, that is," Lenth said as he followed his leader and made his way through the brush. "This ranger would like things easy for once."

"If you wanted it easy," Titus said, his voice floating back to them, "then you should have not joined the Corps. We always do things the hard way."

"Don't I know it," Lenth said.

Aventus shook his hand holding the coins. They clinked as he looked over at Eli. He pointed at the body he had taken them from. "That man just bought us a round of drinks at the next town."

Eli glanced at the body. Blood had spread out across the forest floor and darkened a thick patch of moss.

"Well then, we'll have to remember to raise a mug and thank him properly," Aventus added. The coins disappeared into a pocket, and with a chuckle at his own grim humor, Aventus moved after his comrades.

Mae hesitated, looking in the direction of the shouts and calls, which were steadily growing closer. Gaze distant, she bit her lip.

"What is it?" he asked her, taking a step nearer. Like the rest of them, she was perspiring. Sweat beaded her brow. At some point during their run, she had managed to tie her hair back into a single ponytail with a leather tie. Several strands had come loose and hung over her face. Eli idly wondered how she had managed that feat while on the run. "Tell me. What troubles you?"

"I do not know," Mae said. "I just have—have…" Mae trailed off and scratched an itch on the side of her cheek. She sucked in a breath, then turned her gaze to his. There was a hint of vulnerability within as she searched his face with her eyes. "I have a bad feeling about all of this. An ill wind is upon the air. I do not like it, especially with what we learned in Arvan'Dale."

"I have sensed the same," Eli admitted as he stepped up to her. He felt an irrational stab of desire, and with it, impulse took hold. He pulled her close and kissed her hard. She kissed him back. After a moment, he pulled away. "I love you."

"I thought you felt betrayed by me?" Her eyes searched his face for a long moment, and as they did, a slight, teasing smile tugged at her lips. She leaned forward and kissed him again. Her lips were incredibly soft and he lost himself in the moment, the feel of her pressed against him.

There was another shout, which drew their attention. It was incredibly close at hand, perhaps no more than twenty yards away. The enemy soldier was only concealed by the undergrowth of the forest. Without another word, as silent as ghosts, they turned and moved after the three human rangers, melting into the forest, as only elven rangers could do.

CHAPTER TEN

Eli pulled himself up over the top of the jagged ledge of the ridgetop's crest so that his stomach was pressing against the edge. Despite the chill air, the rock had been warmed by the sun. It felt good against his palms as he, with a grunt, swung his legs up, over, and onto the ledge.

With a crack, an arrow struck the rock a few feet to the left of where he'd just been. The arrow fell back and away, clattering against the rocks and dropping out of sight.

"Bloody gods," Lenth said as he dragged himself over the ledge a few feet from Eli. "They just don't give up, do they?"

Without answering, Eli pulled himself to his feet and took his bow off his back, then hastily shrugged off his pack, dropping it at his feet. Another arrow flew by, only to hit a rocky outcropping to his right.

Eli's anger sparked. Though it was exciting, he had never much enjoyed coming under fire, especially when he could not return it in kind. Mae was still below, climbing. She was also under fire from the enemy. That bothered him too, and not just a little.

He reached down to his pack and undid the ties holding his bundle of arrows to it. Taking a handful from the bundle, he stepped up to the edge.

Carefully peeking over, he saw Mae was ten feet below and steadily climbing up toward him. Titus was just past her and working his way up the rock face, with Aventus a few feet over to the left and moving up as quickly as he could, though his chosen path to the top of the ridge was a more difficult one. It had not been apparent from below, but the last fifteen yards had been a straight-up climb.

There were six men at the bottom, all with bows. They were loosing arrows at the climbers, hooting and hollering as they did it. They were not terribly bad either and had come close to hitting Eli more than once. As if to emphasize that point, one missile cracked loudly into a rock an inch from Mae's left hip. She glanced over at it as the arrow fell away, then redoubled her efforts to get to the top as fast as possible.

"You want to play, eh?" Eli asked those below in a near whisper. "Let us play then. Only, you are about to learn, I am a master at this game."

Not only was his anger growing but so too was his concern for Mae's safety. The longer this went on, the greater the chance one of them would become injured, and Eli meant to stop it. Nocking an arrow, he picked out one of the enemy, drew the string of his bow taut, aimed for a mere heartbeat, then released.

Two heartbeats later, his arrow hit its intended target, driving deep into the shoulder. The enemy soldier fell backward to the ground, dropping his bow in the process. Grievously injured, he was no longer a threat.

Without hesitating, Eli turned his gaze away to a new target, nocked another arrow, and in rapid succession loosed. This shot flew true as well and drove into his target's chest. Already in the process of releasing an arrow, the enemy soldier jerked violently as he was hit and let go of the string early. The errant missile flew off wide and to the left. He tottered for a moment, gazing down upon the arrow that had buried itself in his chest, then vomited blood and pitched forward to the forest floor.

"Get him," one of the men below shouted in rage, pointing at Eli. He was clearly a leader of some sort. His armor wasn't fine enough to be an officer, so that pegged him as a sergeant. "Get that bastard up there. Bring that elf down for me, boys, and I will buy you a drink next time we hit a tavern."

"You're next, my obliging friend," Eli said to himself, a promise to the sergeant below. "Keep standing out in the open, just like that."

As he nocked his bow yet again, an enemy arrow hissed menacingly by Eli's head. Ignoring it, he kept his gaze fixed upon the sergeant.

"Make your shots count, boys," the sergeant encouraged as he nocked an arrow of his own. "Aim carefully. I want them brought down."

Another arrow hissed by, this one uncomfortably close as well. Eli felt the wind of its passing against his neck. He aimed and released. The sergeant had been in the process of raising his own bow when Eli's missile hit him square on the forehead, with an audible *thunk* that carried clear up to the crest of the ridge. The sergeant immediately crumpled.

Bow in hand, Lenth was there next to him. He loosed an arrow and hit his mark, taking a man in the upper arm. The wounded enemy soldier dropped his own bow and began screaming in both agony and panic. With that, those below scattered, seeking cover of the trees and boulders. Lenth released a second arrow, which hit the screaming man nearly square in the chest. The strike drove him back two steps. With a dumbfounded expression, he stared down at the arrow sticking out of his chest for a long moment, then fell over onto his side and lay twitching amidst the brush in the clearing below.

Emerging from the forest, another soldier appeared. This one, though a skirmisher like the rest, was wearing the trappings of an officer. He even wore a white-plumed helmet that set him apart from the others.

"Get down, sir," one of the sheltering men called urgently. "They're uncommonly good with those bows."

The officer did not hesitate. He dashed for cover. Eli tracked the leader, following him with his bow, leading a little, then released. His arrow shot downward, punching clean through the man's right thigh, just a hair before he reached cover behind a large boulder. The officer cried out in surprise as he staggered behind the big rock and collapsed.

"Bastards," the officer called out a few moments later. "Bloody bastards."

Eli nocked another arrow but relaxed a little. No one was shooting back, and the enemy seemed content enough to cower behind whatever cover they could find. He blew out a relieved breath.

"I thought you elven rangers never miss." Lenth had his bow with an arrow ready and was gazing down at the enemy. Eli noted Lenth was carefully scanning the ground and trees around where the enemy had taken shelter.

Mae pulled herself up to the ledge, and as she did, Eli reached down and offered her a hand. She clasped his firmly, and he hauled her up and onto the rock, while feeling an incredible sense of relief that she was uninjured and no longer being shot at.

"Eli, you missed," Lenth said again.

"I didn't miss," Eli replied with a tinge of indignity as he reached out a hand and pulled Titus up and onto the rock.

"Thank you," Titus said, looking back down. "That was one heck of a climb."

"It was," Eli agreed.

Lenth focused as he raised his bow, aiming. A heartbeat later, there was a twang as he released. The arrow shot downward. There was a resulting cry of pain. Eli glanced over the side and saw one of the enemy, an arrow lodged in his stomach, dragging himself behind a tree. He left a trail of blood on the forest floor behind him.

"He made the mistake of exposing himself to take a shot," Lenth said matter-of-factly. "I guess you could say I showed him the error of his ways."

"It certainly seems that way," Eli agreed. "Let us hope the rest take the lesson to heart and leave us be."

"That would be good," Lenth said. "I believe I would like that."

Mae stepped forward and offered a helping hand to Aventus, while Lenth nocked another arrow and stood ready. The enemy below did not come out from cover. Though Eli could hear the enemy speaking urgently amongst themselves, he could not catch what was being said. That frustrated him a little, for he would have dearly liked to eavesdrop on that conversation.

"What do you mean, you didn't miss?" Lenth pressed as he stepped back from the edge and out of sight from those below now that their entire party was up. "That officer still lives. You hit him in the leg."

"I wanted him to live," Eli replied smugly. "It was intentional."

"Right." Lenth's tone was clearly disbelieving. "You expect me to believe you wanted to just wing him and not kill him? He is an officer."

"I desired only to injure."

"Why not go for the kill?" Aventus asked curiously. "We've always been instructed to go for the officers and sergeants first. Heck, you taught Titus and me that, literally beating it into our heads. Go for the officers first."

"As you should," Eli said.

"I don't understand," Lenth said.

"That officer down there," Titus explained patiently, "is gonna be more concerned with saving his own hide than skinning ours, especially now that he's been wounded." Titus looked over at Eli. "That was a good move and quick thinking. It might just slow down the pursuit or even downright discourage it."

"Thank you," Eli said with a slight bow, then glanced around the crest of the ridge they had climbed up to, studying it with a critical eye. The ridgetop was only about twenty yards wide. Much of the soil had eroded away, revealing mostly weather-worn bedrock. There was only a handful of trees, and those appeared stunted, likely the result of the wind and elevation.

The ridgeline continued to the south for another two hundred yards before climbing steeply higher. Stepping over, Eli was pleasantly surprised to find the reverse side of the ridge was not as steep as the one they had just climbed. It had more of a gentle grade and would be easy to negotiate back down, to a point where they would be able to slip into the forest and hopefully disappear, losing their pursuers.

Eli smiled to himself at the thought of that. Frustrating the enemy was always a good thing, and disappearing was one way to do that.

Aventus followed Eli's gaze. "Well, that's lucky. We will be able to make tracks."

"Yes," Eli said, "I was just thinking the same."

Titus looked over at Aventus and a sour expression crossed his face. "Perhaps I was wrong, but I thought we had an understanding."

The other ranger looked back over at him, at a loss. Then things clicked and he understood. "You were serious about that?"

"I am," Titus said. "No more tempting fate. It will only serve to cause more trouble."

"You are too superstitious, Titus," Aventus drawled, "really…"

"Uh," Mae said, drawing their attention. There was a note of worry in her tone. She was looking over the ledge and down at the enemy. "We might have a slight problem here."

Eli and the others moved over to her.

"Oh," Titus said as he looked meaningfully over at Aventus with some heat, "this is just great. See?" Titus gestured with a hand. "What do you say to that?"

"You can't blame this on me," Aventus said.

"I can't?" Titus asked.

"That's not fair," Aventus protested. "They were already chasing us."

Shaking his head slightly in disbelief, Eli stared at the enemy. Down below them were more than a hundred skirmishers. Dozens had already begun the climb up the ridge. Eli could see more under the tree canopy beyond those that were in view. But that was not what had caught his attention or caused him concern.

"Shoot them," came a shout from below. It was the officer Eli had wounded. The arrow still stuck out of his thigh. He was being supported by another man.

"He looks pissed," Lenth said, glancing over at Eli. "Don't you think? Perhaps winging him was not the wisest of moves after all, eh?"

"You may be onto something," Eli said without looking over. "I believe what we are dealing with here is the law of unforeseen consequences."

At Eli's side, Titus's jaw gave a tick. "Or it could just be Aventus tempting Fortuna to screw with us."

"I said, bloody shoot them," the officer roared from below.

A group of ten men with bows was standing off to the side. Almost in unison, they raised their bows skyward.

"We might want to step back now," Aventus said hastily as he took several steps away from the edge. With the others, Eli moved back, and as he did, arrows arced upward at them. Several clattered loudly against the rocks of the ridge beneath the ledge. A few sailed harmlessly overhead, arcing high and then falling out of sight in the trees on the other side of the ridge.

Eli looked over at Mae. "Not only are there skirmishers down there, but also Castol foresters. I saw two of them. You are correct. We are in some trouble."

"Foresters?" Titus exclaimed and moved back up to the ledge and peered quickly down. He stepped back, and a heartbeat later, more arrows flew upward. He shot a glare over at Aventus.

"Titus, really," Aventus protested, holding both hands up, "how was I to know they would have foresters with—?"

Face incredibly stern, Titus raised a finger at the other ranger, silencing him. "Not another word, Aventus. Not another word."

With a snap, Aventus closed his mouth.

"Those foresters are almost as good as we are," Lenth said.

"I recognized Kyber amongst them," Eli said, knowing Titus would know the man.

"This is getting better and better," Titus groaned. "Why does it have to be Kyber? Of all foresters, why him? Why here? Why now?"

"You forgot, why me?" Eli said.

"Who is Kyber?" Mae asked.

"He is a real mean bastard," Titus said, "and we are in trouble, deep trouble, if Eli's right."

"I am right," Eli said to Titus and then turned to Mae. "Kyber is a captain of the foresters. I have had one or two, maybe even three, encounters with him."

"Encounters?" Mae asked, her eyes narrowing suspiciously. "And he lived?"

Eli gave a nod of confirmation. "Oh, and he is quite good at his trade, quite good."

"Which means," Mae said sourly, "he's better than good."

"You also might say he and I, well, uh"—Eli laughed lightly in a manner that conveyed some embarrassment— "we are also not on the best of terms, if you know what I mean."

"Of course you're not," Titus said, his tone heavy with irony. "I mean, who wouldn't immediately take to you, Eli? You are just so loveable."

"Right?" Eli said. "I found it shocking too that he tried to kill me not once, but twice now."

"Uh-huh," Titus said. "Any chance Kyber didn't recognize you? I don't need him finding extra motivation at tracking us down, not now. You sort of tend to bring out the best in people, where they actually want to go out of their way to kill you."

"I seriously doubt that," Eli said. "Most people just love me."

"And cows can fly," Aventus said.

"So, do you think he saw you?" Titus asked.

"Well," Eli said, "he was sort of looking right at me a moment ago. But, honestly, it is a goodly distance down. He might have mistaken me for another elf."

"As if there are very many other elven rangers about?" Titus asked him.

"HULLOO THERE, ELI!" came the shout from below.

"On second thought," Eli said, "and some reconsideration, I believe he did recognize me."

"So, what was your first clue?" Titus asked.

"Now, I want to kill you, husband," Mae said.

"I think there's a line for that," Lenth said to Mae.

Eli stepped toward the edge, exposing his head as he looked down. The enemy were still climbing. It took him a moment, but he spotted Kyber standing under cover of the boulder and exposing just his head a little. It was the same rock the officer had taken shelter behind. Eli judged that even if he took a shot, he would likely miss, as Kyber was smart enough to duck should he raise his bow. Besides, it would take at least two heartbeats for his arrow to reach Kyber.

No, it was not a practical shot. Eli knew he would need all his remaining arrows in the hours to come, especially if Kyber was on their trail and scouting for the skirmishers, who were trained scouts in their own right.

"Ha," Kyber called, "I thought that might be you."

"Kyber," Eli called back down in a genial manner. "I wish I could say it is a pleasure seeing you. But then I would be lying, would I not?"

There was a harsh bark of a laugh from Kyber. "Trust me, the pleasure is all mine. Or soon it will be."

"Coming after us, then?" Eli asked.

"Oh yes. And this time, I am going to get you. I will take real pleasure in gutting you, real pleasure. Then I will take your ears as a prize, a keepsake that I will wear around my neck."

Eli almost grinned as he gazed down at Kyber. "You and what army?" Eli paused dramatically and made a show of studying the skirmishers climbing the ridge. "Oh wait. You have an army."

Mae stepped forward and pulled Eli back and away from the edge.

"Why did you do that?" Eli asked. "Things were just getting interesting."

"There is no sense in playing with him," Mae said.

"Of course there is," Eli said. "Think of the fun of it."

"I don't believe we need to piss them off even more," Lenth said as he peeked over the edge. "They're getting closer, Titus. Can we just go now?"

Massaging the back of his neck, Titus stared at Eli for several heartbeats, his expression unreadable, then turned his gaze southward. "He's right. We have to get moving and take advantage of the lead we have. There's no time to waste. Come on."

Without waiting, Titus began moving southward along the ridgeline. Aventus and Lenth followed after him. After a few feet, they broke into a brisk jog.

"Is he that good?" Mae asked.

"You mean Kyber?" Eli asked.

Mae gave a nod.

"Yes," Eli said, "and he is holding a serious grudge against me—well, maybe more than one grudge, to be honest."

"I can well understand why," Mae said. "I am thinking that wit of yours is a constant source of trouble."

"You are looking at it the wrong way." Eli shrugged on his pack and picked up his bundle of arrows.

"Wrong way?" Mae asked. "How?"

"Think of it as generating a little excitement now and again."

Mae eyed him for a long moment. "If Kyber does not kill you first, then after we get out of this mess, I just might, husband of mine."

Feeling his heart begin to beat with the excitement of the moment, Eli grinned at his wife.

Shaking her head in clear exasperation, Mae turned and started after the human rangers. Eli followed and Mae picked up the pace to a matching jog. They moved along the ridgeline, heading southward, in the general direction of the border, which was still some miles off.

"Did you really intend to wound that officer?" Mae asked curiously, after they had gone a hundred yards.

Eli glanced over at her and flashed her another grin. "That's my story and I am sticking to it."

CHAPTER ELEVEN

Dipping both hands into the stream, Eli cupped them together and drew forth some water. He brought it up to his lips and drank, draining all that he held in both palms. The water was bitterly cold and, in the chill air, made his fingers ache slightly. Yet, it was also fresh, clean, and more than welcome.

Mae sank to a knee by his side and lowered a cupped hand to the stream. Leaning over, she closed her eyes briefly as she drank. Then she dipped her hand again and drank some more.

"That is some *good* water," Mae said, straightening back up. She wiped her lips with the back of her arm, then looked over at him, caught his look, and offered up a slight smile that spoke of weariness but also great affection. The smile was only for Eli and he treasured it.

Like him, she was clearly tired, worn, and quite dirty. A smear of dirt marred her left cheek, as did a spot on her chin. They both needed a bath, and badly too. Had they come across a lake or pond, despite the cold, Eli would have readily jumped in and scrubbed himself clean. But they were still in the heart of the forest. There were no lakes or ponds nearby, at least any that he knew of.

Mae turned her eyes skyward. Eli followed her gaze and briefly studied what could be seen of the sky through the thick canopy of leaves that hung high overhead. Then his gaze returned to Mae as she continued to look upward. Studying her, Eli suddenly felt his heart stir, beating faster, as she absently moved an errant strand of hair from her face and tucked it behind an ear. As his desire for her unexpectedly surged, his breath caught in his throat.

Gods, she was magnificent. Just truly magnificent... absolute perfection.

Though he doubted she realized it, in nearly every movement, there was a natural grace about her. She always seemed to use an economy of motion, never taking more steps than were required. It reminded him of how a large forest cat moved, a predator beyond compare, one that one would not willingly turn one's back on.

And there was no doubt, she was not only dangerous but also at times completely unpredictable. He loved that about her. Direct in her intentions, but also volatile and dangerous... excitement embodied in a single spirit.

Eli stilled, stunned to his core. While so many others faded to nothingness, this moment would remain seared into his memory. Until the day he passed from this world, he would recall it perfectly, for it was when the puzzle of his attraction, his desire for Mae, finally revealed itself. He saw it plainly. It was so obvious he could not believe it had not occurred to him before.

Her spirit was strong and unquenchable, a fiery aspect of her being that made her who she was. He loved that she always took the direct approach to things, to people, and especially to him when he intentionally poked at her. Subtlety was not something she bothered to play with. Direct and to the point, that was Mae.

Back home, despite the elevated position her mother occupied, Mae had been considered somewhat awkward, at least socially. That was especially true for the top of their society, those with long, venerated lines who looked down their noses at others they viewed as less fortunate.

Despite being well off, Mae had been nearly an outcast from her peers, those her own age. And yet, she had never allowed that to slow her down in pursuing her own goals. That she did not quite fit in had not seemed to bother her overly much.

Still, having gotten to really know Mae over the last few months, he suspected deep down it troubled her a great deal, and maybe even had been painful. She concealed it well. Eli found that bothered him, for he had come to care deeply for her. As much as he hated to see her in pain, he knew pain was an integral part of life. There was simply no avoiding it.

With him, she was at home in her own skin, comfortable, confident beyond belief. But in her mother's court, not so much. He recalled the shy awkwardness at their first meeting, when they had been formally introduced many years before. At that moment, he had not thought much of her. He had judged her harshly and then turned his attention to someone else. How could he have ever known?

How wrong was he? Eli chided himself for being so superficial. There was a strong lesson here. One he decided to take to heart.

In truth, Eli himself had not exactly fit in either, at least in polite society. After many years of effort to be what his father expected of him, he had eventually given up. A lack of acceptance was one of the things that had motivated him and driven him into this life of being a ranger. That and his desire to irritate his father. But Eli would admit that to no one else but himself.

In the end, he had concluded the opinions of others mattered little to him in the grand scheme of things. He was his own person and that was all that mattered. In Eli's estimation, the only ones who counted were his wife and those precious few he had named friends. To those individuals he would listen.

After years of service to his people, he was now excused his eccentricities, mostly. They, his people, and his father to a degree, had come to respect his desire to be left alone, especially after he had proven himself one of the finest rangers to have ever walked the forests. And Eli was content with that, even if his father wasn't.

Eli continued to gaze at Mae as she took a sip of water from her canteen, then filled it. He suspected her peers would adjust to her in time, just as they had to him. She was not only good at what she did, but also had become, like him, dangerous.

Mae didn't see that in herself, not yet, but given time, experience, and some worldly seasoning, she would begin to understand. That it was necessary for such a process to play out was a tragedy, for she was a gentle soul. Mae was someone who did not enjoy hurting others or being hurt in turn. That was one of the qualities that made her such an excellent ranger.

And though he had not seen it at first, there was no doubt about it, not anymore. He and she were soul mates, for not only their similarities but also the differences that had forged them into who they were. That much was now abundantly clear. Perhaps, Eli considered, they had always been destined to not only come together but to *be* together as well, two souls meant for one another.

Blinking and feeling stunned at this revelation, Eli shook his head slightly. His heart was hammering in his chest. With no little amount of effort, he tore his gaze from Mae and studied the area around them. The forest was old in these parts and filled with hardwoods. The leaf canopy blotted out much of the sky, creating an artificial twilight below.

The stream, as if lost and trying to find its way, cut through the forest in a meandering manner. The water was fast-moving and pleasant to listen to. Eli found himself enjoying its voice. Unpolluted, the water was crystal clear. He could see right down to the stream's rocky bottom. But for the agreeable sound of the rushing water, the forest around them was utterly silent, almost grim.

Just behind him and Mae, Titus, Lenth, and Aventus were crouched down a few yards away. The three human rangers had laid out their rations upon the forest floor, unwrapped them, and were sharing.

"It is too quiet," Mae whispered to him, as if she were afraid to disturb the trees around them. "It is much too quiet for my liking."

"I know it," Eli said in the same low tone, his mood shifting. She was right. It was too quiet. "There are few animals about."

"It is as if many of the animals fled or went into hiding," Mae said. "They are afraid of something."

"I have never seen the like either, other than in a Gray Field," Eli replied, then took another drink of water. He shrugged off his pack and untied his canteen. Eli unstopped it and dipped the metal canteen, a gift from a human, beneath the surface of the water. He patiently waited for it to fill. His canteen had gone dry several hours before. This was the first stream they had come across since leaving Arvan'Dale and it had been a welcome sight when they had chanced upon it.

A gust of wind blew through the trees overhead, causing the leaves to whisper amongst themselves and the limbs to creak. Mae glanced skyward again, watching them. Biting her lower lip, she turned her gaze to him and at first did not speak. "We have maybe two hours until nightfall, maybe less."

"That seems about right." Satisfied his canteen was full, he stopped it with the cork, sealing it tight. The canteen was dripping wet. He shook it, shedding some of the water, before reattaching it to his pack, tying the knot tight so that it would not come loose during travel. Eli then pulled out his spare waterskin and filled that as well.

"Perhaps," Mae said, "when the sun sets, we might be able to rest some. With these old trees, even if there is a moon tonight, it will be quite dark under the cover of this forest. As you said, human eyesight is poor. Without magical means, it will become impossible to track us, at least until dawn. That should provide the respite we need."

"There is that, yes." Eli opened his pack and pulled out his haversack, which was becoming alarmingly light. He fished around inside for a moment, then pulled out a cloth-wrapped bundle. Unwrapping it, he revealed the remains of their supply of dried fish. He offered it to Mae, who took a small piece and popped it into her mouth, chewing as she watched him.

Eli selected a piece as well and ate it, finding it surprisingly flavorful. He was very hungry, and at times, hunger made the best cook. The fish was the last of what the caretaker had provided, and he had been saving it, for it had not only been dried, but was also well-seasoned and tasty. By comparison, most of their rations were quite plain and unappealing. They were in essence nothing more than fuel to keep going.

"Beyond that, what do you have left for food?" Mae asked as she swallowed and took another piece of fish.

"Not much," Eli said, "some strips of dried venison, half a loaf of bread, and a few hunks of hardtack. At best, maybe two days' worth of food. What about you?"

"About the same," Mae said. "We are going to have to replenish our supplies soon."

"Yeah," Eli said. "We are." He glanced around at the trees. "The animals may be onto something. It may be unwise to spend the night out in the open and under the trees."

Her eyes fixed on him, Mae had frozen in the act of chewing. After a moment, she swallowed the piece of fish. They said nothing more after that, but finished the rest of the fish in silence.

With canteen in hand and still chewing on a hunk of biscuit, Titus stood and moved over to them. He knelt by the edge of the stream and refilled his canteen.

"We seem to have lost them," Titus said, when he had finished. He took a long pull from the canteen, then dipped it into the stream and refilled it. When he was done, he stopped the canteen closed. "For the moment, at least."

"For the moment," Eli agreed.

"You are thinking they will pick up our trail again?" Mae asked.

"Kyber will not give up that easy," Eli said, "especially now that he knows I am out here. There are likely other foresters with them."

"I suspected," Titus said, almost regretfully. "Like a dog with a bone, he will keep on after us. Still, they must be as spent as we are. They too will need rest."

"Agreed," Eli said.

Titus blew out a weary breath. "They have driven us farther to the southeast than I would have preferred. Yes, we're closer to the border, but we need to be heading south-southwest toward Astrix."

"The Castol army is likely already at the town's gates," Eli said, pointing out what they both surely knew but had until this point not voiced. In truth, with the pursuit, there had not been time. "Nothing we do now will likely matter to Astrix's defense. The town is on its own."

"Yeah," Titus said, with a regretful note. "By sending Maran, we might have done all we could for them. But still, I can't help but feel—"

"We need to look to ourselves now," Mae said, interrupting Titus.

The human ranger gave a weary nod, scratched an itch on his right ear, then began idly scratching in his beard. He seemed to suddenly perk up. "The town is far from defenseless. More importantly, they are led by a good man."

"Prefect Deverex?" Mae asked.

"The camp prefect is a tough one," Titus said, "with more than thirty-five years of service behind him."

"It sounds like you respect him," Mae said.

"I do," Titus replied. "Before his retirement, he and I crossed paths a time or two. He has certainly earned my respect. Still, I would like to see if we can yet do something to help them."

"Honestly, there is nothing we can do about Astrix at the moment," Eli said. "On the other hand, look on the bright side. We are diverting a goodly number of the enemy from participating with the main effort against the town."

"There is that." Stifling a yawn, with one hand, Titus reached down into the water and splashed some on his face. He splashed some more, washing away the dust and grime that had accumulated. He wiped at weary eyes as he leaned back. Titus sniffed at the air. "It smells like snow is coming, especially with the temperature dropping over the last few hours."

Eli felt himself scowl. He had thought the same. From what he could see of the sky, it had clouded up, making the twilight at the forest floor darker than it should have been at this hour. He glanced to the east and saw only trunks of trees, very little undergrowth, and beds of moss.

"I've never known you to carry a sword, especially a legionary short sword." Titus gestured at the weapon belted to Eli's side.

His hand finding the hilt, Eli glanced down at the sheathed sword. After a moment, he looked back up. "It was a gift."

"A gift?" Titus cocked an eyebrow. "Really, from who?"

"From a…" He glanced at Mae, whose face had lost all expression. "From an *old* friend," Eli said carefully. "I guess you could say it is an honor to bear this weapon. I carry it at his request."

"Then it must be special to you, and he must be some friend. From that hilt, it's as plain a sword as I've ever seen, a common soldier's weapon. And from what I've seen, you seem to prefer to carry weapons with a little more personality to them. This friend must have made a real impression upon you."

Titus seemed to lose interest and looked over at Aventus and Lenth before scanning the trees carefully around them. Eli and Mae shared a look.

"You have no idea," Eli said in a near whisper as he turned his gaze eastward once more and brought his mind back to the matter at hand, which was thoroughly eluding their pursuers and finding a place to rest for a few hours. He was about to suggest an option he knew he really did not want.

"What?" Titus asked, having returned his gaze to Eli. "I know that look of yours. You are going to tell me something I do not want to hear. Or at least you are considering a course of action, something you know I will not like."

"I know a place that is not too far off," Eli said after a long moment. "We might be able to find shelter there. But, ah, there could be some complications to doing that."

"That figures, doesn't it?" Titus looked over at him with a healthy dose of concern. "Whenever I am with you, it always seems like we do things the hard way. Why is that?"

"You have noticed that as well?" Mae asked. "I thought I was the only one."

Titus gave a chuckle. "So, Eli, tell me of this place you know."

"Well, I did know it," Eli said. "The passage of time changes all things."

"How long ago were you last there?" Titus scowled slightly.

"A few decades at most."

"Decades?" Titus asked, his skepticism clearly growing.

Eli felt himself scowl as he thought on it some more. "Give or take one, maybe two…perhaps, now that I am thinking on it, thirty, or really forty years. Sometimes it is hard to be sure how much time has passed."

Titus did not look happy at that news. "So, this place you are thinking of taking us to might not be there anymore."

"That is entirely possible," Eli admitted.

"There still might be some shelter to be had?" Mae asked, to which Eli gave a slow nod.

"Maybe," Eli said, "if some of the structures still stand. Though, I suspect the place is still inhabited."

"What kind of place are we talking about?" Titus asked. "A farmstead? I am not aware of any towns or villages in this area. If there were any, I would know, as we are close to the border."

"Well, it is not quite a village, but more of a cluster of homes, four to be exact. You might call it a forest settlement. The people who live there chose such a remote location on purpose."

"They don't want to be bothered," Mae surmised.

"Yes, that is correct," Eli said. "There, they set down roots and carved out a life for themselves."

Titus rubbed his beard and jaw. "I guess it is too much to hope that they are the friendly sort?"

"Well," Eli said, "friendly is such a relative word, is it not?"

"I'm not liking this option, Eli," Titus said. "I'm really not. But then again, when you suggested it, you knew I wouldn't very well like it."

"There is a bright side," Eli said.

"I would love to hear what you consider to be the bright side," Titus said, then looked at Mae. "I can't wait to hear this."

"Even though they live on the Castol side of the border," Eli said, "they detest their overlords. Actually, I think it is the taxes they do not like paying that drove them to such an isolated life."

"This may come as a surprise, but no one likes paying taxes, Eli," Titus said. "Not me, not anyone."

"Anyway," Eli said, "we would be bringing them the knowledge that there are Castol soldiers in their neck of the woods."

"Eli," Mae said, "we led those soldiers this way. They might take issue with that."

Eli adopted an innocent expression. "You know that, and I know that, but they do not know it. So, why bother with such small details?"

"That is a rather big detail, Eli," Titus said.

"You want us to lie to them?" Mae asked.

"I would not call it lying, exactly, perhaps omitting a key detail or two, misleading at best. But honestly, we would be warning them of a potential threat, and in truth, they may just welcome us for it."

Titus eyed Eli for several long heartbeats without saying anything.

"They don't like being disturbed, do they?" Titus finally asked.

Eli gave a nod. "I believe that is a good way to put it."

"What are the odds they might, say, try to kill us at first sight?" Titus asked.

"Honestly," Eli said, "I do not know."

"How about giving me your best guess at that, eh?" Titus asked.

"If I were a wagering sort, and keep in mind I am most definitely not," Eli said and made a show of thinking on it some, "maybe an even chance."

Titus brought his hand to his face and scratched his beard as he seemed to contemplate what Eli had just told him. "Those are not the kind of odds I like betting my life on, Eli."

Eli gave a half shrug of his shoulders. "It is better than a hundred percent chance. If they invite us in for a drink and some food, that is a positive sign. I mean, why waste good food on someone you are going to kill, eh?"

Titus just shook his head. "Can you think of another place we can hole up, at least for a few hours? There are no elven shelters about? No better places?"

"Not within a day's hike, at least," Eli said. "There is one closer, but that is back the way we came, and I do not believe you want to go that way."

A drop of water landed on Titus's arm. Scowling, he looked up, his eyes searching. A few heartbeats later, it began to rain lightly, the sound of it pattering pleasantly on the leaves overhead. The canopy would protect them from the worst of it, but still, given enough time, they'd become thoroughly drenched, and that was not good.

"The temperature is still dropping." Eli ran his gaze over the two other rangers a few feet away. They were still eating. Both looked thoroughly worn out. "If it does snow, Titus, without a doubt, we will need a dry place, at least for a few hours to rest and recover before pushing onward. Our pursuers have the advantage of camping anywhere they wish, pitching tents, and lighting fires. We, as the hunted, do not."

"I know that." Titus's shoulders slumped. He let out what could only be called a resigned breath. "So, what's this place called?"

"I do not believe it has a name," Eli said, "one I know at any rate."

Titus did not speak for several heartbeats. "I am not happy about this, Eli. You know that, right?" Titus paused and shook his head. "Of course you do."

"We could chance it and ride out the weather in a make-shift shelter." Eli ran his gaze around the forest. "There is plenty of material around to construct one. But after we push on and the pursuit continues…"

"The enemy could easily find evidence of us having been there," Titus said. "At the very least, they'd find our shelter. And it could put them right back on our trail."

"Correct," Eli said. "If we shelter in the forest or go to the settlement, tomorrow we could head directly east for the Tibexra River. I know a good place to cross about half a day's hike from here. I doubt Kyber knows of it. Once across, we could follow the river to the imperial border. There is a town out that way, two days' further travel."

"Mekhet," Mae said.

"Yes," Eli said. "That's the name of the town. We might even gain a lead on them to the point where he will break off the pursuit."

"That would take us farther east," Titus said, "away from Astrix."

"Yes, it would," Eli agreed.

"How badly does Kyber want your hide?" Titus asked.

"Knowing Eli, probably pretty bad," Mae said. "He has a way of bringing out the best in people."

Eli looked over at his wife with an unhappy expression, then turned his attention back to Titus. "Right now, they do not know exactly where we are. We have an advantage for the moment, but given enough time, there is a strong chance Kyber will find our trail, whether or not we go to the forest settlement or make our own shelter and then push on in the morning. The advantage of the forest settlement is that we might find support there. It will certainly be dry, warm, and if welcomed, we might even be able to replenish our supplies."

"Then again, they may not be so welcoming," Mae said.

Eli gave a shrug. "We also need to consider what has been happening throughout the region."

"You are speaking of Lutha Nyx," Titus said unhappily.

"You have noticed the lack of animals about?" Eli asked.

"We have," Titus said. "It has been like this in every place that has seen attacks. It's unnatural."

"A roof over our heads and some stout walls may not be a bad thing then," Eli said. "I am thinking it would be better than remaining outside when the sun goes down."

"All right. That decides it, then." Titus stood with a groan. "Our supplies are running low too and it is possible a storm is on the way. The forest settlement it is. Let's not waste any additional time and see if we can get there before the sun sets."

"If they are not welcoming," Mae said, "a forest shelter may be a foregone conclusion."

"Maybe." Titus glanced around them and drew in a deep breath that seemed to contain his concern. "Eli's right though. I do not wish to be in this forest after dark, not after what we've seen. Now, let's get moving."

CHAPTER TWELVE

With an arrow nocked in his bow, Eli knelt just to the side of a tree. Partially exposed, he scanned the field before him and saw no threats, then glanced over at Titus, who stood a few feet away to his left. Dusk was fully upon them, and it was growing darker by the moment. Titus turned his gaze from the field back over to him. Eli gave a firm nod to the human.

Titus turned to the two rangers who were waiting behind him and flashed a series of curt hand signals that Eli could not fully see. With that, he, Aventus, and Lenth stepped forward from the tree line, first emerging from cover and then moving out into the cultivated field.

Crouching low, they spread out into a line ten yards across with their bows out and ready. Titus made another signal, and all three started forward through the first rows of crops toward the forest settlement.

Heads swiveling and eyes scanning what lay ahead, they moved slowly, deliberately. They were headed across the field toward a cluster of buildings that lay slightly more than a hundred yards distant, on the other side of the field. Their immediate objective was the closest building, a grass-roofed barn.

Mae was at the next tree over to Eli's right, an old hemlock. She also had taken a knee. Both he and she had their eyes peeled and were watching ahead of the human rangers, providing an overwatch should things go bad.

With no lights of any kind, the buildings of the settlement were dark and uninviting. A cold sensation slithered down his spine. It had nothing to do with the plummeting temperature or snow, which had begun to fall in place of the rain that had plagued them as they'd made their way through the forest to the settlement. No, this was a serious concern.

Something here, at the settlement, was clearly not right. In fact, Eli's gut was telling him things were quite wrong. The first clue had been the settlement itself and the fields that surrounded it. They had watched for almost an hour, looking for any indications of life, any people inhabiting the place, of which there should have been dozens. They had seen no one.

Not only that, but the fields had long been ready for harvest. Though Eli was not a farmer and had never been one, even he could tell they should have been picked weeks ago.

What was going on here?

Afraid he already knew the answer to that question, Eli glanced ever so briefly up at the overcast sky. About an hour before, the rain had shifted first to a snowy mix, then full-on snow, which now fell in large, fluffy flakes, drifting slowly downward. It was already beginning to stick, not only on the ground, but on the plants in the field, coating the leaves in a dusting of white and giving the view before him a picturesque quality.

Turning his gaze back to the rangers out in the field, Eli scanned the growing darkness ahead as the three men continued to advance across the field. Nothing moved. But for the occasional gusts of wind, the forest behind was utterly silent and still.

One slow step after another, the rangers continued forward. Halfway across the field, Eli glanced over at Mae and flashed her a sign in fingerspeak to proceed. She had expected it and stood. Together, they started after the rangers, emerging from the shadows of the forest.

Nothing happened.

No shout of alarm came. There was no sign that they had been spotted...nothing. Eli almost felt as if he would have been relieved had an alarm been sounded, for the alternative was one he did not wish to contemplate.

Before he even reached the first row of plants, the sweet, almost grassy, summerish smell of tomatoes was strong on the air, filling his nostrils. For lack of a better description, he would have called it a green smell.

Then, before he knew it, he was brushing past the first few plants, which grew waist-high and were heavily loaded with dozens of tomatoes. Shedding their light covering of snow, the leaves whispered quietly against his thighs and waist as he passed, following after the human rangers ahead.

He spared a glance down at the tomatoes. All were ripe, with a goodly number having split open. A few had begun to pass beyond this stage, going bad. He could smell that too, the rot.

Eli glanced over at Mae, and their eyes met. He held hers for a protracted moment. The knowing look they shared conveyed worry for what they would find ahead. Then Mae broke eye contact as she turned her gaze ahead, clearly scanning the buildings amidst the growing darkness. Almost regretfully, Eli turned his own gaze back to the task at hand and focused on scanning for threats.

After about twelve feet, the rows of tomatoes gave over to long string bean plants. They too hadn't been harvested. Eli knelt and examined a beanstalk. Between his fingers, the beans felt slimy to the touch, which told him they were beginning to rot as well.

Eli straightened and continued onward, scanning ahead, searching out places someone might hide amongst the buildings, a shadowed doorway, the corner of the barn, stacks of firewood, a pile of dirt. Of the few windows he could see, all were shuttered.

Still, he saw nothing, no movement, no hint of a threat. There was no indication of life. The settlement appeared abandoned.

With every third step, turning to look behind, he searched the forest carefully. Nothing moved there either. Other than the gusts of wind and stirring of leaves, there was no sound about. It was unnaturally silent. Eli did not even hear the bleat of sheep or mooing of cows coming from the barn. Nothing … no sound … no life … just nothing.

Ahead, the rangers had reached the first building, the barn. There were thin, slit-like windows just above eye level. Stepping on his tip toes, Lenth peered in one for a long moment. He relaxed, dropped back down, and shook his head to both Titus and Aventus.

With that, Aventus went to the left side of the barn and Titus the right. Both men poked their heads around the corners, peering off into the darkness. After several long heartbeats, Titus turned and motioned to Eli and Mae to come forward.

Picking up their pace, they moved quickly across the rest of the field and reached the barn. With Mae following right behind him, Eli moved up to Titus.

The ranger had returned to looking around the corner, clearly studying what lay ahead. The darkness around them was near absolute. The snow had begun falling harder and the wind was even picking up a little. The first real snow-storm of the season was likely in the offing.

"Nothing's moving, at least that I can see," Titus hissed in a whisper to Eli and Mae.

The wind took that moment to gust strongly about them, swirling the snow in a near complete whiteout. Eli closed his eyes against it and felt the snow and wind sting his face. Around the corner, what sounded like a door banged loudly several times.

As the gust died down, Titus glanced around the corner again. After a moment, he pulled back behind cover. "It's a window shutter on the next building over that's come loose. Either the latch broke or someone forgot to secure it."

"Where are the people who lived here?" Mae asked from behind Eli.

"It's like every other settlement, village, and town we came across in the region," Titus said unhappily. "I suspect all we're gonna find inside these buildings are bones of the deceased."

Eli silently agreed with Titus.

"Coming here was a mistake," Mae said.

"Maybe, maybe not," Eli said. "We need to investigate further and be certain. The people who lived here might have just left, like those others you told us about, Titus."

"That was farther south," Titus said. "You knew them, these people who lived here. How likely is that?"

"That they just quit, upped and left?"

Titus gave a nod, to which Eli did not reply.

"That's what I thought," Titus said grimly.

Eli was silent for a long moment. This was rapidly becoming a nightmare returned to life, one he had firmly thought was well behind him. He had seen so much evil done, there were times he wondered how much more he could take. With no little amount of effort, he forced such feelings aside, along with the trepidation of what lay ahead.

"Well?" Titus asked, when Eli did not reply. "You've dealt with this kind of thing before. What do we do?"

Eli gave that some thought and was silent for several more heartbeats. "We select the most defensible building, get out of the snow, start a fire, get dry, and remain inside till morning or the storm passes."

"And if we're attacked by whatever is going after the people in this region?" Titus asked. "What then?"

"Then we use fire to defend ourselves," Eli said.

"Will that help?" Titus asked. "Did it help that last time?"

"It did," Eli said, "somewhat."

Titus gave him a long look that reeked terribly of unhappiness.

"Do you really want to remain out here?" Eli asked the human. "In the open? Those things like to hide in the darkness and shadow. They will be on you before you are even aware of it."

"You've seen them?" Titus asked, then straightened slightly. "You've fought them too, haven't you?"

"I have." Eli gave a slight nod, and with that, memory flashed of hideous, alien monsters, both large and small, with sharp teeth and razor-like claws. He well recalled the excited gibbering noise they made as they attacked, the sound of their powerful jaws as they broke the bones of their victims, the screams they made when injured. The sight of a woman, an innocent, being devoured alive. Her screams…

He tried to suppress an involuntary shudder and mostly failed.

"What are they?" Titus asked.

"No one's really sure." Though Eli had his suspicions, he was not ready to share them with Titus. In fact, he knew he was not.

"That's not terribly helpful," Titus said.

"They are monsters that eat people," Eli said, "and everything else that's living, crawls, slithers, or generally walks the land. They do not seem to discriminate overly much. Their hunger is insatiable."

"High Father protect us against such evil," Titus said.

"As far as I understand it," Eli said, after a long moment of silence, "to summon the creatures, a priest or some type of special follower of Lutha Nyx's faith is required. They also must be close, supposedly really close, to control them, the creatures, that is."

"So," Mae said, "if you are correct, this settlement and Arvan'Dale were specifically targeted?"

"Yes," Eli said, glancing around as he thought it through. "Yes, I would think so."

"That means someone had to know this place existed," Titus said. "They were familiar with it."

Eli felt himself scowl slightly. Titus had a point. Whoever was behind the attacks would have had to know of the settlement, which few were aware even existed. It was so remote, Eli even doubted Kyber knew about this settlement. But doubt was not certainty.

There was another possibility. So little was known about the goddess. Was his understanding of Lutha Nyx and her cult wrong? Could the creatures roam freely and hunt on their own without close supervision? It was an interesting question, one that bore thinking on. It was also one that was quite worrying.

"And if we kill that person?" Titus asked. "Does it end the madness?"

"No," Eli said, "unfortunately not. Killing the controller only sets the creatures free, at least until sunrise. Any inhibitions they had are lost."

"What happens then?" Mae asked. "When the sun comes up?"

"They return to wherever they were conjured from," Eli said. "They do not seem to be able to handle daylight or bright light. I once saw a paladin call holy light in the dead of night. It banished the creatures quicker than you could blink."

"We don't have a paladin on hand," Titus said.

"We do not," Eli said.

"I don't like this, Eli," Titus said.

"That makes two of us."

"What now?" Titus asked.

"We need to explore and make certain this place is thoroughly abandoned," Eli said. "If a few of the people who lived here are still alive and in hiding, they might pose a risk to us. We cannot have that."

"I don't suppose we can," Titus said as he sucked in a deep breath. "What are the odds of there being survivors?"

"At best, it is doubtful any survived such an attack," Eli said. "But we need to be certain. Stranger things have happened."

Titus nodded. "All right. Let's get this done."

"I'll go first," Eli said, to which Titus did not even protest.

Eli moved past the human and, holding his bow up, advanced around the corner of the barn. With the snow and the growing darkness, it was rapidly becoming more difficult to see, even for him. He knew the humans would be having a difficult time of it too.

With Mae and Titus following, Eli made his way silently along the side of the barn and to the front. Stopping there, he studied the settlement before him. It was much as he recalled it from his last visit, even though it had been decades prior. There was a central rectangular yard bordered by six buildings. A stone well was in the direct center. Covered with snow, a bucket lay on its side next to the well, as did a coil of rope.

The buildings, as far as Eli could determine in the darkness, consisted of another barn that was off to the left, what looked like a storehouse, a cold house, and three other structures that were clearly homes or communal living quarters. All three had chimneys from which no smoke emerged. None of the buildings were taller than a single story, but from what he could determine, they all looked well maintained. Or, they had been until recently.

Eli moved around the corner to his right and came to a stop before the barn door. His heart almost froze in his chest, for the door had been clawed apart and torn open. It lay at his feet, snow-covered pieces all over the ground. He glanced back at Titus, whose face had grown grim. Mae was looking just as grave. H

"I believe we know what we will find inside," Titus said quietly.

"Death," Mae breathed.

"Yes, they've been here," Eli said. "There's likely no one left alive. But still, we will want to check the buildings just the same."

"Do you think the monsters will come back?" Titus asked, glancing around and lowering his bow a little.

"I do not know," Eli said. "I hope not."

"That is the problem, then." Titus sounded frustrated. "Lately, there is a lot of that 'we simply do not know' nonsense."

"Nonsense or not, life is full of mysteries that are just begging to be uncovered," Eli said.

Titus shot Eli an unhappy look. "Was that your attempt at putting a positive spin on this? Are you trying to make me feel better? Because if you are, it's not helping."

"We should search the buildings," Eli reaffirmed, just as the wind gusted strongly, "and make sure no one is hiding inside. We do not need any surprises, not on a night like tonight."

Titus gave a nod.

"We need to do this quickly," Eli said, "then identify a building that is defensible, where we can start a fire and hole up for the night."

"So, I take it you do think there is a chance they will come back, then?" Titus asked.

"Again," Eli said, "I do not know. But as I am no gambler, best to take no chances, eh? More importantly, we are all wet and need to dry off. I do not believe we can afford to continue on without seeking shelter, even if there is risk."

"Right, better safe than sorry is our motto this night." Titus turned around, just as the wind gusted again. Aventus and Lenth were waiting behind them at the corner of the building. The snow swirled about as he motioned for the other two rangers to come up and gather around, which they did.

"I believe we know what happened here." Titus gestured at the remains of the door. "Eli says someone controls the creatures that did this. Though that person is likely no longer here, we need to search this settlement and make sure no one is hiding, especially survivors. They were not the friendliest of sorts to begin with. If there are survivors, they might pose a risk to us. Aventus, you take that building there to the right. Lenth, take that barn over there. I will take this barn." Titus patted the wall next to him. "Mae, that one there across the way is yours. Eli, go for that one to the left of it that looks like a cold house." Titus paused, and his gaze fixed upon the last building. "I am thinking that home over there"—he gestured to the structure on the far right where he was gazing—"will be the best place to hole up for the night. It is small and the walls look thick. More importantly, there is a chimney, which means we can start a fire. There's also a good supply of wood stacked out front. We will rendezvous there and then search it. Any questions?"

There were none.

"Let's get to it, then," Titus said.

They split up.

With Mae, Eli made his way across the yard, their boots crunching softly in the growing snow, which was now almost half an inch thick. Eli caught Mae's eye and flashed a sign in fingerspeak.

Be careful.

Always, came the reply from her, as did a confident grin.

Then Eli returned his attention back on the task at hand. His structure was indeed a cold house. It was half buried in the ground, with walls made completely of field stone that had been mortared together. The roof was arched, with moss growing on its wooden shingles.

The wind gusted again, and with it, the loose shutter behind him began to bang once more. The sound of it grated on his ears as he moved quickly across the snow-covered ground to the door of the cold house, which was intact.

Hand on the latch, he carefully opened it and peered inside. Blackness greeted him, as did the stench of mold and mustiness. Eli waited several moments, allowing his eyes to adjust to the darkness. Even when they had, he could barely make out the granite steps that led downward, but saw the impression of dark, square-like shapes at the base of the stairs, which he took to be stores of some kind.

Without a source of light, there was no sense in proceeding. Anything could be lying down there in wait, concealed. But for some reason he could not state, he knew there was not a living thing in the cold house. Eli was about to take a step inside, when he stopped.

Something caused him to turn. The last building, the one Titus had identified for them to meet at, drew his attention. It was only a few yards away. The door was intact and closed. So too were the shutters. A hint of yellowed light betrayed itself from one of the shutters. The light had just flickered, then flared, and finally died down for a moment, before vanishing altogether.

Someone was inside.

Raising his bow, he began moving toward the building, which was ten yards away. To his right, Titus emerged from the barn he had been searching. He spotted Eli with his bow up and clearly surmised something was not right. His own bow came up as well.

Eli kept moving forward toward the door. The light returned, this time brighter, showing through more seams in the shutters and the door too. Eli got the sense someone inside had started a fire in the hearth or was working to get one started. As if to confirm this, a thin stream of smoke began to emerge from the chimney.

He spared a look at Titus, who had seen the same thing and had also begun to move forward. As quietly as he could, Eli closed the last few feet and moved up to one of the shuttered windows, from which the light shone out into the darkness.

Peering through the cracks, he saw a man kneeling before a fireplace that had the beginnings of a fire going.

The room was mostly dark, and Eli could not get a sense for how the man was dressed or see his face. The man suddenly stiffened, before straightening. On his knees, he looked around toward the window. It was almost as if he could sense Eli's presence, which was surprising, for Eli had been terribly quiet as he approached. Immediately, Eli ducked down and out of the way.

Titus had moved up to the door and stood just to the side of it. Across the way, Mae emerged from her building. She saw them. Eli motioned for her to hold where she was. She gave a nod and remained still. A moment later, Aventus and Lenth stepped from their respective buildings. Eli gave them the same signal. Both dropped to a knee and waited as the snow continued to fall around them.

Taking incredibly slow steps on the fresh snow so that it did not make a crunching noise, Eli joined Titus at the door and flashed a series of signs that indicated one individual was inside. Titus gave an understanding nod and began reaching for the latch, when a strong voice, speaking the common tongue, rang out from inside.

"I know you are out there, strangers." The voice had a distinctly imperial accent to it and a cultured one at that. "I mean you no harm. You're welcome to join me and share the warmth of my fire. That is, if you mean me no harm."

Eli looked to Titus, who gave a shrug of his shoulders, on which snow was beginning to accumulate. After a moment, Titus reached for the latch on the door as Eli brought his bow up. The ranger lifted the latch and swung the door wide. Arrow nocked, Eli moved forward, surging inside.

He found a middle-aged man sitting on a stool, hands resting in his lap. One hand held a small glass vial with a cork stop. The glass of the vial was a light blue. He was clean-shaven and wore a heavy gray cloak over a forest green tunic and brown leather boots. A well-worn wooden staff lay in the corner, along with a short sword and traveling pack. The traveling pack looked broken-in, for its leather was faded and cracked.

Keeping his bow trained on the man, Eli flicked his eyes quickly about the room. The structure was a single-room dwelling. There was a rope bed, a table, and several trunks. He saw no one other than the man present.

"There is no one else here," the man said, "and as I said, I mean you no harm, elven ranger."

"You have seen the High Born before?" Eli asked as he moved farther into the room. He kept his bow trained on the man. Titus came in next, his boots thumping on the wooden planked floor.

"I have," the man said as his eyes flicked to Titus, "just as I've seen and met imperial rangers. Interesting that imperial rangers are traveling with elven rangers this day, especially in Castol territory, interesting indeed. One would think momentous events are afoot."

Oddly, the man seemed wholly unafraid. That troubled Eli.

"You are imperial," Titus said, deigning not to reply to the man's statement.

"Aye," the man said. "I am. My home is a small villa, just outside Mal'Zeel, a humble dwelling at best."

"What are you doing here?" Titus asked as the fire in the hearth began to grow, lighting up more of the room. "You are far from the capital. I am suspecting there is more than meets the eye with you."

In the dim light, the man's eyes seemed like dark voids absorbing all of the scant light from the fire. Eli felt chilled by them and their mile-long stare. It was as if those eyes had witnessed terrible things. Though he did not understand what he was dealing with here, the man before them was dangerous. Eli was sure of it.

"He asked you a question." Eli had not lowered his bow.

The man's dark eyes shifted to Eli, and within them, he sensed resentment, and distaste. "I could say that I am a traveling merchant, but that would be a lie, which you would ultimately see through."

"Then tell the truth," Titus said. "What is your business here?"

"I suspect the reason I have come to this settlement is ultimately the same as yours and those of your companions, who are waiting outside … all three of them."

Titus shot a worried glance at Eli. Titus recovered rapidly and turned his gaze back to the man. "And what is that? Your interests?"

"I came north to find out what's been happening here," the man said, "in places like this settlement. That is my business, ranger."

"I want more," Eli said, deciding a plain approach was best. "Tell us."

"Speak plainly," Titus said, drawing the man's gaze. "By the High Father's blessed majesty, my patience with you is nearing its end."

"My interest is really my own," the man said, then gave a mirthless chuckle, as if he had amused himself, "but in the interest of trust and the hope that you will lower those bows, if you must know, I have been sent to put a stop to the madness here in the north. It has gotten out of hand and my mistress dislikes when that sort of thing happens. It draws far too much attention to her. Such attention can cause complications."

"And what would you know of what's happened here?" Eli asked plainly, not liking the direction the conversation had taken.

The eyes, which were colder than ice, shifted back upon Eli. "More than you can possibly know, elf."

"Try us," Titus said.

"Yesterday, I buried those who sadly perished in this farming settlement, as well as others I have come across in my pursuit of answers. It is the least I can do for the injustice visited upon them. They…they did not deserve what was done to them."

Eli and Titus shared a troubled look.

"What is your name?" Titus asked.

"Before I give it, for there is power in names, will you at least lower your bows? I ask that we act civilized, show each other some common courtesy and respect." He gestured at the hearth, where the fire had begun to snap and pop. Despite the door being open behind them, Eli could feel the heat within the room growing. "After all, I invited you to share my fire."

"I don't like him," Titus said to Eli in Elven, "nor trust him."

"Normally," the man said, speaking fluent Elven, his tone growing as cold as his eyes, "you should not trust me or any like me. That said…I swear upon *High* that no harm shall come from me unto you this night or for as long as our interests align and you do me no harm, ranger. After that, I promise nothing, for priorities shift and change, sometimes in unexpected directions. Such is the way of things."

There was a moment of silence as both Eli and Titus stared at the man sitting upon the stool. That he spoke Elven was a shock, and telling too, for it meant someone had taught him. His accent was not perfect, but it was good enough to be fluent. The man's words were also concerning, at least Eli found them so.

"You swear?" Titus gave a light chuckle. "Did you hear that? He swears not to harm us and we're the ones armed."

Eli had the uncomfortable feeling the unarmed man sitting on the stool could do immeasurable harm, and without any weapons at all. His gaze was once again drawn to the glass vial in the man's hand. He was caressing the vial lightly with his index finger as if it was a treasured possession.

"I do swear," the man added, his tone growing grave. "I swear upon my lady, my goddess, that I will do you no harm this night. My word is my bond, and should I break it, I will suffer my mistress's wrath, and that will be a terrible thing, for Lutha Nyx takes such broken vows very, very seriously."

CHAPTER THIRTEEN

Staring at the man sitting on the stool, Eli found himself utterly frozen. It was a first for him, as if an invisible force held him in a tight and unyielding grip. Horror twisted at his guts.

Then, the initial shock at what he faced wore off, and as if in a bad dream, realization sank in. His gaze flicked to the glass vial in the man's hand. It looked very fragile. Mae was just outside. His fear for her safety was suddenly great.

Eli suspected he knew what the vial was, and though he did not want to, very slowly, he lowered his bow. As he did, he relaxed the string until the tension was gone and took the arrow in hand, then switched it to the hand that held his bow.

"Titus," Eli said, quietly, and without daring to take his gaze from the man before him, "will you kindly lower your bow?"

"What?" Titus asked, looking sharply over. "You heard what he just said. He's with Lutha Nyx, an enemy. We should kill the filth. He's probably the reason every village and settlement for miles around is empty of life."

"Lower the bow," Eli said, firmly.

"No." Titus turned his gaze back to the man on the stool and pulled the string back farther, increasing the tension.

"I think I am going to kill him and let the gods sort things out."

"Lower it," Eli repeated, hardening his voice. "If you attempt to kill him, we all die."

The man sitting on the stool, his unblinking gaze resting on Titus, did not move as he spoke. "He's quite right, my boy. You should lower the bow. It will be healthier for all of us if you do."

"Shut up, you," Titus said, "or by the High Father, I will put an arrow through your heart."

"Titus," Eli said, tearing his gaze away from the man and looking over. "Please, for all of our sakes, just lower the bow." Titus did not respond. "I am asking you to do it, Titus. Trust me on this."

With a pained expression, Titus let go a heated breath. He then released the tension on the bowstring and relaxed. "This goes against my better judgment, but I'll do it."

"If we want to live, this is the way," Eli said.

"Finally," the man on the stool said, slapping his thigh with his free hand, "we are making progress on trusting one another. Progress, indeed. There is nothing so effective as a good deterrence, eh?" He raised the vial for both of them to see and held it there a moment, then placed the hand with the vial to his chest. "I am Davin, and it is my great pleasure to meet you both."

"I hope you know what you are doing," Titus said to Eli with a sidelong glance.

"So do I," Eli said, then turned back to Davin. "Is that your real name?"

"Does it matter?" Davin asked.

"I suppose not," Eli decided. "You may call me Eli, and this here is Titus."

"Those are our real names," Titus fairly growled.

Davin inclined his head slightly, then his gaze shifted to the door, and he gave a shiver as a light gust of wind blew in a chill draft, along with some swirling snow. He waved at the door with a hand. "Would you mind inviting your companions inside and then closing the door? Now that the sun is down, the temperature will continue to drop. I would like to build up some warmth in here. A little heat will make the night pass more comfortably, don't you agree?"

Titus did not look like he wanted to comply, but Eli moved anyway to the back wall to his left. Slowly and carefully, he leaned his bow and arrow against the wall next to the rope bed. Then he turned around and moved back. He stared for a moment at Davin, studying him closely. Though the man was middle-aged for a human, his face was a kindly one. The eyes, on the other hand, spoke of cruelty and the propensity for great evil. Eli supposed he might be imagining that, but the mile-long stare said otherwise.

"The door," Davin prompted, "if you would be so kind?"

"Bring everyone in and close the door," Eli said to the human ranger, deciding the matter for him, as if Eli were still senior and in command. At one point, when he had trained Titus and Aventus, he had been. Titus eyed him unhappily for a long moment.

"Bah," Titus said. "This is what I get for listening and coming here." His boots thunking on the wooden planked floor, Titus went to the door and leaned out, waving for the others to join them. "Eli, next time you have any bright ideas like coming here, I'm not listening."

Within moments, Mae, Aventus, and Lenth had crowded into the small home, stamping their feet to get the snow off as they moved inside. They eyed Davin warily as Titus closed the door behind them with a bang, the air helping to suck it shut.

"He is a follower of Lutha Nyx," Titus said unceremoniously as he pushed past them so he stood in his original position before Davin.

With a look of horror on his face, Lenth froze in the act of leaning his bow against the wall in the corner. His jaw dropping, he looked like he wanted to go back out the door, but instead straightened. His bow clattered to the floor, even as he found the hilt of his sword.

"What?" Aventus asked, looking over at Titus and then to Eli and back again. "Say that again? Titus, did I hear you correctly?"

"You did," Titus said, with an unhappy glance thrown to Eli. "It seems we have a temporary peace with Davin here and, dare I say, his god."

"Now that," Aventus said, the arrow in his bow loosely nocked, "I do not believe."

"He swore upon his god to do us no ill," Eli said. "I expect him to honor such a vow."

"Do we dare trust him?" Aventus asked. "I mean, can we afford to? His god is a dark one."

"You can trust me," Davin said in a calming tone and offered up a disarming smile. The black eyes softened ever so slightly.

The smile did not seem to sit well with Aventus, who took a menacing step forward. Arrow nocked in his bow, he began to raise it.

"You will do him no harm," Eli said firmly. "I mean that, Aventus."

Aventus shot Eli a sidelong glance, then shifted his gaze to Titus, who gave a firm nod. With that, the ranger turned away, took the arrow from his bow, and leaned both next to Eli's against the wall.

"We are *all* going to act very civilized," Eli said. "There will be no harm done by anyone to anyone this night. Our side will not break the truce here."

Mae moved by Lenth and closer to Eli. She drew Davin's gaze, which latched onto hers. It was as if he was studying her closely and Eli did not like it, not one bit. Her gaze had not flinched from Davin's and she returned the look evenly, as if in challenge.

After several heartbeats, Davin blinked, then gave her a nod that was filled with what seemed like respect. In response, as if she had tasted or smelled something vile, a look of utter disgust slowly twisted her expression. She remained there a long moment, just staring, then, as if it were physically difficult, she tore her gaze away from the human sitting on the stool and looked directly at Eli.

Though no words passed between them, he felt as if she was questioning his decision-making process. Her concern was plain, and for a moment, as he gazed back upon her, Eli wished fervently that she was anywhere but here in the small house.

In fact, he wished they were all somewhere else, rather than stuck in the same room as a worshipper of Lutha Nyx. But, as he had told Titus, wishes were like daydreams. They were all in danger. Then, Mae shifted her gaze back to Davin.

"Why would you willingly follow such a vile and cruel goddess?" Mae asked curiously. Her tone was touched with a hint of horror. "I—I just do not understand."

"Not many can understand," Davin responded.

"Try me," Mae said.

"She, *the* goddess, is not what you and most others commonly believe," Davin said. "That is why you do not understand."

"Oh?" Mae arched an eyebrow. "How would you describe her then?"

"Misunderstood would be the most appropriate word."

Mae gave a disbelieving grunt. "There is a reason your kind is hunted and generally killed on sight."

"Which is a great tragedy." Davin spread both hands outward before him. "We are simply misunderstood by those who do not take the trouble to understand."

Feeling like Davin was toying with them, Eli moved his gaze again to the glass vial in the man's hand. His heart chilled that Davin was holding it so casually, for within it was contained death.

"The cruelty of Lutha Nyx's followers is beyond question," Titus said. "We've seen firsthand what your kind does. There was no misunderstanding that senseless butchery."

"We, the Brethren," Davin said carefully, "who control the twisted and gifted, only put them upon those who have earned their fate, crossed our goddess, or interfered with her designs. Never do we commit senseless butchery or harm the innocent."

"Is that so?" Aventus asked.

"It is," Davin said plainly, his tone taking on a slightly dangerous note.

"Then," Aventus said, "explain to me what's been going on along the border, here in the north. All those people slaughtered—you can't tell me they all deserved it, they all crossed your goddess, the families, the children?" Aventus's lips twisted in distaste. "We saw their remains, what was done in your goddess's name. I will remember—be haunted by it for the rest of my life."

"I would love to hear an explanation as well," Titus said.

"Unfortunately, I cannot offer a satisfactory one." Davin scowled slightly and glanced down at the floor before looking back up at them. "What has been done disturbs me, just as it does you."

"Somehow, I seriously doubt it," Titus said.

"Believe me or believe me not," Davin said. "I really do not care. The fact is, my mistress has called me here to rectify the wrong that has been done in her name. And … after what I have seen, I've personally sworn to make things right."

"For all we know," Lenth said, "you could be the root cause of it and are just playing with us."

"I could see how you might think such a thing possible," Davin said, "but in this instance, I am truly here to help. I will locate the individual who is responsible and end the madness." He paused for a heartbeat. "Upon my goddess, I swear it is so."

No one spoke after that.

"I believe him," Mae said, causing the others, including Eli, to turn their gazes to her.

"What?" Titus snapped. "How can you believe him? He likely lies as easily as he speaks."

"From what I know of his goddess," Mae said, "she is not a forgiving sort. He swore in her name, and if he is a true follower of Lutha Nyx, then he will do as he has said he would."

"And if he's not?" Lenth asked. "A true follower?"

"Then he better pray Lutha Nyx does not come after him," Mae said.

"Thank you, my lady," Davin said.

"Do not thank me," Mae said. "I am not your lady. I am just stating what I believe to be true."

"Regardless, you are correct. Lutha Nyx is not the forgiving sort. She expects service to be performed in honor."

"Honor?" Aventus asked. "What do you know of such a word?"

"A great deal, actually," Davin said. "The Brethren follow a code, one set down by the divine. We live by its mandates."

"So, whoever is behind the attacks, they broke your code?" Titus asked. "Is that it?"

Davin gave a slight nod, but said nothing.

"And you are hunting him down?" Titus asked. "That's why you are here?"

Davin once again gave a slight nod but said nothing.

Titus took a step toward Davin. "What will you do when you catch him?"

"The one causing the havoc in these parts?" Davin asked.

"Yes."

"I will send him onto my mistress." Davin offered up a smile. It was without warmth, and Eli felt a cold chill run down his back that had nothing to do with the room being chill and his clothes wet. "Before I do, I will make certain he suffers. He will wish he had never been born by the time I am done with him. Then, once I send him onto the next life, it will be Lutha Nyx's turn. And my punishment will pale in comparison to what she will do. He shall suffer a torment without end."

Eli shifted uncomfortably. He knew he dare not trust Davin, but at the same time, his gut was telling him there was truth to the man's words, some truth at any rate. Besides, it was not wise to falsely swear in a god's name, especially one such as Lutha Nyx. Many of the gods were known to hold grudges, and to say they were not the forgiving sort was an understatement. And Lutha Nyx was one of the worst of the bunch, at least in Eli's estimation.

"Why have you come here?" Davin asked. "I have explained my reasons. I would hear yours. Truth for truth, please."

"We are being pursued," Mae said before Eli could speak, "by Castol soldiers. They are intent on invading the imperial province. We were discovered observing their army marching south. For the moment, we have lost them, but there is a good chance they might pick up our trail at some point. We came here, seeking shelter from the storm."

"They must be good to be able to track you," Davin said, "perhaps even beyond good."

"They are led by a Castol forester named Kyber," Eli said. "And I assure you, he is quite good at what he does."

"Kyber?" Davin asked, as if testing out the name. The fire took that moment to pop loudly. "I've not heard of him, but then again, this is my first time in the north." Davin raised his chin up into the air as he sucked in a breath. "So, the rumors of war are true then."

"It would seem so," Eli said.

Davin glanced down at the glass vial in his hand, rubbing it with two fingers. "They, the Castol, will ultimately fail in such an endeavor."

"You can always rely upon a Castol to make the wrong decision," Aventus said.

"Yes," Titus said, "it seems you can."

"I will enjoy seeing that happen," Davin said, "the Castol crushed by the might of the empire."

Titus's brows drew together slightly.

"Oh, come now," Davin said, "just because I worship a god different than yours, I am still an imperial citizen and loyal to the empire."

"You worship a dark god," Lenth said, as the wind gusted strongly. Outside, the shutter began banging again. "How can you ever be loyal to the empire?"

"Our differences are a matter of perspective only," Davin said. "Just as the High Father is, Lutha Nyx is a goddess of the empire."

"That is a mighty big leap," Aventus scoffed.

"Is there not a temple to her majesty in Mal'Zeel?" Davin asked.

"A temple without priests," Aventus said, "a temple without followers."

"So you and many others believe," Davin said.

"Just because we honor all gods," Titus said, "doesn't mean your goddess supports the empire."

"Of course, not in all things," Davin said, "but she harbors the empire no ill will. Not only am I one of the Brethren, but I am also a loyal, proud citizen. I have always been. I support the emperor, and the senate, though those rich bastards in that august body are terribly corrupt to the point of contemptibility. Sometimes, I find it difficult to stomach their pious pretentions on one side of their face, while with the other they rob and steal."

Titus gave a disbelieving grunt.

"I, like many other citizens, honor the empire, just as we honor the goddess," Davin added. "The cult of Lutha Nyx is strong within the empire."

"By the High Father," Titus said, "I hope not."

The wind took that moment to blow strongly, seeming to pull at the small house. Air whistled through the gaps in the door and shutters. The fire guttered briefly, then surged back as the gust died off.

Deciding the danger for the moment was past them, Eli shrugged off his pack and placed it next to his bow. "Now is not the time for a theological, let alone a political discussion. We have a temporary peace and shelter, a roof over our heads to ride out the storm."

As if in thanks for the words, Davin inclined his head slightly to Eli, just as the wind gusted again.

"You are now my guests," Davin said. "Please make yourselves at home."

Titus hesitated and ran a hand through his beard, then removed his pack as well. The others did the same, dropping them to the floor and sliding them out of the way.

Eli stepped closer to the warmth of the fire. His clothes were wet, almost drenched, from the rain and then the snow. He felt chilled, but the room about them was growing warmer by the moment.

"Lenth," Titus said, turning away from Davin. "You've got first watch outside." He looked around at the others. "We will take turns every hour until dawn."

"No need for that," Davin said. "My pets are watching, not only the settlement, but the forest too. If anyone ventures too close, they will let me know in short order."

"That is how you knew we were here," Eli surmised, looking over at the human sitting on the stool. Davin had an incredibly relaxed air about him. "Your monsters were watching us."

"Monsters?" Lenth asked, glancing around. He shifted his stance as a realization seemed to slam home. It was as if he had not truly considered what they were dealing with in Davin. "You're talking about the things that killed all the people—devoured them? They were watching us? The monsters?"

"Monsters—I guess you could call the twisted that," Davin said to Aventus, then turned his gaze to Eli. "As you approached the settlement, my servants, my pets, spotted you in the forest and reported your presence. Though they are not the ones who have wreaked such havoc in these parts, they are similar enough to the monsters of which you speak."

"Why allow us to come closer?" Titus asked. "Why not just kill us and be done with it?"

"I thought I had already made that clear," Davin said. "You are not my enemy, nor my goddess's. Besides, you are the first living people I have come across in more than a month. I wanted to learn what you knew. I was also curious as to what rangers of both the High Born and empire are doing on the wrong side of the border."

"That makes some sense," Mae said. "And if we had proven hostile? What then?"

"You would have died, quickly. I—I would not have let you suffer—overly much."

Titus shot Eli an unhappy look.

"So," Mae asked after several heartbeats, "have you learned anything from us, then—anything useful?"

"Yes, I have," Davin said. "You confirmed the Castol mean to war on the empire. And now, I am left wondering if this invasion of the imperial province is perhaps connected to the killings."

The pieces of the puzzle suddenly clicked for Eli. He saw the direction Davin was heading. "As in someone is intentionally depopulating the area."

"So that the army can pass through undetected and arrive at Astrix's doorstep, without warning or spies getting wind of it," Titus finished.

"That is certainly a possibility," Davin said, "one I intend to follow up on. The purpose may have also been to spread fear, terror... Whatever the reason, it may take some time, but whoever is responsible for the acts committed in my goddess's name, I will find."

There was another uncomfortable moment.

"And how do you know that a follower like yourself— one who is loyal to the Castol instead of the empire—is not working for your goddess?" Titus asked.

Davin's lips turned up in a smile. "That would not happen."

"How can you be so sure?" Titus asked again.

"Oh, I am certain," Davin said, sobering. "Trust me on that."

"Like we should trust you at all," Aventus said. "Lying must be second nature for you."

"Continue to offend," Davin said dangerously, "and I may forget my manners, perhaps even revoke the hospitality I have generously offered."

"Enough of this," Eli said to Titus and then shot a meaningful look at Aventus. "I mean it."

"Sir," Lenth said, moving toward the door, "about that watch, I will get right on it."

"As I said, there is no need." Absently, Davin stroked the glass vial in his hand.

Eli's gaze flicked to the fragile-looking vial again. He had seen the like before, and when it had shattered, he and his companions at the time had faced a horror beyond imagining.

"You all have the look of being exhausted," Davin said, his tone changing to one of geniality. "My pets will keep watch this night. Sleep. In the morning we will go our separate ways and hopefully never see one another again. At least, I will pray for that."

"We can't trust him," Aventus said to Eli.

"Trust me?" Davin's genial nature slipped away. "If I had desired it so, you would have been dead already."

The man before them was incredibly dangerous. Eli was certain of it.

Not only that, Davin was powerful too, and a priest of some kind. That was something that offered Eli no comfort, for despite his protestations otherwise, the god he worshiped was a dark one.

Eli's gaze went to the man's sword and staff. Perhaps he was even a warrior priest? That was something he found even more concerning. Eli had not known Lutha Nyx had such fighters in her service.

Eli made a snap decision, one born from his gut. He had long studied humans, lived and worked amongst them, and seemed to be able to tell when one of them was lying or bluffing.

"Titus," Eli said, drawing the ranger's attention. "I believe we will be good this night. There is no need to post a watch. We will take him at his word."

"You trust him?" Titus's mouth dropped open slightly. "That is a follower of Lutha Nyx you are putting our faith in. You realize that, right?"

"We need rest and he's offering to provide the watch, and no, I cannot bring myself to fully trust him, but in this instance, I do not believe he is lying. He has sworn on his goddess's name, and what I know of Lutha Nyx's followers, though detestable, they are sticklers for such things."

"I don't like it," Titus said.

"I don't like it either, but the elf speaks true of my kind," Davin said. "You are quite safe here. Please, rest. Consider it a reward for the information you provided. Besides, we are allies of sorts."

"Allies?" Titus scoffed. "You may consider yourself an imperial, but I don't. Imperials honor the High Father and his alignment."

"This day, Lutha Nyx is firmly aligned with your revered god," Davin said. "Take some comfort in that knowledge."

Mae yawned. With the fire and the bodies in the room, the heat was continuing to build. "I could use some sleep, and badly."

"I took the liberty of helping myself to some of the dried meats I discovered here in the settlement." Davin gestured over at the table, upon which were several wrapped bundles of varying sizes. "Help yourselves. There is plenty to be had, and regrettably, the people who once called this settlement home have no more use for it. Take as much as you require for traveling rations. You need not worry. Before I leave in the morning, I will find more for myself."

Eli moved over to the table and unwrapped a bundle. He found a hunk of beef jerky. Bringing it up to his nose, he smelled it to make sure it was good to eat, then took a bite. It was dry and salty, but overall, quite good.

Davin stood and dragged his stool over to the wall, next to the fire. The wind gusted loudly again, whistling through the shutters and door. The fire guttered for several heartbeats. He sat back down and leaned his back against the wall.

"Now, if you will kindly excuse me, I will grab some sleep myself. There are blankets over there by the bed. I can't promise that they are pest-free, but they should keep you warm during the night. That is, if you need them." Davin yawned, and with that, he closed his eyes and said no more. He was still holding the glass vial.

"Are you certain about this?" Titus asked Eli.

"Certain? No. But I don't see that we have a choice." Eli glanced over at Davin. "If he is what I think he is, well then, he is very dangerous."

"I *am* dangerous," Davin affirmed, without opening his eyes, "especially when roused, but not to you all, not tonight, and certainly not tomorrow. Now, kindly stop talking and let me get some sleep, for I need it as well."

CHAPTER FOURTEEN

"Wake up," Davin snapped.

Eli opened his eyes. He was warm, comfortable, and nearly fully rested. Her arm thrown over his chest, Mae was snuggled tightly against him on the floor. Withdrawing the arm, she rolled onto her back, gave a soft groan, and pulled aside her blanket. Eli almost protested as she broke away from him.

"Get up," Davin said, more insistently this time, and with that, Eli threw his blanket to his side and sat up. Putting aside the last vestiges of sleep, he shook his head and stretched.

"What's going on?" Titus asked groggily. He had taken the rope bed. Sitting up and swinging his legs to the floor, the ranger rubbed at his eyes. "What's wrong?"

Back ramrod straight, Davin was still sitting upon his stool by the fire. Eli blinked. Davin's eyes had rolled back into his head. All that showed were the whites, which stared blindly ahead. The wind took that moment to howl, almost supernaturally, tugging at the shutters and door. Outside, the loose shutter began banging again, this time more violently.

"What's wrong?" Titus asked again, standing. The other two rangers were moving too, getting up from where they had slept on the floor.

"We have company," Davin said, "twenty men, possibly more, coming in from the northwest."

"Kyber," Eli breathed and climbed stiffly to his feet. His legs protested strongly at the movement and so too did his back. He was terribly sore from the exertions of the previous day's pursuit. They had come many miles through difficult and broken terrain. Now, it seemed Eli was feeling every single mile. "How far out are they?"

"No more than a half mile," Davin said, the whites of his eyes still showing and staring into nothingness. Eli gave an involuntary shiver at the sight. "They are making a beeline for the settlement. The snow is slowing them down some but not overly much. At the pace they are moving, we have maybe half an hour, at best—maybe even less."

"I thought you said Kyber didn't know about this place," Titus said to Eli.

"I said I doubted he knew about it. Honestly, Titus, there is a world of difference between what I say and what I mean. You should know that by now."

"You don't say?" Titus asked. "You just don't say."

"We need to get out of here." Mae, on her knees, began rolling up her blanket. "And quickly."

"That does seem like a wise and considered move," Eli said to her. "Very wise indeed. I mean, why make Kyber's job easier and just wait for him, eh?"

Mae stopped the rolling of her blanket and looked up at him, fire in her gaze. She raised a warning finger and wagged it in a threatening manner. "Do not start with me, husband. I am giving you fair warning. Do not start with me if you know what is good for you."

"I like her," Titus said as he rapidly finished rolling his own blanket. "You know, Eli, you married the right girl there. She calls you on your bullshit."

"Do not start with me either, Titus. Just because I give him some slack does not mean I give you humans the same latitude."

"You give me slack?" Eli asked as if thoroughly shocked by the suggestion, though his attention was still fixed on Davin. Mae did not reply, but returned to rolling her blanket tightly.

As Eli watched, Davin closed his eyes. When he opened them a moment later, they were their normal black color, the pupils at any rate. The white around them was bloodshot, as if he'd not slept a wink throughout the night.

Davin stood from his stool. He turned around and grabbed his sword harness, which was hanging from a peg on the wall. He slid it over his head and onto his right shoulder. With a smooth move, he picked the scabbard up, with sword inside, from where it leaned against the wall and dropped it into the loop, fitting with an audible click.

"At least our clothes from last night are dry," Lenth said, having moved over to the fire. He was holding his tunic, which he had hung over the mantle. They all had a spare set of dry clothes and had worn them to sleep.

"Lenth, toss me my tunic there, will you?" Eli pointed to a stool where his tunic had been hung to dry. Lenth tossed it to Eli, who caught it and began folding it. Lenth then did the same for the rest, including Mae.

Aventus retrieved his boots and felt inside. "My boots are still damp," he said unhappily before slipping one on.

"What happened to those elven boots you were gifted with upon completion of your training?" Eli asked curiously, looking up. "They were made special for you and would have stayed dry even if it had been a full downpour." He glanced over at Titus. "I see he still has his."

"It's a long story," Aventus said.

"Long story, my ass," Titus said. "He lost them in a game of dice. Probably tempted fate and got screwed doing it."

"Dice?" Eli asked, feeling not only surprise, but also some amusement at Aventus. "Really? You gambled away a pair of nearly priceless boots? Those would have taken years to wear out and you'd have never found the like in the empire."

Aventus did not answer, but instead almost sullenly turned his gaze down to his pack, into which he was placing a wrapped bundle.

"Really," Titus confirmed as he slipped his own boots on. "Some days he plays the fool well."

"I guess someone has to," Lenth said.

"The prize was worth the risk," Aventus grudgingly said, "at least it seemed so at the time. Though, thinking back, the bastard I was playing against likely cheated."

"Ah," Titus said, "the loaded dice excuse again. I've heard that one before. I'm thinking the truth is simply that you're a magnet for fate. You just tempt it too often and the result is trouble."

Eli turned his attention away from Aventus and back to Davin, who was busy securing his own bag. The leather was cracked and had a used look about it. "Any idea on what time of day it is?"

"A couple of hours before dawn," Davin said. "Maybe a little less. We've gotten about four inches of snow outside, with more coming down."

Though he was still dog-tired, Eli realized they had nearly managed a full night's sleep. Still, it did not make up for what they had lost over the last two days, but sleep was sleep, which was better than none.

"That's not too bad," Aventus said. "I can deal with four inches—not too bad at all."

"It is when it makes it easier for the enemy to not only track you but hunt you down as well," Eli said as he packed his blanket into his pack, then tied the flap closed. Like the rest, he had taken the precaution of going to sleep fully clothed. Unlike the rest, his boots were already on.

Aventus gave an unhappy grunt.

Eli reached over to the where he had left his daggers and sword, all within arm's reach. He grabbed the daggers and slipped them into their sheaths, then reached for the sword. As his hand closed around the scabbard, a shock of some kind ran quickly through him and he almost jumped. He looked down at the sword, studying it, while the others continued busily to ready themselves.

Had he just imagined the shock?

No, something had indeed happened. The little hairs on his arm were standing up. Had it been the magic of the sword? He glanced over at Davin and wondered. Had he just been sent a warning of some kind from the sword? Eli did not know what to think. It was yet another mystery, a puzzle to solve.

Mae tapped him lightly on the arm. "Come on, we do not have much time."

Eli had never felt anything like what had just happened. He found he was slightly shaken and that surprised him. Deciding to ponder some more on it later, when there was sufficient time, he began moving again and belted the sword tightly about his waist.

Even though the weapon looked like a legionary short sword, it had come with a belt instead of a harness, which usually slipped over the shoulder with the sword hanging at the hip of the average legionary. He had never much cared for the legionary setup. The belt suited him just fine and, in Eli's opinion, made it easier to move through the forest.

With a sword belt, there was less of a chance of a strap getting snagged on a branch or caught in some brush.

Next, Eli picked up his pack and shrugged it on, settling it into place and then tightening the straps so that it was a good, comfortable fit. He reached for his bundle of arrows and untied it, looking at the contents sourly. He had only three arrows left. Three was not a whole lot. It was fewer, given their situation, than he would have preferred. Still, Eli found himself looking on the bright side. Three was better than none at all.

"Titus," Eli said, looking up as he removed the three missiles. "How many arrows do you have left?"

"Two," Titus said, pausing in his work of returning his haversack to his pack.

"I have three," Mae said.

"One," Lenth said.

"Two," Aventus said. "Well, that's not good."

"Try to make every shot count, then," Titus said to them all, "and I mean every shot."

Using the leather ties, Eli secured the empty arrow bundle to his pack, then took the arrows in his hand. When the time came, in the heat of the moment, having the missiles handy would make it easier to shoot them rapidly at the enemy.

Taking his bow, Eli moved to the door and, hand on the latch, looked back at Davin. The man had just put his own pack on and had taken the staff, a simple piece of shaped wood about six feet in length, that had been smoothed by excessive use. Eli had the feeling it was well loved.

"How close are they now?" Eli asked him.

Davin closed his eyes again, then opened them. Only the whites were showing, which Eli thought incredibly unnerving. He had never seen anything like it.

The man stood rock still for several moments, then closed his eyes and opened them again, his dark pupils showing this time. Blinking, they were unfocused for a heartbeat, then they settled back on Eli. Under the flickering glow of the firelight, Davin's eyes seemed particularly dark.

"They've nearly reached the tree line," Davin said.

"Time to go then," Eli said and opened the door. A gust of wind blew inward, along with some swirling snow. It was still dark outside, especially made so by the storm and falling snow.

The dim light from the fire inside the house fell on the snow just beyond the doorstep. Eli took a step outside. His boots crunched down into the fresh snow. The temperature was bitterly cold against his cheeks and exposed skin, the wind making it almost painful.

Lenth emerged next, head swiveling left to right, bow nocked as he searched for threats. Aventus followed and did the same. Titus and Davin stepped out into the snow. Titus surveyed the snow-covered settlement, a look of deep unhappiness on his face. Tugging on her pack, Mae was the last one out.

"Which way?" Titus asked as the wind gusted again, causing a near whiteout for several heartbeats.

"Gods," Aventus said as he averted his face and turned partially away, "why couldn't the weather have held off for just one more day?"

"Eli," Titus asked again, this time more insistent, "which way do we go?"

Eli had been staring at the snow, which had fallen across the yard before them. There were faint indications of tracks that the falling snow was doing its best to cover up. They looked like the prints of small animals. Eli doubted animals would have ventured out in such a storm. No, they would have sought shelter, or been snug in their burrows—besides, he well recalled the absence of them in the forest, the strange and unsettling quiet.

"Eli," Titus said. "You know the area. Which way should we go?"

Pulling his attention from the fading prints in the snow, he looked over at Titus. Eli glanced around, thought for a moment as to the best course of action, and pointed behind the house they had sheltered in. "We head east and into the forest, away from Kyber and his men."

"That's in the direction of the river crossing you mentioned," Titus said, having to raise his voice above the wind, which had whipped up around them again. "With this cold, fording a river may not be the wisest idea. Besides, Kyber is going to follow us easily enough. Our tracks will lead him right to it. He won't have to work too hard to follow." Titus paused. "And I have to be honest, I'm not much liking the river idea."

"You are correct," Eli said. "Water and extreme cold do not mix well. I believe the river will be our last option. More importantly, to the east, say three to four miles from here, the terrain becomes rugged and climbs over a series of small ridges. We will have the elevation on them. That might give us an advantage to any fight that is coming."

"It's going to be a race once they find out we've left." Titus rubbed the back of his neck.

"That is when it becomes exciting," Eli said.

"Honestly, I could do with a little bit less excitement," Titus said. "But I like the idea of some elevation. Perhaps we might even be able to ambush them. A few well-placed shots from above might slow them down a little, get them to think twice about following."

"That is what I was thinking," Eli said.

Titus rubbed the back of his neck again as he looked at Eli. "I'm gonna tell you plainly, Eli, I am tired of being chased."

"Me too," Eli said.

"We need to get moving," Davin said with a note of urgency. "The more time we waste here talking, the closer they get."

"Time to go, then." Titus clapped his hands together. "Aventus and Lenth, you both have point. We're moving due east. Get a move on."

"Got it, boss." Aventus started forward with Lenth at his side.

"And, Aventus?" Titus said almost as an afterthought, causing the other ranger to pause and look back after he had taken just a couple of steps. "No more tempting fate," Titus said. "Stop mentioning the gods, will you? I am thinking they have been listening to you of late."

"Perhaps he should instead start praying," Eli suggested, half serious.

"Why would I ever do that?" Aventus asked and grinned back at his leader before continuing onward around the side of the house, following after Lenth.

"Why indeed," Titus said, shaking his head, then turned his attention to Eli. "Why am I saddled with the sinners and the godless like him? Can you explain that to me? I would really like to know."

"Perhaps it is simply fate," Eli said, resisting a grin.

"Fate?" Titus said, eyeing Eli dubiously.

"Yeah," Eli said, "maybe it is really your job to convert them and get them to see the light. Have you thought of that?"

Titus's eyebrows drew together as he stared at Eli. Then he suddenly grinned. "You are full of shit. You know that, right?"

"Oh?" Eli asked.

"Aventus's nature," Titus said. "It's why he and I get along so well together and make such a good team. I was just like him—before I saw the light and way."

"I know," Eli said.

"You do?" Titus asked, seeming surprised, then shook his head. "Of course you do."

Eli's attention was drawn to his wife. Mae was staring toward the northwest, trying to peer through the driving snow. She wore a troubled expression and that bothered Eli.

"What?" he asked her.

"Did you really think Kyber knew not of this place?" she asked him, looking over and searching his face with her eyes.

"He might have known," Eli admitted, "but I do not believe he did. I could be wrong, but I think not."

"Then," Mae said hesitantly, and glanced over at Davin, "he might have used other means to track us."

Eli took a step back and looked sharply over at Davin as the wind gusted lightly again. It swirled the snow around them. "Is that possible? Could he have used your goddess's creatures?"

Davin frowned, then hesitated a heartbeat before answering. "I suppose it is possible. There are some that have the ability to hunt and track, not only animals, but also people."

"That just figures," Titus said, "doesn't it?"

"Go," Eli told Mae. "Keep an eye on Aventus and Lenth. Make sure they do not get into trouble. We will be right behind you. There is something that needs to be sorted first."

She looked to him, her gaze flicking to Davin, then gave a nod. She started off, leaving them.

Eli turned his gaze to the settlement's yard once more and pointed with his bow. "Those tracks out there are from your pets, right?"

Davin looked and gave an unhappy nod of confirmation. "They are."

"Great High Father," Titus said. "There must be dozens of them."

"And there are tracks like that out in the forest too, right?" Eli asked. "Tracks that Kyber and his men will happen across?"

"Yes," Davin said. "They are from smaller conjurings, harmless creatures really. They are my eyes and ears and alert me to problems, threats, and things of concern."

"When your eyes went white," Titus said, "you were communicating with them?"

"In a manner of speaking, yes," Davin said. "I was seeing through their eyes, which are not the same as ours. The view is—for lack of a better explanation—twisted."

Eli and Titus shared a brief look. They were both unhappy with what Davin was telling them, let alone what he represented.

Eli turned back to Davin. "So, if Kyber or someone with him is using a similar magic, there is a strong chance they have seen the tracks? They will know what they represent, yes?"

"That is correct," Davin said. "The twisted that killed everyone in this settlement did the same to the animals in the surrounding forest. Someone who is familiar with their use will recognize the lack of animals, the twisted's distinctive tracks and their mark."

It was as Eli had expected. "Our pursuers, can they see them as you do? Can they communicate with them? I am speaking of the pets you control. Please answer honestly."

"No," Davin said, "they are only able to see and communicate with those they have personally conjured. Unless mine are uncovered from the shadows, which is unlikely, all they will discover are their tracks."

Eli gave a nod. It was as he suspected. He sucked in a breath as he thought through what he must do next. "You are planning on coming with us?"

"You'd leave me behind?" Davin asked, looking between Eli and Titus as the wind picked up again. A note of concern and surprise had crept into his voice. It turned to outrage. "With the enemy almost upon the settlement, you'd abandon me? After I gave you advance warning of their approach? You'd still leave me?"

"I would," Titus said, "without a second's thought. You wanted to confront whoever had done this…" Titus waved to the northwest. "Well, he might be out there."

"And he might not be," Davin said. "This Kyber could have known about the settlement and guessed you'd come here, camped a distance away, rested some, then set out well before dawn in the hopes of catching you by surprise."

"I am not so convinced," Titus said.

"He's coming with us, Titus," Eli said.

"What?" Titus asked. "Why?"

"I believe he will be useful. He has already proven so by alerting us to the threat of Kyber and his men approaching."

"He's also dangerous. Did you forget that?"

"Forget? No," Eli said. "He also understands these creatures. We do not. It is something we will need to deal with."

"There is that," Davin said. "My knowledge may just prove useful, my unique skills too, especially in the coming hours if a conjurer is with them."

"Is that what you call them?" Titus asked. "Unique skills?"

Davin gave a shrug of his shoulders. "Call it what you will."

"We are going to move fast," Eli said to Davin. "You will have to keep up."

"I am accustomed to adversity," Davin said. "You need not worry about me. Moving with rapidity will not be a problem, even over rugged terrain."

"I'm not happy about this," Titus said. "By bringing him along, we're inviting trouble, which we already have in plenty. We should just go our separate ways and be done with him."

"Do you swear to continue the peace we have in place?" Eli asked Davin, pointedly ignoring Titus.

"I do," Davin said, "while we travel together, and as long as you and your people don't break it, we have an accord."

"Done, then." Eli turned to Titus. "He has my protection."

"Bah." Titus waved a disgusted hand at Eli, then scowled as the wind gusted once more, this time strongly. He turned to Davin after it had died down. "Say, why don't you just take Kyber and his boys out with your pets? If your goddess is so strong, what do you need us for?"

"It's not the right time." Davin averted his gaze.

"What do you mean, it's not the right time?" Titus gestured in the direction the enemy were coming. "If not now, when?"

Davin turned his gaze northwestward and for a moment it seemed like he would not answer. "I cannot fully explain it to you, not with the time we have here. I may even be prohibited from doing so. But part of what I have ready to release can only be used once, and it must be triggered near the target, what I want attacked and killed."

"So then, get close to them," Titus said.

"You don't understand," Davin said with a pained expression. "Releasing the twisted is just as much of an art as it is calling and controlling one."

"You are right," Titus said. "I don't understand."

"Controlling, let alone conjuring, takes a lot of effort," Eli explained, gesturing at Davin with his bow. "While he works to unleash the unnatural, he will be vulnerable to attack. If he's interrupted or distracted, even slightly, the monster could escape his control if the conjuring has gone far enough. That could easily mean the death of everyone, starting with himself."

"Correct to some degree," Davin said, and held up the glass vial, "except for what has already been conjured and bottled."

Eli eyed the vial warily. "Which is why they like to work in the shadows, on their terms, and not at the spur of the moment, like you are asking him to do."

"Again, that is correct." Davin shifted his staff, planting the end in the snow. "We are also trained in the use of small arms so that we are not put in that position during a desperate moment. If it comes to it, I can fight with some skill."

Titus did not look wholly convinced. He appeared about to say something more when Eli abruptly turned away toward the house and smiled slightly.

"What?" Titus asked him, with no little amount of concern. "I know that look. What nonsense are you thinking of doing now?"

Feeling a bubble of amusement, Eli stepped back inside and up to the fire that was crackling pleasantly in the fireplace. He reached down for a blackened chunk of wood that had long since burned itself out.

The piece had spilled from the fire and lay on the stone just before the blaze. He touched it gingerly to make sure it was not dangerously hot. Satisfied it wasn't, he picked it up and stood. Turning to the wall opposite the door, he stepped forward and used the charred chunk of wood to write in the common tongue, making sure the letters were not only large enough, but easy to see from the door. After a moment, he stood back, admiring his work.

"Really?" Titus asked from the doorway. "*'Sorry we missed you. Please feel free to make yourself at home.'* That's the best you could come up with?"

"I believe it conveys the message splendidly," Eli said.

"I'm surprised you didn't sign it," Titus said.

"Oh, right," Eli said, and hastily wrote his name. He turned around. "That was a good idea. Thank you, Titus." Eli turned back and admired the message once more. "I sure hope Kyber appreciates my effort."

"And you think there is something wrong with *me?*" Davin asked as he eyed the message.

"I know there is something wrong with us both," Titus said, gesturing at Eli. "We wouldn't do the job we do if there wasn't."

"You really want them to follow us, don't you?" Davin said.

"I hope so." Eli spared the message written on the wall one more look, then turned and made his way out of the building, making sure to close the door behind him.

Amidst the falling snow, he gazed around the settlement one last time, peering for several heartbeats to the northwest. He saw nothing, no movement.

The enemy were close.

He could almost feel it on the wind. With that in mind, he turned and started after the others, following their tracks around the building and toward the east. Titus and Davin moved with him, their feet crunching in the snow. After they had gone a few feet, Eli felt his heart quicken to a new beat, one that spoke of excitement to come.

The hunt was on once more.

CHAPTER FIFTEEN

The snow had tapered off shortly after sunrise. Within an hour, the sky had cleared, becoming a vibrant blue with not a hint of a cloud in sight. The wind had also died down and now only blew in light, gentle gusts that brought a touch of winter with them.

Eli glanced up at the sun, which hung in the sky at its zenith. It shone brilliantly downward in a vain attempt at bringing the day some warmth. He supposed the temperature was hovering somewhere just above freezing, for the snow that clung to the nearest branches had begun to melt, sending droplets of water to fall to the ground, making little holes in the snow.

Eli rubbed his hands together to generate some warmth, his breath steaming on the air as he exhaled. His clothes were damp from their travels through the snow-laden forest, and Eli was cold.

He would have liked to have had a fire, for it seemed like the moment they had stopped for an extended break, a cold chill had started to set in. But a fire wasn't a wise option, not when there were people after you, especially if you had left a trail through the snow that even the worst scout could follow.

Still, the cold wasn't all that bad, and he had experienced worse. Just as he had in the past, he would endure, for it was only a matter of mind over body. Ranger training taught one how to put physical discomfort aside. Besides, they would begin moving soon enough again, and once they did, the physical exertion would warm him up.

Having pushed straight through from the settlement, with hardly a stop, they had chosen the top of a steep hill with a bald top as the place for their first extended break. The hill rose at least a hundred feet over the forest and was part of a series of small ridges that ran north and south for a few miles in either direction.

To reach the summit, they'd had to do some climbing, which made the crest the perfect place to hole up for a bit. The hill was as safe a place as any, at least Eli thought so. Titus had agreed. So, they had called a break.

Anyone attempting to reach them would be spotted long before they could get to the top. And yet, what their current position offered in temporary security, the elements took just as much their due. There was a consistent gusting wind at the summit. Exposed as they were, each gust mercilessly attempted to steal what body heat they had and chilled them further in their damp clothes.

A few feet away, Mae had cleared the snow from a rock that abutted a boulder. Sitting on the rock, her back against the sun-warmed boulder and her legs stretched out before her, she was dozing, occasionally shifting in an attempt to get more comfortable.

Upon leaving the settlement, the pace they had set and kept up had been a punishing one. Despite the cold snow and damp clothes, the respite had been a welcome break for everyone. The others lounged wearily about nearby. Davin had found a spot a few feet away from Mae and, lying upon his thick woolen cloak, also appeared to be sleeping. He was using his pack as a pillow.

The man had been as good as his word. He kept up with the rest of them, and without complaint too. For a moment, Eli found himself wondering, despite what the man had sworn, how far Davin's word carried.

Had Eli done the right thing by allowing him to come along?

Sitting upon a cloak that had been laid out over the snow, Aventus and Lenth were seated on a large, flat rock off to the left. They had taken shelter between two large boulders. While they shared rations, both men were talking quietly amongst themselves. Titus had positioned himself on the opposite side of the hill about ten yards away and, like Eli, was standing watch.

Eli was keeping an eye on the side of the hill they had climbed a short while before, while Titus watched the reverse slope and the ridges just beyond.

So far, Eli had seen no hint of pursuit. That was becoming somewhat troubling. His gaze moved from the slope to the forest below, which was draped in a blanket of fresh snow. The view was magnificent. It spread out for as far as the eye could see, and Eli loved it all.

A quarter of a mile away, an eagle soared above the trees. The bird was clearly on the hunt. It was the first animal he had seen in days. Eli tracked its flight, watching as the bird circled gracefully.

Despite the tension of the pursuit, his aches and pains, Eli felt himself relaxing. He sucked in a breath of the cold, unpolluted air and then let it out through his nose. His breath steamed before being whisked away by the light breeze.

There was incredible beauty in the view, and his heart almost broke at the display before him. This was one of the true perks of being a ranger, traveling, seeing the world's beauty as most never were able. He felt honored, privileged even, for such moments were gifts to be not only savored but cherished and enjoyed to their fullest.

A crunch of snow drew his attention. Mae had gotten to her feet. Like a cat rising from a good nap, she stretched out her back, then moved over to him. She offered a private smile that was meant only for Eli, then turned her gaze outward, seeming to soak up the view. She was silent for a number of long heartbeats.

"It is so peaceful-looking, so perfect, do you not think so?" Mae asked without turning away from the view.

"Our world is a beautiful one. That is for certain."

"Sometimes, I forget to look, to search for the beauty." Mae gestured before them. "Then something like this comes along and not only surprises but delights me. I find I enjoy such surprises. It is as if the Great Mother is reminding us of that for which we fight and struggle."

"Yes. When least expected, such things can creep up on you."

"Hard to believe there are people out there, somewhere, intent on doing us harm." Mae shook her head ever so slightly. "I find it at times difficult to fathom."

Eli turned his gaze away from her and back out to the vast forest, then shifted it to the slope of the hill they had climbed. Though nothing and no one was in view, Eli felt more than a little troubled, and the feeling was growing. They had been on the hilltop for nearly an hour. Kyber and his men should have closely followed. He would have expected to see them by now. That they hadn't was beginning to bother him.

"Agreed."

"What do you think it means?" Mae asked after a brief silence. It was as if she had read his thoughts. He well knew what she questioned.

Where was Kyber?

"The lack of close pursuit?" Eli asked and then continued before she could answer. "I do not know. I really do not."

"Titus told me of the message you left," Mae said.

Eli had expected disapproval but, instead, did not sense it. So, he decided to play it safe and offer only a noncommittal grunt.

"At first, I was not too pleased with you," Mae admitted. "Then, I thought it humorous, and I do not even know Kyber."

"You did?" Eli was honestly surprised. "Really?"

"Yes." Mae laid a hand upon his shoulder. "It was a jest well played, clever even."

"So, you are finally beginning to appreciate my humor. That did not take too long."

Mae withdrew her hand from his shoulder, took a step back, and eyed him closely. "I did not say that, not fully. Let us just say your humor still needs some work."

"Work? I am shocked, just shocked you would even think that, let alone suggest such a thing." Eli injected a hint of hurt into his tone. "I will have you know that over centuries of work, my humor has been carefully developed, tempered, and honed to a fine point. It needs *some work*? Haa."

"I do not believe much ever shocks you, husband," Mae said in an amused tone. She laughed lightly. "But there are times when you amuse me, and this is one."

Eli was silent for a moment as he studied her and she him.

"Do you think Kyber got my message?" Eli asked seriously after a moment and turned away, his eyes raking the slope of the hill once more, then the forest below them, searching for even the tiniest hint that the enemy were drawing near or lying concealed somewhere below. He spotted nothing.

"I believe he did," Mae said.

"Then where is he?" Eli allowed some of the frustration to show. "I would have expected him to be right on our tail. The more we sit here, the more I begin to think I am missing something, something important."

"Perhaps he took your advice and made himself at home in that house. It was rather a cold and snowy night. The fire might have been too much of an opportunity to pass up."

Eli looked over at her and blinked. "I had not considered that. You know, I did not expect him to take my suggestion literally."

"I can see how you would think that. No one in their right mind should ever take you literally."

"Hey!" he protested. "That's not fair."

Mae shot him a grin. "It is but one possibility, though."

"One?" Eli thought on it some. "Perhaps he and his people needed rest or decided to wait out the storm, especially, as you said, since we left them a warm house with a good fire."

"If he was foolish enough to do that," Mae said, "he will not catch us, not now. We're nearly at the river. Once we reach it, we can turn south and make for the border, hopefully crossing it by nightfall."

"That is right. Another day and a half's travel and we will be at Mekhet," Eli said. "I doubt he would have the strength to overcome the town's garrison or even risk such a venture—that is, if he follows us that far. To do so would not be the wisest move."

"He may have called off the pursuit. We dragged them well away from Astrix, which is their army's objective, at least an initial one. I would assume the foresters, along with those skirmishers, were supposed to be the eyes and ears of the army. They may have been called back or prohibited from pursuing us too far."

"There is that." Eli tapped his chin with a finger. "But I just do not see the man giving up so easily, not him. He can be like a stubborn dog with a bone that he does not want to give up."

"But he might have done just that," Mae said, "especially if someone ordered him to do so."

"True," Eli conceded, but was still far from convinced. "That is very true. Even Kyber has superiors. Whether he listens to them or not is another matter altogether."

"Care to tell me about the history between you two? Why does he hate you so?"

"I killed his father," Eli said simply.

"Did he deserve it?" Mae asked.

"He earned it," Eli said and fingered the hilt of one of his daggers.

Mae gave a nod but said nothing.

"It happened in a small fight about twenty years ago," Eli said. "We were out in the middle of nowhere and had been ambushed. It was one of those by bow, daggers"—Eli's hand came to rest upon his sword hilt—"and sword moments, a desperate fight where you use and do whatever you have to, just to survive." Eli paused. "I lived to see another day. He and his companions did not."

"How did Kyber find out you killed his father?" Mae asked.

"I made sure to tell him," Eli said and turned his gaze back out into the forest. "He earned the right to know."

"And now," Mae said, "he hunts us over it."

"Because of that and a few other little things that occurred over the years. But then again, he might not be hunting us. Like you suggested, he may have been forced to turn back."

"What then if he did?" Mae glanced over at the human rangers. "What do we do next?"

"You mean after we reach Mekhet?" Eli asked, while searching the sky for the eagle again. It took him a moment, but the bird had climbed much higher and was now no more than a tiny speck amidst the great expanse of blue that stretched overhead.

"By helping Titus," Mae said, "we have deviated greatly, been diverted from our main mission."

Eli searched the slope below them once again, raking it carefully with his eyes. "Mik'Las. I fear running down him and the Atreena will prove more challenging than I had initially anticipated."

"You know Mik'Las, likely better than anyone else I know," Mae said. "When we set out, did you expect the hunt to be anything but easy?"

"Easy? No. I expected it to be a challenging task, perhaps as difficult as I have ever faced. But now, I am beginning to wonder on just how challenging it will prove to be. I also suspect…" Eli trailed off, not quite sure he wanted to go there with Mae just yet.

"Suspect what?" Mae asked, drawing his attention back once more.

"I suspect your mother planned well."

"What does she have to do with this?" Mae asked, frowning slightly. "Other than it was her who set us on the hunt?"

Eli stared at his wife for a long moment. She deserved his honesty. Going forward, when it came to serious matters like this one, he would strive for nothing short of that.

"Si'Cara might have chosen me another partner," Eli said. "There were several readily available and with more experience too."

"You are suggesting I was chosen for a reason?" Mae asked.

"Yes. Why you? Why not someone else?"

Mae eyed him for several heartbeats, her eyes searching his face. "You believe she knew there was a chance of what might develop between us? Or hoped something would grow and bear fruit? Is that what you are trying to tell me?"

"I am beginning to think that is a strong possibility."

"No," Mae said firmly, her disbelief plain, "it is not. That is not Mother's way."

"Are you so sure, so certain?"

Mae did not immediately respond, but it was clear he had given her a great deal to think on. "By assigning me to such a dangerous mission, she was making a point. Mik'Las stepped over a line that should never have been crossed. Not only did he kill, but he took something of incredible value to our people, the Atreena. By choosing you, the foremost ranger amongst our people, and her own, me, she was making a statement to the council and everyone else."

"If you think it so," Eli said.

"I do," Mae said, a slight suggestion of heat entering her tone.

"Okay, I do not know your mother as well as you. Perhaps you are correct, and it is as you say."

Mae gave a nod, looked out at the forest, then turned her gaze back to him. "I must admit, I have been a little worried when it comes to Mother."

"About what?" Eli asked, wondering where she was going and why.

"Us."

"Oh," Eli said.

"Once Mother learns you have taken me for your wife, I fear it may serve to provoke her to rashness."

"I hope not." Though it had yet to be directed at him, when roused, the warden's temper could be a fierce thing, for he had witnessed it. In truth, Eli had worried about the same, and it was not a small concern either.

"I have become, shall we say, somewhat fond of you, husband. I would not wish to see you executed."

"I do not wish to be executed either," Eli said, somewhat amused, though it was a real concern, one she was right to voice. "It would sort of be a rather disappointing end to the fun."

"Yes, it would," Mae said. And with that, they fell silent for a short time.

"We will eventually find him," Mae said. "We will run Mik'Las to ground and complete the mission my mother set for us."

"Yes," Eli said firmly. "We will not fail."

"I know we will not," Mae said with a resolute nod. "Still, I cannot help but feel by assisting Titus we are prolonging the hunt... making things more difficult for us in the long run."

Eli turned his gaze away from her and back to the forest. He scanned first the steep slope again, then farther out to what he could see below in the gaps in the tree canopy, before turning back to her once more.

"Once we reach Mekhet, you wish to leave them?" Eli jerked his chin toward Titus, who was gazing outward in the opposite direction. He, like the rest, was too far away to overhear their conversation. "To continue the hunt?"

"I do not know," Mae said. "Perhaps it is the right move, maybe not. On one hand, we need to track Mik'Las down. On the other, there is war to think on, a war that could ultimately affect our people and—this business with Lutha Nyx. I do not like it. None of it is any good in my view. Then there is your grandfather to consider."

"There is that," Eli said. "Grandpappy put us on the trail that led to this point. There can be no doubt about that."

Eli turned his gaze back to the forest and its wintery beauty. He sucked in a cold breath and blew it out through his nose.

"In all honesty, though I am being selfish, I do not mind prolonging our mission, allowing Mik'Las to gain more of a lead on us."

"What do you mean?" Mae asked, her brows drawing together. "Why would you wish to drag things out?"

"When we finish, capture or kill him, and return, should we—or really I—survive your mother's wrath, we will undoubtedly be broken up. There is no way either of us will be permitted to continue to serve together and remain in the Corps."

"No," Mae said, her voice a near whisper, "at the very least we will receive new partners."

"So, I have no desire to return, not any time soon. The longer the hunt lasts, the more time we have together. Out here, it is just us, and I find I rather like it that way."

Mae cleared her throat. "I—I appreciate that, but there is duty to consider, a higher responsibility to our people, and then there is the Atreena."

"Duty," Eli said, "yes, it is always there, hanging like a dark cloud on the horizon. Yet, for you, I would willingly give it all up, set it aside. How could I not want that?"

"Can you, the redoubtable Eli, even do that?" Mae asked, her eyes on him. They watered slightly as she took a step nearer. "You would give up everything, for me?"

"I—I…" Eli paused, and his hand, almost as if it had a will of its own, traveled down to the sword belted to his side. He patted the hilt lightly. "I want to and would, but I do not know if I will be able or ultimately permitted such a luxury. You well know what lies ahead for me in the centuries to come. I do not believe I will be permitted to shirk what is coming in light of what it means for our people. Could I afford to be so selfish?"

Mae did not immediately respond. The silence between them grew. Then her hand returned to his shoulder, and she gave it a squeeze. He looked back at her and their gazes locked.

"No matter how long it takes," Mae said, "let us catch Mik'Las, then decide what to do next. Whatever happens, we will do it together, you and me. I will allow no one else to interfere, not even my mother, when it comes to that decision. It will be us, and us alone that decides what is to come."

"Together," Eli affirmed.

"Perhaps, when we are done with this mission, we will both choose to step aside for a spell, to spend time with each other, maybe even start a family of our own." She glanced down at the sword and her brow furrowed slightly. "Then, when the Last War finally comes to Istros, we do what is needed or required for our people. After that, who knows…?"

Eli thought on that for a moment, wondering what such a life would look like, having their own home, a roof over their heads, waking up next to Mae every morning, spending the days with her … that wouldn't be so bad … A child … children possibly … he could not see himself as a father … yet … but honestly, the rest did not sound so bad. "A family? I think I might like that and spending time with you."

Mae smiled. "I would too."

"If we are fortunate, we may have two or three centuries together," Eli said.

"Well more than the average human's lifetime."

"Yes." Eli's gaze traveled to Davin and then Titus. "And what of them? What of this war we are facing, and Lutha Nyx?"

"All right," Titus called, "rest time is over."

Biting her lip, Mae glanced over at Titus. In the same quiet tone only Eli could hear, she said, "I think we stay with them, for a time, and see if we can help, as your grandfather clearly wishes us to do."

"And if there is nothing we can do for them?" Eli asked. "What then?"

"Then we continue after Mik'Las."

"Okay," Eli said firmly. "It is decided, then. That is what we shall do."

Mae shifted her gaze back to Eli and eyed him for a moment more, then turned away toward her pack and bow, which she had left where she'd been sitting. Eli bent down and picked up his own pack and slipped it on. He grabbed his bow next, along with the precious few arrows he had left, then stepped over to Davin, who had made himself ready and was waiting, staff in hand.

"I have seen no sign of pursuit," Eli said to him. "I am wondering if your pets have picked anything up."

"I was forced to release my pets," Davin said. "They are no longer watching and have not been since we left the settlement."

"What?" Titus asked from a few feet away. "That might have been helpful to know, don't you think?"

"Why?" Eli asked curiously. "Why let them go when they could be useful?"

"Like all things, their time was up," Davin said. "To keep them longer would have been unwise, maybe even a little dangerous for us. I do not enjoy taking such risks, unless it is absolutely needed."

"Can you conjure new ones and send them back the way we came?" Titus asked. "I'd like to know where the enemy is, especially if they're still following."

"Not until nightfall at the earliest," Davin said. "They, like me, need some time to recover."

Titus expelled an unhappy breath and glanced around from person to person. He spared Davin another look, then turned to the others.

"Eli and I will bring up the rear," Titus said to them all. "Davin and Mae in the center. Aventus and Lenth will have point. We move down the hill, toward the river. Once we hit it, we're turning and traveling south, following it all the way to the border. Any questions?"

There were none.

"Let's go, then," Titus said. "I'd like to be well on our way to Mekhet and the safety of its garrison before the sun goes down."

Holding their bows loosely, Aventus and Lenth started down the other side of the hill. Mae turned to Eli, gave a nod, then looked to Davin and raised an eyebrow that was a clear invitation. With his staff used more as a walking stick, Davin started forward with her, and together they made their way after Aventus and Lenth, following their tracks in the snow.

Eli started to go too, when Titus grabbed his arm and held him back. He shook his head before flashing a sign to hold.

"What?" Eli asked, after Mae and Davin had made their way down from the crest and into the trees. They were no longer in sight.

"I don't trust him," Titus said.

"And you think I do?" Eli asked, becoming amused by the suggestion. "Honestly, Titus, I thought you knew me better than that."

"Having him along with us is a serious risk."

"Yes, it is," Eli admitted, growing serious, "but in my mind a necessary one."

"You realize he could be the one responsible for all that's happened along the border," Titus said. "You know that, right?"

"I do know it, but I think he is what he says he is, and also why he has come to the north. It sounds crazy, but I believe someone is misusing his goddess's power."

"I'm buying it too, but I still can't help but have a bad feeling about this, him traveling with us." Titus rubbed the back of his neck. "Even amongst your people, there is a standing death sentence for followers of his cult. You know there is a reason for that. Regardless of the reason, we should not be trusting him, let alone permitting him to travel with us."

"Which is why he is with us."

"I am not following you," Titus said.

"This way, we can better keep an eye on him," Eli said. "And if he proves useful, all the better."

"And if not?" Titus asked. "Do we break our word and kill him? When this is all over, do we send him onto his goddess anyway or just let him go? I'll tell you plain, Eli, I don't much like the idea of someone with his power and abilities running freely around the empire. He and those like him are one of the reasons we rangers exist in the first place. Just like for yours, we are the first layer of protection for our people, for the empire."

Eli was silent for a long moment as he gave it some thought. Titus had made some very good points, ones that could not be easily dismissed. His gaze traveled in the direction Davin and Mae had gone. All that remained were their tracks in the snow.

"That," Eli said finally, "is a bridge we will cross when we come to it. Now, come on, Titus. Let us get moving before the others get too far ahead."

CHAPTER SIXTEEN

"That's a long way across." Titus whistled softly. "A bloody long way."

"It is," Eli agreed as he stared at the river before them. The Tibexra was fifty yards across from one side to the other. As a result of the rains that had preceded the snow, the water had been churned into an ugly brownish color that was far from welcoming.

Having risen and climbed the banks, near the point where it was threatening to overflow, the river was also fast-moving. More concerning, there was a lot of debris in the water, limbs both large and small, along with logs and even entire trees that had been uprooted and washed away. And as if in a race and hurtling toward the finish line, the debris rushed past, almost quicker than one could sprint.

"There is a lot of shit in that water," Aventus said.

"Thank you for that observation, Mister Obvious," Eli said to the human. In truth, Eli was feeling disappointed by the dangerous conditions of the river, and Aventus's continual comments had begun to annoy him, which didn't help either. He had hoped, if need be, especially if it was an emergency, they might use the ford to cross. That did not seem like an option now.

Eli shifted his attention to their surroundings. They were standing on the western bank, in a small clearing that abutted the river. On both sides of the river, the forest seemed thick and uninterrupted. A carpet of snow was draped over everything.

Once they had climbed down the ridges toward the river, the forest life had become abundant and plain to see. There had been fresh rabbit, deer, and hog tracks in the snow, the complete opposite of the forest on the other side of the ridges.

"I'd not want to cross that"—Aventus gestured at the river—"even with the ford you mentioned, Eli. You couldn't pay me to even try."

"Where is that, by the way?" Titus asked, looking over at Eli. "How far are we from your crossing?"

Eli gave it some thought, looked down the river, then up it. He sucked in a long breath and let it out through his nose. "I believe maybe a mile or two, south of our current position."

"With the height of the river, there is a strong chance we won't be able to use it, Titus," Aventus said. "I'd willingly make a wager on that and happily take your money too, when you lost. But then, we might be dead, eh, so what would be the point?"

"A chance?" Titus asked him unhappily as he eyed the rushing water skeptically. It was loud, for there were a couple of large rocks in the center of the river, around which the water rushed. "Aventus, I'd say there was no chance and I'm not taking your wager. Only a fool would attempt to cross that, even in a boat."

"We're stuck on this side of the river, then," Eli said.

"You don't say," Titus said. "Not, mind you, that I was overly eager to cross anyways, what with this cold."

"It is but one option removed from us." Eli glanced over at Mae, who was studying the far bank with a troubled and distant look. Biting her lip, she turned and scanned the forest behind them. "What?" Eli asked her. "What are you thinking?"

"We have seen no evidence Kyber is pursuing us," Mae said. "If he was, he should have caught up by now, especially after our stops to rest."

"Yeah," Titus said. "Maybe he gave up. So?"

"So," Mae said, "perhaps, after he came upon the settlement and found us gone, his goal was never to pursue us in the first place."

"I'm not following you, my lady," Titus said. "Care to elaborate?"

"Maybe Kyber knows of the ford as well," Mae said. "Then there is our destination. It is easy to deduce where we are headed, at least I think so."

"Mekhet." Lenth shifted his stance as he said the town's name.

"It is the nearest imperial town with any semblance of safety," Mae said.

"Oh, that is great," Titus snapped, looking at Eli with deep unhappiness. "Isn't that just great? After he turned up at the settlement, I should have suspected as much. Instead of following, he might have gone straight to the ford. Or he might be waiting for us somewhere downriver, between here and Mekhet."

"He may still not know of the crossing," Eli said. "I found it only by accident and no one lives within the area. At least, no one did when I last passed through."

"Yeah, but he certainly knows of Mekhet." Clearly thinking, Titus looked southward as he scratched in his beard. "Still, I don't see that we have much choice in the matter."

"There is always a choice," Davin said. "The gods give all individuals free will. The priests of the High Father even teach of that."

"Oh really?" Titus asked. "Then what would you suggest?"

"We do not have to go south," Davin said. "We could go north. There is a ferry two hard days' hike from here. I came through that way."

"I know it," Titus said. "The problem with that route is that there is a Castol garrison stationed there to collect tolls. Granted, it's small, but it will prove tricky getting past them, especially since Aventus and I are wanted by the Castol authorities, not to mention Eli here." Titus waved at him with his bow. "With the invasion of the province, that garrison may have even been reinforced and ordered to detain all imperials. Heck, Kyber might have sent word to them about us. No, that is one option we simply can't chance."

"We might be able to find a boat there or nearby," Davin said, "and borrow it. I saw several when I passed through a couple of months back."

Titus stared at him for a long moment. "That is a possibility, but with the garrison there, it is still risky and a long way off too. Then there is the river to consider. In its current condition..."

"We could go back the way we came," Aventus suggested, "circle around the ford and make our way overland to Mekhet, avoiding the river entirely."

"Backtracking might see us blunder into Kyber and his men," Titus said, "if they are following, that is. I don't think that is a viable option either."

Titus turned his gaze to the river, which was continuing to rush by. A great big tree, complete with green oak leaves still attached to the branches, was being carried down the center of the river. He tracked it with his eyes as the monster of a tree passed by.

"We go south, then." Eli pointed in the direction they needed to go. "We stick with the plan but play it very, very carefully."

"Follow the river all the way to imperial lands, then travel to Mekhet," Titus said, looking in the same direction. He scratched at his beard again.

Eli gave a nod. "That is what I am suggesting. It is still the easiest path open to us at the moment."

"And if Kyber is there, waiting," Titus said, "we try to go around him and his men without being detected."

"Yes," Eli said.

"If it comes to a fight?" Lenth asked. "Honestly, I've never been overly fond of running. I'm already more than a little tired of it."

"I believe we all are," Aventus added.

"We go through them if it comes to a fight," Mae said quietly.

"All right," Titus said firmly and eyed Mae for a couple of heartbeats. "So that we are clear, this is what we're going to do. We are not that far from Eli's crossing. Since there is a chance Kyber may be there waiting, we move carefully up to it, make certain there is no ambush, then, if there isn't, we will pick up the pace some and press on through the night, traveling south. Any objections to that?"

No one said anything.

"Good," Titus continued. "We will see how far we can make it without taking an extended break. I'll take point, with Lenth. Aventus, you take our right flank with Eli, about ten to fifteen yards out into the forest. That way, we have a good, broad front as we move along the river."

"If anyone's hidden along the river's edge then we're bound to find them," Eli said. "It is as good a plan as any, I guess."

"Got it, boss," Aventus said to Titus.

"Mae, you hang back with Davin, say about thirty to forty feet," Titus continued. "Try to keep him from making too much noise. We don't need to give ourselves away."

"You need not worry about me, ranger," Davin said. "I will be like the dead in a cemetery, betraying no noise."

Titus eyed Davin for a long moment, then ran his gaze around the party. "We're going to take this nice and slow and quiet-like. As soon as we reach the ford, and find no one's there, as I said, we will pick up the pace and continue south. If we encounter anyone along the way, we will stop and pull back, assess the situation, then try to work our way around them without being discovered. If that's not possible, we fight."

Eli could tell Titus was not only nervous about their situation, but also deeply worried, for the scout usually did not repeat himself. That was one of his few tells.

Titus paused and looked out across the river, studying the far bank. It was clear to Eli that the ranger captain wished to be on the other side, with the river between them and the enemy. Then Titus turned his gaze southward and a look of grim determination settled upon his bearded face. "All right, no sense in delaying things further. Everyone knows what they need to do. Let's get moving."

Raising his bow, he motioned curtly to Lenth. The two men moved forward and began making their way out of the clearing and into the forest, paralleling the river.

Mae stepped up to Eli and grabbed him one-handed by the tunic. Her other held her bow and arrows. She pulled him close, pressing her lips against his in almost desperate desire. It was a deeply impassioned kiss, and kissing her back, Eli lost himself once more to her. After several moments, she broke the kiss by pushing him back and away from her, roughly so. His heart beat wildly in his chest.

Mae eyed Eli fiercely and spoke in a low tone that was meant only for him. "If it comes to it, you fight like it's a bow, daggers, and sword moment, understand?"

"You do the same, wife," Eli said. "I will not lose you to someone like Kyber."

She gave a firm nod, her gaze flicking briefly to the sword belted to his side. He sensed her unease with the magical weapon.

"Now go," Mae said to him, "and mind what I have said."

"I will." Eli turned away and jogged over to Aventus, who had moved into position and was waiting for him a few yards into the forest.

"How very sweet." Aventus flashed him a mocking smile. "You two young lover birds just lighten my heart and give me hope for the future, a brighter future. Yes, you do, sir."

"Aventus, I am older than your great-great-great-grandfather and then some." Eli flashed the ranger a closed-mouthed grin. "And I will be getting it up with her long after you are gone from this world, and nothing more than a memory and a fading one at that … as I may have with your mother's mother."

Aventus stared at him, saying nothing at first. He blinked several times while his mind processed what Eli had said. It was clear to Eli that Aventus was suddenly discomforted by Eli's comment and age. Eli had discovered it was not a unique feeling amongst humans. They were peculiarly sensitive about their short lives and their matrons. It seemed to remind them of their own mortality, and so he had just pointed it out to set the human straight.

"Yeah—right," Aventus said after a long silence.

"Come on." Confident he had made his point, Eli raised his bow and loosely nocked an arrow. He began moving forward slowly. "Let us get this done and do it right."

"You believe they're waiting somewhere ahead?" Aventus asked after a few steps, raising his own bow and nocking an arrow as he moved along with Eli.

"I do not know." Eli looked over at Aventus, who had begun to place some distance between them. "But I do not wish to be caught by surprise."

Aventus gave a nod, then turned away and scanned the forest as they started moving deeper into it. Off to Eli's left and just ahead, he could see Lenth steadily working his way forward. Along the river's edge, the trees had thinned some and as a result there was more undergrowth. Eli was only able to catch intermittent flashes of Titus as he continued forward a few feet to Lenth's left.

Taking another step, Eli glanced back and saw Mae, with Davin, watching them. She made a show of winking at him. Then, almost with effort, Eli turned back forward and scanned the forest carefully as he took another measured step.

The day's light was beginning to dim. Dusk was upon them, and in a short time, night would fall. The forest ahead was already beginning to fill with shadows that seemed to tease and trick the eye.

They advanced two hundred yards, then three. The river, thirty yards away, continued to rush noisily by. Eli had a flash of large rocks in the center and some whitewater.

He found the sound of the rushing water pleasant, but also distracting. Without any interference, he wanted to listen to the forest clearly, cleanly ... to hear it and become one with the natural sounds. It wasn't just the eyes that were critical to detecting threats, but also the other senses. That included one's gut too. Taken altogether, it allowed one to sense when something was off. And if one had a feeling something was not quite right, then it usually wasn't. The sound of the water was making that more difficult.

Slowly, almost painfully, they moved forward silently, stepping over fallen trees and low-lying brush and making their way around bushes when required. The forest, in Eli's eyes, was the perfect place for concealment, especially at night when the light was poor. Even during the daytime, there were plenty of places and shadows to conceal oneself in.

He enjoyed the challenge of not only sneaking through the forest unobserved, but also finding those who did not want to be found. He was a master of both skills, as he was an elf and the forest was his home.

Eli moved around a large bush whose leaves were beginning to change color from a light green to a bright yellow, its limbs bent heavy with snow. On the other side, he came nearly face-to-face with a red squirrel sitting in the snow a foot from him. The little creature had been digging. It froze, straightened, and looked up at him with eyes that did not blink. Then, almost angrily, the squirrel began chattering loudly before making a break for it and dashing off to the safety of the nearest tree.

Still chattering at him, it climbed around the side of the trunk and higher before reappearing on a thick branch high overhead. The animal continued to chatter away in a disapproving manner, as if the little creature was admonishing him for startling it.

Eyeing the squirrel, Aventus looked amused as he glanced over at Eli. For his part, Eli gave a shrug of his

BY BOW, DAGGERS & SWORD

shoulders, and then, without saying a word, he and the human ranger continued onward, advancing through the trees.

With every step, it seemed the forest was growing darker, as the day's light began to steadily fail. The temperature was beginning to drop too, presaging another cold and unforgiving night. Overhead, birds in the canopy sang and called out to themselves as they settled in for the night, becoming a constant backdrop along with the rushing water of the river.

The forest around them was healthy, vibrant, strong, and nothing like the one around Arvan'Dale. It teemed with life. He could faintly hear the Mother's song too. She called to him, sweetly, almost seductively. He loved it and wanted to embrace her, but at the same time he refused to be distracted by the enticement. Kyber might be out there, somewhere, and the man was as dangerous as they came. This was one time Eli could not afford a distraction.

He stepped over a snow-covered snag and paused briefly as a natural clearing came into view before him. Inside the clearing the light was slightly brighter. A large, ancient tree had fallen some years ago. It had taken down several others with it, which had opened this portion of the forest floor to the sky.

He glanced over at Aventus and motioned for him to skirt the clearing. The human ranger gave a nod and proceeded to do just that. As he did, Eli stepped out from the tree line. Startled, several birds sheltering in the brush of the clearing took flight. Eli sank to a knee as they scattered into the air, squawking loudly in protest. A moment later, they were gone, and relative silence once again returned to the forest.

He took several moments to listen, straining to hear over the sound of the river and the birds singing in the trees around them. He detected nothing out of the ordinary, so he rose and continued straight through the clearing to the other side. A glance showed him Aventus was halfway around the side of the clearing and moving steadily forward toward the other side.

The fallen tree had truly been a giant, with a thick, gnarled trunk, marking it as an elder of the forest. With the tree on its side, the roots alone stood fifteen feet in height. For a moment Eli eyed them and the old tree, now merely a snag, and felt some sorrow that such a long-lived being had finally passed from the world. In time, the forest would reclaim it, recycling it as it did all living things, and when that happened, several more trees would blossom in its place and be given a chance at life. Such was the cycle of things, the natural way, and Eli was okay with that.

Turning away, Eli proceeded through the clearing until he reached the trees on the far side. Like an ominous veil hanging over everything, twilight once again spread out before him and across the snow-covered forest floor.

Ahead, there was much less vegetation as the trees shifted to hardwoods, and older ones too, like the fallen giant he had just passed. He scanned carefully, his eyes raking everything, and again saw nothing out of the ordinary. Then something to his immediate left and slightly behind him in the clearing caught his attention. Eli looked over and felt himself scowl as he studied what lay next to the fallen tree. With the snow, it was almost perfectly hidden from view. He'd almost missed it.

How interesting … how fascinating … how unexpected!

He motioned for Aventus to hold. The ranger nodded and sank to a knee. Eli looked around and spotted Titus.

He and Lenth had just moved into the hardwoods and were making their way forward. Eli made a hooting call from a rare owl that did not live in these parts. It was a distinctive call and one he had taught Titus to listen for. The ranger immediately looked around. So too did Lenth. Eli signaled for them to hold. They moved rapidly to the nearest tree and, sinking to a knee, took cover.

Through the brush that grew up in the clearing, Eli couldn't see Mae and Davin but saw Titus clearly signal to them. Eli turned to his left and moved back into the clearing toward the fallen giant and a tangle of brush, or really a pile of branches. Surprised at his find, he looked up and caught Titus's gaze, then signaled for the human to join him.

Titus deftly slunk over and knelt before him.

"What's up?"

"I found us a boat," Eli said with no little amount of surprise and gestured to the pile of brush and branches.

Titus looked where he indicated and blinked in clear surprise, then reached out and lifted a pine branch heavy with snow, revealing more of the boat. "Why, it's a canoe, and a large one at that." Titus pulled off another branch and set it aside. "This thing looks old, like it's been here a while."

Eli agreed with that assessment. The wood of the canoe was beginning to gray with age and exposure. He moved more of the snow-covered branches off and set them to the side. Together they worked at uncovering the find, and in moments, the entire canoe was free of coverings. Then, they both turned it over onto its back, rolling it right side up. A couple of paddles fell out. These too looked aged, with a few cracks having formed in the wood.

Eli studied the inside of the canoe critically. It looked solid. He did not see any holes or rot. He turned the canoe back over and onto its side, then brushed the snow off the bottom with his boot.

"It looks sound to me," Eli said to Titus.

"There's a lot of debris in that river, Eli," Titus said. "This might get us across, but with the current moving as it is and all that shit in the water, it would be very dangerous."

"Where is your sense of adventure?" Eli asked, only half teasing the human.

"I'm serious," Titus responded. "Crossing that river is a sketchy thing to do."

"Continuing forward as we are might be just as dangerous, especially if Kyber is waiting," Eli pointed out. "Have you considered that?"

"Then again, he might not be waiting," Titus said, though he did not sound convinced. They both knew Kyber was not one to give up. "Once we cross the border, there is a nice bridge on the other side of Mekhet. It's guarded too. That will be a much safer way of crossing."

"I know," Eli said, then glanced around the clearing as a thought occurred to him. "Why here?"

"You mean the canoe?" Titus asked.

"Who put it here and then hid it?" Eli asked.

"I know fur trappers paddle up and down the river," Titus said. "They use large canoes like this one. It allows them to carry their wares back to the market in Mekhet or north to the town of Drange."

"Why didn't he come back for it? A canoe, like this one, is valuable. Even an old one is worth trading for, especially out here in the middle of nowhere."

"I dunno," Titus said, regarding the canoe for a long moment. "But it has been here for a while. There is no doubt about that." He looked toward the river. "The water isn't as rough over there. This was likely an easy place for a landing, and the hiding place here by this snag, it's well out of view of anyone traveling on the river who might want a new canoe."

"Yeah." Eli glanced in the direction of the river. He could see it through the trees. As expected, there was a lot of debris moving downriver. Any attempt at a crossing would be, as Titus said, dangerous. Eli had no real wish to test the river either.

"I think we should proceed as we had planned," Titus said.

"And if Kyber is waiting just ahead?" Eli asked.

"Then we either come back and use the boat or go around him. Do you see any other good options?"

Eli shook his head, then glanced around. It was growing darker. "It will be night soon. Do we push through for Mekhet, or make camp somewhere ahead?"

"I am thinking we push on through and stop for nothing," Titus said. "Setting a fire tonight would not be advisable, and the sooner we get there, the better."

"All right," Eli said. "Let us get back to it then."

"I'll tell Mae and Davin why we stopped and what we found here. You fill Aventus in. Then we will push onward."

With that, Titus moved off. Eli glanced down at the canoe and wondered again what had happened to the owner. Sparing another glance over at the river, he turned and made his way to Aventus and sank down on a knee next to him.

"I saw you flip that canoe over," Aventus said in a whisper. "Good find. With all that snow and those branches covering it, I didn't even see it. Strange that it's all the way out here and was just left."

"Yeah," Eli said. "We were thinking the same, and it has been here for a while, years even."

"So, it wasn't sound?"

"Oh, it was, but the river is up and crossing in a canoe may not be the wisest thing to attempt."

"You know, I kind of agree with that assessment." Aventus glanced in the direction of the river. "Besides, I've never been overly fond of boating…you might recall that."

"I almost forgot about that," Eli said with a chuckle.

"My dislike of boats began that time you decided to take me fishing on that lake," Aventus said. "And you knew I didn't know how to swim."

"You learned quick enough when the boat rolled," Eli said, thoroughly amused at the memory.

"No thanks to you," Aventus said sourly.

"That is a matter of perspective."

An owl hoot caught their attention. Titus was back with Lenth. He pointed southward with his bow, and they started forward once more.

"Time to earn our pay," Aventus said, rising.

"You get paid?" Eli asked with an innocent tone. "Really? I want to get paid."

"You elves don't believe in the value of coin," Aventus said, looking down at him. "What do you care if I get paid or not?"

"It is a matter of fairness," Eli said.

"It's a matter of bullshit on your part," Aventus hissed back at him, and with that, the human ranger moved out.

Eli stood and shifted a few feet to Aventus's left to spread out from him. As they worked their way deeper into the forest, the snow crunched softly under their feet. After three hundred yards, the twilight that lay over them seemed to lighten. In the gloom, there was another clearing ahead, a big one.

They moved toward it, and after a few more steps, Eli saw what looked like a structure of some kind. Scowling, he wondered what it could be. Titus came to a stop and looked over at him. He pointed at the building in question. Eli gave a shrug of his shoulders to say he did not know what it was. Titus turned to Mae and Davin. He held up a hand, a clear signal for them to hold, then snapped a series of signals to Eli, Aventus, and Lenth in fingerspeak.

We go forward. Scout.

Eli gave a nod of confirmation. Then, more slowly this time, Titus and Lenth started forward. A few heartbeats after, Eli and Aventus began moving too. They all had their bows ready, eyes raking over everything in view.

Using the trees for cover and leapfrogging from one to the next, they closed the last few yards to the large clearing. It became plain someone had built a log cabin in the middle of the forest and then cleared a patch of land around it.

Eli stopped at the edge of the clearing, behind a stand of brush, and took a knee. Aventus, a few feet away, did the same. The cabin was of simple construction, mean-looking and only a single story, with a grass-thatched roof that looked like it had grown wild. There was an untended feel to the place. No light came from the structure's windows, which were glassless and shuttered. A couple of the shutters hung at odd angles, revealing a dark interior.

The area that had been cleared around the house was overgrown with brush. There was even an axe at the edge of the clearing. It was embedded in a thick chopping block that had been used to split logs. The wooden chopping block was covered over in ivy, as was a small pile of split logs next to it. Some of the snow had melted and the split wood had long since grayed with age.

Whoever had gone to such an effort to build in the middle of nowhere had either abandoned the place, giving it back up to nature, or had long since died. There were no cultivated fields and not even a hint of what could have once been a garden.

Eli decided it must be a hunting cabin of some kind, or a place where a trapper had set up shop while he worked the river in these parts. He glanced behind them and wondered if the canoe had belonged to the person who had put down roots here. He suspected that there was a very good chance of that being a correct assumption. Maybe it had indeed been a fur trapper.

Eli glanced toward the river. What he could see of it through the trees seemed to be rougher than where the canoe had been stashed. There were several large boulders and some whitewater in view.

He studied the area around the cabin and saw no movement, no hint anyone was in hiding. He studied the snow around the cabin and didn't see any tracks either. The place looked deserted, completely abandoned.

Titus looked at Eli and flashed a signal. Eli gave a nod of understanding, and with that, Titus stepped forward and emerged into the clearing. As he did, Eli shifted his gaze, scanning the trees beyond the clearing again, on the other side of the cabin, and saw no threats. Titus crept forward and up to the house. When he reached it, he motioned for Lenth to join him. Lenth moved quickly forward and up to the cabin.

Once Lenth had joined him, Titus moved around to the other side, while Lenth went up to the corner and watched beyond, covering Titus with his bow. Eli supposed the door to the cabin was where Titus was headed and that it was on the other side. He glanced over briefly at Aventus, whose attention was fixed forward, watching.

They waited, with Eli scanning all that could be seen. Nothing moved. He scowled slightly as something began to nag at him. He gave it some thought. Then it hit him. Even though it was nearly dark, the forest around them had gone silent, too silent, and not like what they had encountered just a few miles back and over the ridges toward Arvan'Dale or by the settlement. In the distance, he could still hear birds singing and calling to one another. So why were they not doing that here?

Eli ran his gaze around the clearing again, then out into the forest around them. He saw nothing out of the ordinary. Titus reappeared and, stepping around the house, rejoined Lenth. They put their heads together. Something was said between them, then Titus flashed a signal in fingerspeak.

No one here. Clear.

Eli gave a nod. He began to search the trees around them again, and then around the cabin and clearing, looking closer. Darkness was falling and the shadows were growing deeper. Still, he saw nothing. Something wasn't quite right. He could feel it in his gut, but what that was, he had no idea.

Titus signaled them to come forward.

"Do not move," Eli said quietly to Aventus, who froze as he was starting to stand. "Whatever you do, do not move or make a noise. We are not alone in this place. I am sure of it."

Instead of looking at Eli, Aventus tensed, then, as Eli was, began scanning the area.

Still, Eli saw nothing. He was becoming frustrated by that.

He wanted to signal Titus, to warn him, but dared not. Any movement might give their position away, and he was now convinced some sort of a threat lurked in the growing shadows and darkness. But where that was or what it was, he had absolutely no idea.

Titus scowled at their lack of response, then stiffened slightly as realization struck him. He turned to Lenth, said something, then the two of them, as if nothing was wrong, began moving casually back toward the trees.

Eli tensed himself as they drew nearer. Then, just five yards before they reached cover, something shot downward from above and through the gloom of the coming night. Eli almost missed it, but there was a meaty thwack, a surprised grunt, and Lenth was spun violently around. Crying out in agony, the human collapsed to a knee. An arrow stuck out of his shoulder.

Eli turned his gaze toward the tree canopy to the right and cursed himself for missing it. There were men up in the trees. They had walked into an ambush, one Kyber had set.

CHAPTER SEVENTEEN

Eli's gaze was drawn up to the tree canopy off to his right. Someone was up there, legs straddling a thick limb. Having concealed himself with leaves, the man had been perfectly camouflaged and clearly had a bow. Eli cursed himself for not thinking to look up before now. He had been the one in the trees often enough to know better.

Aiming, Eli pulled back on the string and released. His bow twanged powerfully. One of his precious arrows hissed away. It flew true and Eli was almost immediately rewarded with a cry of pain. A mere heartbeat later, the assailant dropped from the tree, at least thirty feet to the ground below, where he landed heavily on his stomach in the snow with an audible *thud*.

"Bloody gods," Aventus whispered, seemingly to himself. "They're in the trees."

Another arrow zipped through the growing darkness and flew right past Titus's head to hammer into the ground next to him, kicking up a small spray of snow. The end of the arrow quivered with unspent force.

To Eli's right, Aventus raised his bow toward the canopy and released. His arrow hissed away.

"Titus," Eli shouted as he nocked another arrow. "Get Lenth and yourself under cover!"

Titus reached down, grabbed Lenth by an arm, and hauled the injured ranger to his feet. Together they began what looked like a painful jog, at least for Lenth, toward the cover of the trees.

"They're over here!"

Eli looked in the direction of the voice and brought his bow up. Across the clearing, a man had emerged from behind a tree. He was pointing at Titus and Lenth.

"They're over—" His next words were cut off as Eli's arrow took him in the throat. The force of the strike knocked him flat onto his back. Grabbing at the end of missile, which had gone clean through, he tried to yank it out, while his legs thrashed violently about in the snow.

An arrow hissed past Eli, close enough that it caused him to duck involuntarily.

"More up in the trees," Aventus said and pointed, then brought his own bow up. "Two across the way, there. See them on that branch?" Aventus did not wait for a reply. He aimed and released, his arrow shooting away. "Eli, I'm out. No more arrows."

There was a heavy grunt across the way, and a man standing on a thick limb dropped his bow and reached for the arrow that had pierced him clean through the chest, right where the heart was located. He stiffened as he tugged at it, trying to free it. A moment later, without a word, he collapsed, falling forward and off the limb. Arms dangling limply, he hung by a rope, which was tied about his waist.

Eli raised his own bow and aimed at the last man on the branch, who had been next to the one Aventus had just shot. This man had raised his bow and was clearly aiming at Titus and Lenth. Eli let go the tension on the bowstring. His arrow shot away and slammed hard into the man's lower chest.

Struck, he fell back and off the limb, releasing his arrow, which shot harmlessly up into the sky. He dropped all the way to the ground, where he landed with a heavy *thud*. He did not get up or stir, but lay there in the snow, very still.

Half dragging Lenth with one arm, Titus reached the trees. A brown-fletched arrow was lodged firmly in the back of Lenth's shoulder.

"Oh gods," Lenth moaned as he reached for it with his good arm, "it hurts."

"Don't touch it, man," Titus ordered and slapped Lenth's hand away from the arrow. "You might cause more damage trying to yank it out. We will deal with it when we have time, understand?"

"I do," Lenth said miserably.

There were more shouts now from across the way.

"Titus," Eli said, "your arrows. Give them to me."

"Here." Titus handed over his two arrows. Eli tossed one to Aventus, who caught it.

"Thanks," Aventus said.

"What about his arrow?" Eli gestured at the wounded ranger.

"I dropped it back there," Lenth said, "along with my bow. I don't want to lose my bow. Can you get it, Titus?"

"We're not going back for it," Titus said. "I will buy you a new one."

"I made that bow with my own hands," Lenth lamented.

"We're still not going back for it," Titus said. "You can make another."

"There's more coming," Aventus warned. "A lot more."

Eli looked around and saw at least ten men. They had emerged from the trees. All were carrying bows.

Titus, guiding Lenth, moved for cover behind a tree.

"Titus," Eli said, "head for the canoe. We will use it to cross to the other side."

"I told you I dislike boats, Eli," Aventus said. "And only a madman would try to cross the river as it is now."

"Then call me mad." Eli hardened his tone. "I don't care if you like boats or not. We are out of options, and the river it is."

"Eli," Aventus protested, "I—"

"Think of it this way, Aventus," Eli said, cutting him off. "If we survive, you will have one heck of a story to tell." He turned to Titus. "You need to get moving. We will hold them off for as long as we can."

Titus gave a nod, then looked at Lenth, who, despite the cold, had perspiration on his forehead. "Can you walk?"

"I can bloody well run," Lenth said as he gritted his teeth against the pain.

Titus released him, slung his bow across his back, and drew his sword. He gave Lenth a gentle shove in the direction of the canoe and the injured ranger started running. It was more of an awkward and painful jog than anything else, but he was moving under his own power and that was all that mattered.

Titus looked like he was having second thoughts and wanted to join them. An arrow hissed by, just as another thunked into a tree behind Eli.

"Get that canoe to the water," Eli said to Titus. "Take Mae and Davin with you but get to the canoe. We will slow them down and buy you what time we can."

"Right. I will see you there." Titus paused and jabbed a finger at Eli. "Don't keep me waiting. I don't want to be the one to tell Mae you died."

"Never," Eli said with a grin as Titus, crouching low, ran after Lenth.

Another missile hissed by, shooting off into the darkness behind them.

Eli glanced at the enemy through the stand of brush he was concealed behind. There were more than a dozen now at the edge of the trees on the other side of the clearing. It was nearly dark too, and the moon was coming up, just showing itself above the trees to the east. Eli saw only skirmishers. There were no foresters amongst them. They had not advanced farther either, but were shooting arrows in their general direction.

Aventus had his bow nocked and was about loose.

"Do not shoot," Eli ordered as he moved away from the stand of brush and over to the cover of a tree. "Save it a moment."

"Why?" Aventus asked as he moved under cover to a tree ten feet to the left of Eli's. He put his back to it and looked over at Eli. "Why did you stop me? I had a good target in sight."

"When we both loose, there will be no more arrows," Eli said. "We will be out, and when they figure that out, they are going to come after us." Another arrow thunked into the tree Eli was taking cover behind. Yet another hissed between them and off into the forest. "Let us buy Titus more time to get the boat to the water. Our job is to delay them, understand?"

Aventus nodded and Eli began counting. Several more arrows hissed by or thunked into the trunk of his tree. Eli was grateful the tree trunk was so large. One arrow landed uncomfortably near his left foot, the force snapping the shaft as it drove through the snow and into the ground. Eyeing it warily, he moved his foot away and under cover.

When Eli got to a hundred, he peeked back around the tree, then pulled back out of sight. Several of the enemy had begun advancing across the clearing. He counted to ten, then looked again. They were halfway across, with some by the cabin.

"Now," Eli said quietly to Aventus. "Take your shot."

Aventus leaned around the tree, aimed for a heartbeat, and loosed. His bow twanged with the released tension and his shot hissed outward, even as the ranger drew back under cover.

There was an agonized scream. "Oh gods, I'm hit."

"Got him," Aventus said triumphantly.

"Sarge, I'm hit," the man screamed. "I'm hit. Help me. Oh great gods above and below. I'm hit."

"Good shot," Eli said to Aventus. "Now go and help Titus."

"What about you?" Aventus asked as he slung his bow over his back and drew his sword.

"I will be right behind you," Eli said. "No matter how dangerous it is, we have to get that boat in the water and across the river, understand? It is a big canoe."

"I do. But I still don't want to leave. They're going to come after you in a moment. You can use my sword, and besides, leaving you doesn't feel right. That woman of yours might take issue with it. Honestly, Eli, she scares me more than a little."

Eli grinned at that. "There are days she scares me too."

"Then why did you marry her?" Aventus asked. "Seriously, Eli, there are times I just don't understand you elves."

"Don't worry about me or why I married her. That is my business." Eli sobered. "Listen, I am going to shoot and scoot. Once I get a few yards into the trees and the darkness, they're mine. They'll become the hunted. Now get going. You will only get in the way of what needs to be done."

"But…"

"No buts," Eli said. "I know what I am doing. You know that. You've seen me do this before. Trust me, you don't want to be there. You can better help with the canoe."

"All right," Aventus said. "I hope you're right."

"I am."

"Be death," Aventus said firmly.

"I will be." Eli gave a nod, and with that, Aventus turned and sprinted away.

"They're running," someone shouted. "I see one. They're running. After them!"

Eli counted to ten then leaned around the tree to make sure he was visible to the enemy. He picked a target and drew back on the bowstring. Several of the enemy had started running themselves, with the clear intent of pursuing Aventus. Eli picked out the one in front. It was an easy shot. He released, then ducked back behind the tree. There was a deep grunt as the arrow hammered home. A moment later, he could hear his target crash to the ground. Cries of alarm followed.

Eli peeked around the corner again. The charging enemy had stopped, with some seeking cover behind the cabin, others throwing themselves to the ground. Eli ducked back under cover. Slinging his bow over his back, he drew his daggers.

"Time to dance."

He looked ahead and picked out the thick trunk of an oak tree no more than five yards away. He dashed for it and threw himself behind it. An arrow hissed by in the growing darkness. It had been uncomfortably close. Almost without hesitation, Eli moved again and, doing his best to keep this tree between him and the enemy, ran to another tree, deeper into the forest and growing gloom.

"Forward," someone with a note of authority called. "Get your asses moving, boys. I said forward."

Daggers in hand, and hidden behind the tree, Eli fell still as could be and waited. His heart had begun to beat with the excitement of the moment and what was shortly to come.

From around the other side of the tree, he could hear the enemy moving into the forest, brushing aside the undergrowth, feet crunching the snow, coming forward tentatively, if not warily. With the moon rising into the night sky, he had chosen the dark side of the tree and done his best to merge with the shadow there.

He waited.

A man with a nocked bow, peering deeper into the forest, stepped past Eli's tree, coming within three feet of him. Not once did he look over. Eli held himself completely motionless. He even held his breath for fear of giving himself away.

"Do you see him?" the man hissed to someone behind without turning. "I can't see anything."

"No, keep going. We'll find him."

Eli remained perfectly still. He prayed the man did not look to his right. He didn't, but continued onward, taking several steps before the next enemy appeared and came around the tree on Eli's right side. The second man did not look either. Both men were staring out into the forest, scanning ahead of them.

Eli let him continue on too. A third man passed, then a fourth. The third turned to say something to the fourth and spotted Eli. The man's eyes widened with incredible shock. Before he could utter a word or do more than blink, Eli moved, coming up behind him and smoothly slicing his razor-sharp dagger across the neck, opening it neatly up.

Blood fountained, and before the body could even fall, Eli reversed his direction and spun toward the fourth man, who had stumbled to a stop, jaw falling open in apparent shock.

Moving like lightning, Eli slashed one dagger across the man's stomach, slicing it open, and the other across the under part of the man's forearm, with which he held the arrow to the bow. The blade cut easily through the soft flesh and then the tendons, severing them. Then Eli was past, dashing for the shelter of a tree four yards over to the right.

Behind him, his victim began to scream and cry out, not only in pain, but also in horror at the damage that had been done to him. An arrow hissed by Eli's shoulder, flying off into the darkness, a fraction of a heartbeat before he reached the cover of the tree. Then he was around it and had his back against the tree, with the trunk between him and the enemy.

"Did you see him?"

"He went that way," someone shouted. "I almost hit him."

Pushing off from the tree, Eli ran to the next.

"There he is. Get him!"

Eli did not even bother to weave. Head down, he ran for the tree and the safety it provided. He threw himself behind it. A couple of arrows hissed harmlessly by.

The man he'd wounded continued to scream.

"Shut up!" someone roared, then there was the sound of a slap on flesh. "Stop bloody screaming, you fool."

Surprisingly, the injured man stopped his screaming, but instead began sobbing. It was a pitiful sound and Eli found himself feeling slightly bad for what he had been forced to do, for the stomach wound alone would be fatal. That feeling did not last, for Eli shoved it aside and steeled himself for what needed to be done.

"You have to be quicker, boys," Eli called back to them. "Or you will all end up fodder for the worms."

He figured he had just put fifteen feet between himself and the enemy skirmishers. The darkness was growing more absolute the deeper he went into the forest. He knew for his next ambush, he needed to put even more distance between himself and the enemy.

"Oh, Sarge," the crying man blubbered. "I can't use my fingers. My stomach, he's killed me. Oh, it hurts so. What has he done? What has he done?" The sobbing devolved into crying and then abruptly into screaming again.

Using the screaming as cover for the sound of his boots on the snow, Eli ran for the next tree, farther out into the forest. There was no resulting shout of alarm, no call that he'd been seen. Eli put his back to the tree, feeling the rough bark. Behind him there was a sickening sound of what could only be a sword chopping down, and with it, the screaming abruptly ceased.

"You killed him, Sarge." The tone was filled with shock.

"He was already dead," the sergeant said plainly. "He just didn't know it yet. It was a mercy killing, nothing more."

Chest heaving, Eli peeked around the tree and spotted the enemy, some twenty feet away. There were six of them. They had their bows held out before them and were tentatively moving in his direction. A man on the left was several yards ahead of the others. He was hunched over and had his bow ready with an arrow nocked as he moved slowly forward.

Eli looked around to his immediate left and saw a suitable tree a few yards off. If the man continued on his current track, he would walk right by the tree. Eli reached down and picked up a branch. He tossed it in the opposite direction. It landed with a heavy crunch of snow.

"What was that?" someone called.

Eli made a dash for the tree he wanted and was able to make it to cover once more without being spotted.

"I thought I heard something over here," the man nearest Eli's new tree said. Eli held himself perfectly still. He forced himself to exhale and then breathe in. His heart was pounding in his chest as if it wanted to explode forth. It was a wonder they could not hear it.

"Keep your eyes open, boys," the sergeant said.

The crunching of the snow drew closer. Silently, Eli sheathed both daggers. Though the moon was out, the leaves overhead were thick and the light underneath them poor. Once again, Eli was concealed in the darkest of shadows. He took a moment to thank the gods for the poor night vision with which they had gifted humans and then settled down to wait.

The expected crunch of footsteps came closer and closer. Then his mark began to come into view, just around the side of the tree Eli was behind. Eli first saw the bow and nocked arrow. Before the rest of the man could emerge into view, he struck, moving around the side of the tree and hammering his fist into the man's face, while at the same time sweeping the bow down and away from his body. The arrow released harmlessly into the ground, even as blood fountained over Eli's fist as the nose crunched from the power of his blow. Ignoring the pain in his hand, Eli hit him again in the face just to be sure.

Stunned, and blinking, the man took a stumbling step backward. Eli caught him and spun him around to face the others, who were only feet away, while holding on tightly to both arms and pinning the man in place.

"Here I am, boys," Eli shouted, holding his victim firm as he began to struggle. "Who wants me?"

There was a startled exclamation and then an arrow hammered into the stunned man's chest, emerging out the back, the bloodied point touching Eli's chest. Another arrow punched into a leg, and with that, Eli released the man while throwing himself behind the tree again and under cover.

The injured man dropped to his knees and moaned in agony. A moment later, he began gagging and convulsing as his lungs filled with blood. He vomited blood onto the snow in a sickening display and then pitched forward.

"I got him, Sarge, I got him!" someone shouted excitedly and rushed up, just as Eli broke from cover and moved to the next tree over, a few yards away. "Oh gods—"

"You fool, you shot Jessip."

Drawing his daggers once more, Eli peered around the tree and saw five men gathered around the newly injured man, who was clearly dying.

"What have I done?" a voice sobbed. "I've killed him. Sarge, I've killed Jessip."

"Shaddup you." The sergeant cuffed the man on the side of the head. "You idiots need to watch what you are shooting at and keep your cool. Put those damn bows away. Swords out."

"Where is he?" someone else asked.

Eli ducked back under cover so that he wasn't seen by the sergeant, a burly man, who looked in his general direction, searching the forest and darkness with his eyes.

"Sarge, what do we do?"

"We find and kill him."

"What have I done?"

"Get ahold of yourself, man," the sergeant snapped. This was followed by the sound of another cuff. "Or I will kill you myself."

"What if he's one of those daemons?" another voice asked.

The voices were scared and stressed, which was what Eli wanted.

"This isn't one of those monsters," the sergeant replied tersely. "It's one of those bloody elves Kyber told us about. Stick a sword in him and he'll die just like any man. They're just long-lived, is all."

"He's a ranger," one of the sergeant's men said, his awe plain. "They have magic, can do things no man can, like make themselves invisible."

"Yeah, Sarge. It's true. My pa told me. That's what he's been doing."

"Invisible? Bullshit," the sergeant said. "We saw him plain enough. I said, shaddup. We're gonna find and kill the bastard."

"I wish the rest of the company was here, Sarge."

"They'll be soon enough," the sergeant said. "I sent a runner. Now let's see if we can find and kill this bastard before the captain gets here and takes all the credit." The sergeant raised his voice and called out into the forest. "You hear that? You may have gotten a few of us, but we're gonna get you and gut you, you bastard. We're coming for you. You hear me?"

Eli chose not to reply, as he didn't want them to know where he was.

The enemy began moving again, toward Eli's tree, which was what he wanted. He slowly moved around the tree in the opposite direction as they drew closer.

"Keep your eyes open, and stay close," the sergeant said. "This way, boys."

Eli remained still. From the crunch of footsteps, the group had changed direction and were moving slightly away. Perhaps, Eli considered, the sergeant had gotten himself turned around in the darkness. The footsteps began moving away from the man who was now dead but still bleeding out in the snow from the two arrow wounds. Eli peered around the side of the tree and saw them moving in a northwesterly direction. Even though they had their backs to him and were moving away, it still worked for him.

"I am death," Eli said to himself.

Watching the enemy move steadily away, Eli stepped out from behind the tree. He began moving up behind them, timing the sound of his crunching steps to match those trudging through the snow ahead. It was tedious, but Eli kept at it. One slow step after another, he drew nearer, closer.

One of the enemy was trailing slightly behind the others. His bow, which he held at the ready, string taut, was shaking. Eli idly wondered why he'd not drawn his sword when ordered by the sergeant. Perhaps he was just more confident with the bow. It didn't matter. He would be the first to die. Eli took another step closer, then one more. As if sensing something, the man looked back, just as Eli was upon him.

Their eyes met, and as they did, Eli plunged his curved dagger into the side of the man's neck, driving it deep. He felt the blade grate against the spine, then yanked it out, tearing skin, muscle, and tendon as he did it. He turned and lunged, striking at the next man, driving his straight dagger deep into the lower back, aiming for the kidney, and swung away for another enemy, just steps away and to the side.

That man had begun to turn in Eli's direction, just as Eli reached him. Realization sank home and he screamed in terror a heartbeat before Eli drove his dagger deep into his side, eliciting a heavy grunt. Eli gave the blade a twist and received another grunt in reply.

Then the other two men were turning to face him. One was but a youth. The other was older for a human and clearly the sergeant.

Startled, both stepped back in surprise. Then the youth dropped his sword and, screaming, turned and ran. The sergeant raised his blade and, with an inarticulate yell and determined look, charged for Eli.

Having dealt his last victim a mortal wound, Eli threw him roughly aside and ducked as the sergeant swung for him, a vicious attack aimed at Eli's chest. The sword found only air as the blade flew by just over his head. Eli then dodged to the side to avoid the man as he charged by, spinning around like a dancer as he did it. The sergeant may have missed, but one of Eli's daggers, the curved one, found the sergeant's side as the man's momentum carried him past. Eli's blade dug deep, opening him up.

The sergeant stumbled a couple of steps, then turned to face Eli. He reached down a hand to the terrible wound that had torn his side open. Eli knew it was likely a mortal wound, for the blood gushed out, down his side and onto the snow.

"You're a real bastard." The sergeant's voice trembled with terrible pain. He was gritting his teeth, which seemed almost brilliant in a patch of moonlight that shone down from a gap above.

"There are some days," Eli said plainly, "that I wish I was a bastard."

"Time for you to die, elf," the sergeant said with resolve. "I'm gonna take you with me to the next world."

"Many before you have tried the same and failed, for I am death."

The sergeant's eyes narrowed, and with a stumbling effort he started forward from the patch of moonlight and attacked, this time more warily. Eli dodged the first strike and then caught the next on his curved dagger. The two blades rang loudly as they came together.

The sergeant was strong, and sparks flew in the near absolute darkness. Eli felt the blow painfully communicated to his hand. He ignored it and, with all his strength, forced his opponent's sword aside, then drove his other dagger up and into the sergeant's stomach. The man gave an agonized grunt as the blade went in. A powerful flow of blood sluiced over Eli's hand and forearm.

"I'm gonna kill you," the sergeant groaned, spitting bloodied spittle into Eli's face.

"Not today," Eli said to the sergeant. Their faces were almost close enough to touch. In the other's pain-wracked eyes, Eli saw an understanding dawn that death was at hand. Eli gave the dagger in the sergeant's belly a savage twist. The man gagged, and blood stained his teeth as his face contorted in pain. With that, Eli shoved the man backward. He crumpled to the ground. "You won't be taking anyone else with you to the next life, other than those you brought."

The sergeant's mouth worked, but only a fountain of blood emerged. Remembering that there was one more enemy, Eli looked around for the youth. But he was gone, having fled.

Stepping back from the dying man, Eli took a relieved breath and wondered where the rest of Kyber's men were.

As if in answer, behind Eli, out in the forest in the direction of the canoe, there was a shout of warning, then the ring of steel meeting steel. There was another cry, an agonized one. This one sounded like it came from a female. Eli's head snapped around and fear gripped his heart like a vice. A moment later he was running.

CHAPTER EIGHTEEN

Shouts, cries, and the sound of fighting came from ahead. With trees flashing by, Eli ran for all he had. He now understood with terrible certainty why the foresters had not been with the ambush at the house. They had circled around behind and had been waiting for the ambush to be sprung.

He ran and the sound of fighting increased. Then it was just ahead. Through the darkness, he saw a confusing melee at the water's edge. The canoe lay tipped on its side. Davin was swinging his staff against a sword-wielding man, fending off attack after attack. Titus was trading blows with two of the enemy and, with his back nearly at the water's edge, was slowly giving ground. Aventus was there too and engaged.

Where was Mae?

He couldn't see her. Then Eli's gaze fell upon her. She was sprawled a few feet on the other side of the canoe and trying, struggling even, to get up. An enemy was standing over her, his sword coming down to strike a final, killing blow. Eli's heart froze. He was too far away to help, to stop what was about to happen.

"No!" he shouted in horror.

Then, impossibly, Lenth was there, sword in hand and arrow still sticking out of his shoulder. Clearly struggling with the effort of wielding his sword, Lenth caught the enemy's blade upon his own with a ringing clang.

The forester recovered and pushed Lenth's blade aside with seeming ease, then backhanded him hard to the face. Lenth staggered to the side, and as he did, the forester struck out with his sword, stabbing him just above the stomach. Lenth stiffened but did not cry out.

The forester shoved Lenth off his sword, and with that, the ranger crumpled to the ground. Then he turned back to Mae, who had managed to pull herself to her knees. She looked slightly dazed and was staring at Lenth's body in what could only be described as horror.

Still running flat-out, Eli literally flew through the air as he leaped over the canoe. While airborne, he twisted his body and threw his straight-edged dagger. The tip of the blade struck true and cracked into the side of the man's head. He went down hard as Eli hit the ground, rolled, and came back to his feet.

Mae looked over at him, a dazed look to her eyes. She shook her head, and her gaze came back into focus as she blinked at him. She did not have a weapon, even her daggers.

"Catch," Eli called and tossed her his curved dagger, as he drew the sword.

The shock hit him again, and as it did, Eli felt as if someone else, a phantom presence, was there with him, standing at his side or looking out through his eyes. It was an odd feeling that he could not adequately explain. Already an expert with the sword, he spun the weapon in his hand. The blade felt natural, perfectly balanced, like none other he had ever wielded. He seemed to be hyperaware of everything going on around him, as if he sensed the fight through some other means. It was almost as if time had, ever so slightly, slowed down and his peripheral vision had grown wider.

He turned to the nearest of the enemy, one of the two men who were pressing Titus back, and moved to attack. The man closest broke off from Titus and turned to face him. Eli lunged. The other man blocked, and almost effortlessly, Eli moved his blade around the other's sword and sliced a gash across the man's forearm. It seemed like he could do anything he wanted with the sword, and with that came a powerful sense of confidence that reinforced that feeling.

Hissing, Eli's opponent danced back, looked down at the cut, and then back up at Eli. A grim look of determination settled over his face. He moved forward to attack, and as he did, Eli lunged, jabbing out for his right leg, which was extended.

The move caught the forester by surprise and off balance. He just barely managed to block, but Eli's follow-up attack was incredibly fast and took the man in the upper arm. He cried out as the blade cut to the bone. Then Eli stepped in close and, before his opponent could react, stabbed hard into his opponent's abdomen, driving his blade down and into the pelvis.

Choking with pain, the man dropped his own sword and fell off the blade, crumpling to the ground at his feet. Eli kicked the discarded sword away and went for the next opponent, stepping over his mortally wounded foe without a moment's thought.

Eli still had that hyperalert feeling. He seemed to be aware of the entire fight all at once, the positioning of everyone. It was disconcerting to say the least, but it clearly came from the sword, and he would take what the weapon offered him.

There were seven foresters still on their feet. There had been ten, but Davin had just cracked the one he'd been fighting with his staff, hitting the man across the side of the temple and felling him like a tree.

Faced off against Aventus, Kyber was on the other side of the fight. There was an eighth man, who was not a forester. He was standing back from the fighting and dressed in a simple gray robe that was cinched at the waist. He was merely watching. It was then that Eli noticed he was holding a glass vial in his hand and had raised it up into the air. Eli stumbled to a stop, his heart chilling at what he knew was about to happen. The man was too far for Eli to easily reach.

"Davin!" Eli yelled and pointed his sword at the robed figure. Just at that moment, the robed man squeezed his hand, crushing the vial in his grip. There was an audible *pop* that seemed to shake the very air around them. Darkness much blacker than the night upon them flowed from his hand, which shed drops of blood down onto the snow. The darkness began to rapidly coalesce into a figure that seemed to leak black smoke, obscuring its form as something materialized before his eyes.

Then, as if a gust of wind had cleared it, the smoke dissipated.

Eli found himself gazing upon a true monster come to life. It was something that even his past experiences with Lutha Nyx's followers had not prepared him for. Monstrously large, the alien creature stood over eight feet tall. It carried itself erect and had six thick and muscular arms and two legs that ended in razor-sharp claws.

The creature was also completely naked, with rough, purple skin. Its face was a horrific mess, with a large circular maw filled with hundreds of teeth. Its two eyes took them all in, the pupils blacker than the darkest night.

Eli gave an involuntary shiver.

The creature turned its head to look over at the man who had summoned it. The man pointed at Aventus, and with that, the monster gave a screech that clawed at the ears. It was an inhuman sound that immediately stopped all of the combatants dead in their tracks.

For a moment, silence reigned. Behind Eli there was an audible *crunch*, followed by another *pop* that shook the air around them. Then the creature moved to attack, launching itself with terrifying speed at Aventus, who stood rooted to the ground, as if in shock.

The creature knocked the forester Aventus had been fighting aside. He flew into the nearest tree trunk and connected with a sickening *crunch* before sliding limply down to the snow.

That seemed to break Aventus's paralysis, for he took a step back and then another and, with impossibly wide eyes, raised his sword. The creature leaped like a mountain lion onto its prey. It brought Aventus to the ground, and as it did, the human ranger screamed.

The scream was drowned out by another terrifying screech. This one seemed filled with malice, loathing, and torment.

"Savacha Ho," Davin roared from behind Eli and another creature just as large and hideous raced past Eli, running on all fours, and crashed into the first, ripping it free from Aventus. This one resembled a dog, or really a bear, that had been twisted and perverted horribly. Roaring and tearing at each other, the two monsters went tumbling off into the darkness of the forest, both roaring with rage as they fought one another.

Tearing his gaze from the two monsters, Eli turned back to the robed man, knowing he must be stopped before he could conjure another creature. He took a step forward, but before he could take another, there was a series of *pops* that once again seemed to shake the air around them.

Davin roared, "Savacha Ho toacha."

There was a skittering sound and a dozen little creatures, each green and furred, no bigger than a raccoon and just as hideous as the larger monsters, went racing past and around Eli toward the robed man.

"No," the robed man gasped in horror and mounting panic. "No. She promised... NO!" He took two steps back. With teeth biting and claws tearing at the flesh, the creatures leapt upon him. He went down screaming and thrashing as the little monsters began eating him alive.

Everyone, foresters included, was staring on in horror. Then Titus stabbed out at the man he had been fighting, taking him in the back and driving him to the ground. Eli turned to Kyber, and their eyes met. They were still too far apart for Eli to easily reach him. There were two foresters between them.

"Kill him!" Kyber shouted and pointed at Eli. "Kill him now!"

The two foresters turned and immediately charged. Eli met them, and as if someone else were fighting for him, his sword seemed to flash, knocking the first blade aside, catching the next and turning that blade away too. But that wasn't right. Eli knew he was directing the sword, but it seemed almost easy, as if he were fighting unskilled children. He kicked out with a boot and caught the lower leg of one of the men, knocking him off balance. The other pressed the attack. Eli caught the enemy's blade once more and thrust it aside.

Then Mae was there. Screaming with rage, she drove her dagger into the side of the man's neck. He dropped. Eli moved around him and struck out at the other forester, who neatly blocked, the two sword blades coming together in a ringing clang that stung his hands painfully.

Eli recovered and jabbed. The forester blocked again. Eli pressed his attack once more and slipped by the guard of the other and stabbed him in the thigh, driving him to a knee. Eli was about to finish his opponent off, when from behind and close at hand, there was another screech.

Eli's blood ran cold at the sound, and he started to turn. A blink of the eye later, he found himself flying. He landed hard on the ground as the creature screeched again.

"Savacha Ho toacha da," Davin roared.

Aching everywhere, Eli picked himself up onto his hands and knees. He'd lost his sword. He looked up to see the bear-like monster Davin had summoned rip the forester he had wounded literally in two from the torso, then toss both parts aside. The monster screeched loudly again. It shifted its attention onto another forester, who, without a moment's hesitation, turned and ran for his life. Returning to all fours, the monster chased after him. And with that, the rest of the foresters, including Kyber, turned tail and ran. Before he disappeared into the forest, Kyber glanced backward and straight at Eli. Then he was gone.

Eli lay on the ground breathing heavily. He looked over at the sword, which lay a few feet away, and eyed it warily. There was no doubt the sword helped to make one a better fighter, but it also gave one a strong dose of confidence. Eli knew that such confidence could get one killed, for it bred recklessness. He would have to guard against it.

In the darkness, the monster roared. Someone screamed.

"I guess…" Eli dragged himself to his feet. He felt exhausted and drained beyond belief. He looked over at Davin. "I guess it was not such a bad idea to let you tag along, eh?"

Davin did not look amused as he glanced around at the carnage. "We need to get the canoe into the water and across the river. We don't have much time. Hurry."

Eli saw Davin's little pets were still feeding upon the remains of the robed man. With teeth tearing flesh and snapping bones, it was a sickening display. Blood had colored the snow around the feeding site red.

"What?" Titus asked, tearing his gaze from the monsters to look over at Davin. "What do you mean?"

"My summoning will last no more than another sixty heartbeats." Davin tossed his staff into the canoe and then began dragging it to the water by himself. The area along the river's edge was slightly sheltered by two large boulders at the water's edge ten feet upstream.

"And then what?" Titus asked.

"It goes back from whence it came," Davin said.

"He's right," Eli said. "There's a whole company out there and they are coming this way."

Aventus groaned and sat up, looked around for a moment, then felt his arms and legs. "I'm alive. I can't believe I am alive."

"I dunno how," Titus said as he helped the other ranger to his feet. "I thought you were a dead man when that beast took you down."

Aventus's nose was bleeding, as was a wound on his forehead. He had scratches and cuts on both arms too.

"I feel like I was run over by a manure cart." Aventus staggered slightly, almost losing his balance when Titus let him go.

"You smell like it," Titus said.

"Come on," Davin encouraged as he slid the canoe into the water. "Help me."

Eli turned around, looking for Mae. She was still holding his dagger but was kneeling next to Lenth. There were tears running down her cheeks. Eli moved over to her and placed a hand upon her shoulder.

She looked up at him. "He saved my life, at the cost of his own."

"He did," Eli said.

"Why? Why would he do that?"

Eli gently pulled Mae to her feet. "I told you there is worth in man. Now, you have learned that firsthand."

"High Father," Titus breathed unhappily as he took in Lenth's body. "High Father, make his crossing of the great river and into the next life an easy one. Bless him and keep him close, for he was a good man and an even better ranger."

"Titus," Aventus said as Davin climbed into the canoe, which was now in the water. Aventus had moved over and was holding it against the current. Davin had a paddle in hand. "We need to go."

Titus looked around, nodded, then directed himself back toward Lenth's body. "It may be some time, but I promise, we will come back for you and give you a proper funeral. We will also offer up a sacrifice to the High Father upon your behalf. Until then, I bid you a safe journey crossing over, my friend."

Titus knelt and closed Lenth's eyes. He then turned and made for the canoe. Off in the distance there was another screech that sounded different from the others, almost as if it were filled with relief.

"That's it," Davin said, "the conjuring is done. If they've worked with the twisted before, and I suspect they have, they will know what that means and come back."

There was a series of small screeches. This was followed almost immediately by a number of pops. Eli blinked. The creatures that had been feeding upon the robed man had vanished into thin air.

"Right," Titus said, "everyone in the canoe. Let's get going."

Mae was still staring at Lenth's body. Eli grabbed her arm and guided her to the canoe. Almost mechanically, she stepped into it. Eli looked around and spotted his new sword. He went over and picked it up. This time there was no shock, no hyperalert feeling. It seemed as if it was just any other sword. He wondered idly on that and what it meant as he slid it home into the scabbard. Mae's bow also lay at his feet. He bent down to pick it up and tossed it to her.

A paddle lay on the ground at the water's edge. He picked it up as Titus and Aventus pushed the canoe farther out into the water, which was still rushing by and just beyond. In the darkness were various shapes that he well knew were all manner of debris. Eli waded into the water, which was bitterly cold. There was also a strong current tugging at his legs, threatening to sweep him away and down the river, which was close to overflowing its banks. Aventus and Titus jumped into the canoe.

Eli pushed hard, giving the canoe some momentum, then jumped in at the rear. He began paddling. Davin, at the front, dug into the water with the other paddle and did the same. The canoe surged forward from the sheltered area and was caught by the current.

Digging his paddle into the water and steering with all his might, Eli worked to point the nose of the craft downriver while Davin paddled for all he was worth up front.

A large branch bumped against the side of the canoe with a heavy *thud* and turned the bow slightly upstream, even as the rushing water of the river drove them downstream.

Eli dug into the water again, while Davin paddled furiously to help correct their course, and they succeeded, with the bow once again pointing downstream. Eli angled the bow toward the far side of the river and then he and Davin began paddling as hard and as fast as they could.

Another thick branch hammered into the side of the canoe, rocking it and threatening to turn them over.

"I want to tell that story," Aventus said to Eli, "you know the one…about surviving a flooded river, chock-full of debris, in a clapped-out old canoe. I really want to."

"You will," Eli said as he fought to angle the canoe correctly by steering with the paddle. Having succeeded, he began paddling again.

"Tree," Mae called out in warning.

Eli looked around and saw a massive tree coming downstream for them, just yards away. He dug his paddle into the water, turning the canoe directly downstream as Davin continued to paddle madly. The tree bumped the back of the canoe hard, almost tipping them over. Eli leaned to the left hard and the canoe stabilized. Then the tree slid past them and continued down the river.

Eli breathed out a sigh of relief just as something splashed into the water to the right of the canoe. Eli glanced back and saw two men on the far bank with bows.

"Paddle faster, please," Aventus encouraged. "Get us to the other side."

Eli looked around. They were only ten yards from the far bank. He dug in hard for all he was worth and so too did Davin. An arrow thunked into the bottom of the canoe, between Eli and Mae. It punched through the bottom, becoming lodged halfway through. Immediately water began to spurt upward in a small stream.

Then the front of the canoe scraped against the bank. Throwing the paddle aside and grabbing his staff, Davin immediately jumped out.

"Another tree," Mae called urgently as she jumped into the knee-high water. "Everybody out."

Eli looked over as he jumped out of the canoe and into the water, which came up to his waist. A massive tree being carried along with the current was racing straight for them. The roots that were above the surface were scraping along the riverbank, tearing it up. The tree was just feet away from them.

"Oh shit," Aventus cursed as he jumped off onto the shore.

Titus just ran up the center of the canoe and leapt out onto dry land. Having been at the back of the canoe, Eli was forced to slog through the water, which fought against him, slowing him down. The tree came closer and closer as he followed after Mae. She made it onto the muddy shore and then there was dry land under his feet, and with her, he was scrambling up the slope of the riverbank to safety.

A mere heartbeat later there was a massive crash, followed by a splintering as the canoe was crushed by the uprooted tree. Eli glanced back and saw the remains of both the canoe and tree swept away into the darkness.

"That was close," Aventus breathed.

"Yep," Titus said.

"See?" Eli said, wearily to Aventus. He felt terribly exhausted, to the point where it was weighing heavily upon him. "Boating's not that bad."

"This time was almost as bad as the last," Aventus said, then brightened. "But at least I've got a story to tell."

"There is that," Eli said.

"Hey, Eli," Kyber yelled from the far bank.

Without turning, Eli continued climbing tiredly up the bank and staggered up to the nearest tree. Leaning against it, he was thoroughly beat and needed a rest badly. He was also soaked from the waist down and it was bitterly cold out.

"Hey, Eli," came the call again. "Hullo there."

"What do you want?" Eli, out of breath, called back, not terribly concerned about an accurate bowshot. The distance was too great, even for Kyber. But for the moon, which was now hidden behind a cloud, the darkness was near absolute.

"I'm gonna hunt you down like the dog you are," Kyber said. "I'm coming right after you. On that I promise."

Eli glanced around, then gave a sick chuckle that his enemy could not hear over the rushing water. Cupping his mouth with both hands, he raised his voice. "You are forgetting something."

"And what is that?" Kyber called back to him.

"You are on the wrong side of the river. Good luck with trying to catch me."

"Unless he chances upon a boat like we did," Aventus said, "he's not crossing anytime soon, and even then, it was sketchy."

"The hunt, for the moment, is over," Titus said wearily.

Kyber stared at Eli for a long moment, then threw his bow down and stamped upon it with both feet. With that, and feeling terribly satisfied with himself, Eli turned away and moved deeper into the trees. The others followed him.

"Is it done, then?" Titus asked Davin after they had gone a few feet. "You killed that conjurer, right? You ended it? The madness is done?"

"That was not what you wrongly named a conjurer," Davin said wearily. "That robed bastard was just a man with

MARC ALAN EDELHEIT

a vial of badness who was taught how to use it, to direct the twisted at an enemy. He had no defense against my death-lings. If he were capable of conjuring on his own, he would have been able to counter them with ease. No, there is someone else out there, someone I must still find, someone who taught him what to do."

"That is just great," Aventus said. "Isn't it, Titus?"

"How do we find him?" Titus asked.

"We?" Davin looked at Titus curiously.

"Yeah, we," Titus said. "He needs to be found and killed, and I don't think we can do it without you, let alone face the … the twisted by ourselves."

Davin rubbed his jaw as he regarded Titus in the dark-ness. "Honestly, I could use your help. And when this is all over? What then? Do you knife me in the back and call the business done?"

Titus glanced over at Eli before turning back to Davin. "We go our separate ways and never again speak on the mat-ter. I don't tell my superiors about you, and we all try to forget the matter. You have my word on that."

Davin gave a nod and then looked at Aventus. "And what of him?"

Titus looked over at Aventus. "Aventus, are you with me on this?"

"Always," Aventus said. "It's all tied to the Castol inva-sion anyway, and we need to deal with that too."

"What about you both?" Davin asked Mae and Eli. "I know you're after a criminal. Will you put that off for a time and help?"

Eli's heart was still racing. He looked over at Mae and met her gaze. Moments ago, he had almost lost her. But for Lenth's sacrifice, that had been a close thing. Yes, they had a mission to complete, but Eli was no longer in a hurry to do that, not while she was by his side. In time, they would get to Mik'Las. There was no doubt about that. But this thing with Lutha Nyx and the Castol was important too.

Gazing into her eyes, he could tell she felt the same.

"Grandfather," Mae said in a low tone.

"Grandfather it is," Eli said.

"By bow, daggers, and sword," Mae said fiercely and offered him his dagger. The other one was across the river. Eli regretted its loss, for he'd had it for a very long time. He took the weapon and looked down upon it. She had cleaned the blood from the blade. He slid it into its sheath and looked back up at her.

"By bow, daggers, and sword," he said and gave a nod of confirmation.

"What does that mean?" Titus asked.

"It means," Mae said, "we are going with you. We will help you bring an end to the madness."

The End

Eli and Mae, along with Titus, Aventus, and Davin, will continue their adventure in 2023. Look for Part 3 of a Ranger's Tale.

Important Contact Information for Marc: If you have not yet given my other series a shot, I strongly recommend you do. They are all wild rides. Hit me up on Facebook to let me know what you think!

You can reach out and connect with Marc on:

Patreon: Consider supporting me as an author and get special access. Follow the link below to learn more:

www.patreon.com/marcalanedelheit

Facebook: Make sure you visit my Author Page and smash that like button. I am very active on Facebook. The link below will take you right to my Author Page.
Marc Edelheit Author

Facebook: MAE Fantasy & SciFi Lounge (This is a group I created where members can come together to share a love for Fantasy and Sci-Fi)
Twitter: @MarcEdelheit
You may wish to sign up to my newsletter by visiting my website to get notifications on preorders, contests, and new releases. **In fact, I recommend it!**
I do not spam my subscribers.
http://maenovels.com/

<u>Or</u>

You can follow Marc on **Amazon** through my Author Profile. Smash that follow button under my picture and you will be notified by Amazon when I have a new release.

<u>Reviews</u> keep me motivated and also help to drive sales. I make a point to read each and every one, so please continue to post them.

Again, I hope you enjoyed *By Bow, Daggers & Sword* and would like to offer a sincere thank you for your purchase and support.

Best regards,
Marc Alan Edelheit, your author and tour guide to the worlds of Tannis and Istros.

Printed in Great Britain
by Amazon

83441888R00154